BOYD COUNTY
JUN 3 0 2025
PUBLIC LIBRARY

Purgatory Crossing

A NATHAN STARK, ARMY SCOUT
WESTERN

PURGATORY CROSSING

WILLIAM W. JOHNSTONE
AND J. A. JOHNSTONE

THORNDIKE PRESS
A part of Gale, a Cengage Company

GALE
A Cengage Company

Copyright © 2025 by J.A. Johnstone.
The WWJ steer head logo Reg. U.S. Pat. & TM Off.
Thorndike Press, a part of Gale, a Cengage Company.

ALL RIGHTS RESERVED
This book is a work of fiction. Names, characters, businesses, organizations, places, events, and incidents either are the product of the author's imagination or are used fictitiously. Any resemblance to actual persons, living or dead, events, or locales is entirely coincidental. Following the death of William W. Johnstone, the Johnstone family is working with a carefully selected writer to organize and complete Mr. Johnstone's outlines and many unfinished manuscripts to create additional novels in all of his series like The Last Gunfighter, Mountain Man, and Eagles, among others. This novel was inspired by Mr. Johnstone's superb storytelling.
Thorndike Press® Large Print Softcover Western.
The text of this Large Print edition is unabridged.
Other aspects of the book may vary from the original edition.
Set in 16 pt. Plantin.

**LIBRARY OF CONGRESS CIP DATA ON FILE.
CATALOGUING IN PUBLICATION FOR THIS BOOK
IS AVAILABLE FROM THE LIBRARY OF CONGRESS.**

ISBN-13: 978-1-4205-2456-7 (softcover alk. paper)

Published in 2025 by arrangement with Pinnacle Books, an imprint of Kensington Publishing Corp.

Purgatory Crossing

Chapter 1

A lone buzzard circled high above the mesa, too far up to cast a shadow. Like all desert creatures, he survived by adapting to the harsh climate. He moved sparingly in the heat. Took care to drink whenever he could. And patiently observed the stillness below for the movements of creatures that would one day die and upon whose carcasses he would feast. For everything dies eventually, and opportunists thrive in harsh climates.

The buzzard had known many fat seasons. For a time, the creatures in the wilderness below had been frantic in their activities. The buzzard recognized Man and knew him to be different from other creatures, had learned to track and follow his armies for the refuse and bodies left in their wake. For a time, the sands below had exploded in a blood-soaked fury of battles. Those had been the best times for the buzzard. But those days had passed.

The desert had returned to stillness as Man migrated away, back to the softer lands in the East from which he had come. The sands blew, erasing traces of his passage and returning the desert to stillness. For the buzzard, the lean seasons returned.

Now a plume of dust rose from a single man on a horse on the mesa below. The buzzard circled, assessing the creature's relative fitness and the likelihood of survival. Instinct had taught the bird to read the signs of health and vigor, even from this lofty altitude. He could tell the man and mount far below were fit enough, yet it remained to be seen if they would survive the other perils of this wilderness.

He would return later and find out.

Nathan Stark, Army scout, lifted his gaze and tilted back his hat. High above the mesa, a lone buzzard had been circling. Now it peeled away to points west in search of sustenance. Stark knew that buzzards did not hunt but, rather, waited for others to die so that they could feed. And there was plenty of death out here in this desert.

He brought his gaze back down, repositioned the brim of his Stetson, and leaned forward to stroke the neck of his horse. Feeling the sweat beading in the hairs of Buck's coat, Stark reined to a halt, dismounted, pulled one of the large canteens from the assemblage dangling from his saddle horn, and unscrewed the cap. Buck stamped immediately upon smelling water.

"Thirsty?" Stark chuckled, untied the kerchief from around his neck, and removed the Stetson. "We'll take care of you, buddy."

He reversed the Stetson, poured a quantity of water inside, and set it on the ground before Buck, then squatted as the horse leaned down to take a drink. Stark moistened the kerchief in the hat and wrung it out before retying it around his neck. Then he examined his surroundings.

Bleakness.

Nathan Stark was a well-proportioned man with broad shoulders and a steely gaze. A thick shock of black hair framed his lean, firm-jawed face. He moved with the practiced ease of an experienced trail hand and navigated even unfamiliar territory with a scout's professional eye. When his term of service with the Confederacy ended at Appomattox, he continued his chosen profession as an army scout, going to work for the Union forces. He had served under numerous generals as a civilian subcontractor, including the infamous George Armstrong Custer. Hard, blood-soaked trails were familiar to him.

He had journeyed through Arizona Territory before. There had been much cavalry activity here before the War Between the States. Arizona had voted to join the Confederacy . . . a dream that had ended after the Battle of Picacho Peak. Cavalry had played its decisive role in that engagement, as it had throughout the Territory's history. For here was an unwelcoming and unforgiving land whose inhabitants, both human and animal, resisted newcomers.

Stark knew the people native to these sands: the Navajo, the Yuma, the Apache, the Papago. Some farmed, like the Navajo and Papago. Others hunted and gathered, like the Yuma.

And some raided.

Like the Apache, he thought. The harsher the climate, the greater the likelihood of conflict over scarce resources.

Cavalry out this way had their work cut out for them. The Apache were canny, aggressive opponents. They had set to raiding and killing the earliest settlers with brutal efficiency and then engaged the mounted military sent to oppose them. Amazing horsemen, the Apache inflicted coordinated guerilla attacks upon the sophisticated, drilled soldiers they fought against. Dealing with them became something of an art form, a sub-specialization of the grueling and terrible years known collectively as the Indian Wars.

A succession of generals had made their bones fighting those wars. Sherman had served on the frontier, calling for the utter extermination of the Sioux. Sheridan had worked to deplete game on traditional hunting grounds and force hostiles onto allotted reservation land. And men like General Crook had been given the thankless task of fighting the Apache — an enemy well aware of how things had gone for other tribes and determined to resist a similar fate at all costs.

The heat of the day was coming on. The air shimmered as the ground temperature rose. The animals were still and a thick coating of dust lay upon everything. As Stark watched, a lizard crawled to the top of a nearby boulder and paused, its tongue flicking in and out of its mouth seeking moisture in the heat.

The Apache somehow survive in this horrible climate, he thought. *No wonder they're so tough.*

Buck drank his fill, raising his head and shaking his mane. Still squatting, Stark tilted the opening of the canteen to his lips and took a long, deep, grateful pull of water. And as much as he liked a drink of beer or whiskey now and again, the water trickling down his throat in that dry furnace heat was the most delicious thing he had ever tasted, prompting feelings of gratitude within him that were downright religious.

All them fellas in the Bible were always hanging around in the desert, Stark thought. And considered that he might, squatting there in the sand, understand something about how they must have felt. Folks said, *Hard times make hard men,* he remembered.

He stood, dumped water from his hat and replaced it, recapped the canteen, and remounted. Then he and Buck resumed their journey.

Hard men had been the topic of discussion with the man who'd sent Stark on this assignment. He had made the acquaintance of Mr. Alexander Obediah Greerson, Indian Agent, at Fort Billings, Montana. The man had been about as blunt as could be.

"We created the worst possible outcome in the Arizona Territory. Did it to ourselves," Greerson admitted, gazing around the sparsely furnished office the fort commander had placed at his disposal. "The first waves of settlement from down south in Mexico encountered brutal Apache resistance. So when Americans began heading out that way, we were prepared. We sent scouts ahead of the earliest wagon trains. Began building forts and settlements. There was a military presence there before the War Between the States. An effective one. Good men served on the frontier, learned the craft of cavalry warfare, and implemented what they knew skillfully. For a time, we had the frontier under relative control.

"Then the war broke out. We had to bring those units home. Some went with the Confederacy. But those were federal troops out there, so for the most part, they rejoined the ranks of the Union Army. But the ensuing few years caused a great deal of attrition. We lost a lot of good riders during the war with Johnny Reb. When we turned our attention back to the Arizona Territory, it was with depleted ranks. And the game had changed."

The war had given the tribes the time to regroup and become better organized. The resulting war on the settlers approached levels of brutality rarely seen before. A new generation of leaders was emerging . . . men toughened by the experience of first contact with the bluecoats. Men determined to take revenge. One of them was named Geronimo.

Of course, Stark knew the name. Anyone familiar with the war on the frontier did. It was a name to strike naked fear into the hearts of any man living in the Arizona Territory. For here in this sun-baked, coyote-haunted, scorpion-strewn land, it was a name synonymous with Death itself.

Geronimo.

The man was a force of nature. It was one thing for someone to command a room when he entered. But it was another thing for mere mention of that man's name to silence a room in his absence. The Apache war chief had risen from prominence within his own band to a broader prominence within the Apache nation itself. He cast a long shadow over the Arizona territory — a blood-soaked trail of vengeance and death that threatened even the very military itself.

He was the master of the desert these days, a great tactician who fought the war-hardened cavalry divisions to a standstill with a mixture of brilliance and brutality. General Crook had been given command of the region precisely because of his long familiarity with Geronimo and his demonstrated talent for rescuing victory from the jaws of defeat. For the Union Army *was* facing defeat at the hands of a force half its size, commanded by a man who still lived as a primitive savage.

"Your orders are to board a train for Arizona Territory, disembark in Tucson, and journey south on horseback." Greerson had produced a map from the inside pocket of his tweed coat, unfolded it, and pointed at one section with a stubby finger. "When you come down through the hills near Tubac, there is a telegraph station . . . here on the plains beyond this mountain pass." He tapped it twice. "It will take time for you to get there, and the situation is fluid. They will take stock upon your arrival and issue your orders by telegraph. The Army is coordinating closely with Indian agents on this. And we're much obliged for your help."

Now Stark was approaching the last leg of his journey through these hills. His sense of this was confirmed when he and Buck came around the side of a low rise to find a road cutting across the stony plain. Not a track but an honest-to-goodness road someone had taken the trouble to cut through this section of the wilderness to accommodate the increasing numbers of settlers and supply wagons flooding the Territory.

"Well, look here, Buck." Stark patted the horse's neck. "Signs of civilization. We'll be settled somewhere nice and cozy — a hotel room for me and a nice cool stable for yourself — sooner than you think!"

The road was indeed a sign of civilization. And they didn't have to travel it overly long to learn about the state of things in the Territory. Some enterprising soul had attempted to set up a trading post along the road. Keen to be the first to greet those coming into the area, he had built a large, comfortable storefront of hewn logs.

Even at a distance, their charred forms attested to the carnage that had befallen the place. Black smoke drifted lazily skyward from the ruins. Sections of the building had been knocked over, with logs piled in a haphazard heap where they had fallen instead of burning.

This looks fairly recent, Stark thought. He reined Buck to a stop a quarter mile off and looked around. Had the Apaches stormed down from their hidden base in the hills to do this? It seemed unlikely but not impossible. He set his tracker's eye on the road. There were signs of a group coming through here fairly recently. He dismounted and knelt to study the tracks.

A small group, he reckoned. *And shod.* Which meant the riders had been white or Mexican, but definitely not Indian.

That was as far as he got before he heard

a gunshot and a woman's scream. Then he was back on Buck and riding full gallop toward trouble.

Chapter 2

Buck streaked along the road toward the smoking log structure. Stark leaned forward in the saddle, knees tensed against the mount's sides as his right hand swept toward his holster. The building loomed before them now, with Stark urging Buck around the corner with a sharp pull of the reins. They rounded the edge on a greased streak and pulled up short, the scene before them ghastly.

To his way of thinking, it appeared as if the store owner and family had been making ready to light a shuck. For whatever reason, the cost of doing business in the region had become too high, so the father had drawn a covered wagon up to the side door of the building. Stark guessed the family kept their quarters in the rear of the log structure — the man had probably been preparing to load his wife and kids inside the wagon along with some supplies when the marauders struck. And now he lay dead, his body a heap where it had fallen from the driver's box to land in a gory tangle on the grass.

Stark registered the group of men a split second before they saw him and Buck. And that second made all the difference.

The raiding party was eight strong — six ragged and filthy men who stood in a crescent, ranged around two more of their number, who held the dead man's wife by her arms as she twisted and struggled to get loose. A nearby boy and girl looked on, their shoulders grasped by members of the "audience." Stark saw all this in the instant before the nearest men turned. Then their eyes widened in alarm.

Stark palmed his Colt into his hand, swung one leg over Buck, and dropped to the ground. Then all hell broke loose.

Two of the raiders advanced on Stark, fists and voices raised . . . until they saw the gun in his hand, at which point they backed off. Not everyone came armed to the party, but a few did. One man turned, raising a sawed-off shotgun.

Stark's response was instinctive. He turned sideways to minimize his profile, raised his arm, and fired, the Colt like an extension of his hand. A neat round hole appeared in the shotgunner's forehead, and he keeled over backward, collapsing to the grass.

Then three men's guns were parting leather, including one of the two holding the dead shopkeeper's wife. He let go of her arm and she immediately spun, kicking the other man holding her in the shin so sharply that he went down.

Stark's gun spoke: two loud booms that scattered the group. Two gunmen ran, but a third stood his ground, his piece unpouched and coming up, sight centering on Stark a moment before the scout snapped off a shot that tore the man's throat wide open. He died choking on his own blood.

The children chose that moment to act, both struggling against the grip of their captors. The little girl managed to break free, but the boy's efforts earned him a brisk cuffing upside his ear. He yelped, head snapping sideways just as his mother broke free of her assailant. With a low growl that chilled even Stark's blood, she launched herself at the man who had struck her son, teeth bared, fingers clawed wide. She hit the man with surprising speed and force, knocking him off-balance. Then her nails were raking his face, seeking his eyes.

The man screamed, thrashing against the

woman's grip. The little boy tore free and grabbed his sister's hand.

One of the other gunmen fired, drawing Stark's attention from the melee. The gunman had retreated behind the wagon, firing from behind the rear edge. Stark dropped to his knees, scanned behind the wheels, and spotted legs. He aimed and let fly, firing away. The bullet tore the leg in half at the knee and the man groaned, slumping to the ground alongside the amputation. Stark put him away with one in the wide screaming mouth before spinning and launching himself toward the mother and her children.

The man who had cuffed her son was now well and truly beaten. She had wreaked such havoc upon his face that he held his hands up to it now, moaning and sobbing as he sank to his knees. The mother had gathered her kids to her and was spinning around, seeking a place to run.

"Inside!" snapped Stark. He waved at the door.

He only had to tell her once. Grabbing both her children by the wrists, she made for the doorway as the remaining men came at Stark.

His ammunition was almost exhausted. Coolly as he could, he dropped the cylinder and began reloading, staring down the group of marauders descending upon him. Two noted his action and traded a glance. With a grin, they turned toward the doorway through which the family had disappeared.

One man found his courage — and his weapon. He snapped off a shot that narrowly missed Stark. A moment later, the scout had his Colt loaded and was spinning the cylinder back into place before triggering a shot of his own.

The gunman stiffened and collapsed. And the other men scattered. Two took to their heels while the other leaped into the rear of the wagon, possibly hoping to find a weapon. But somehow Stark doubted that he would. The father seemed to have been preparing his family to go hide in the wilderness for a spell . . . get away from whatever had been bedeviling his business. Most likely, it had been this gang of marauders Stark was set on finishing off. With that in mind, he stepped around the rear of the wagon.

A steel skillet flew out of the wagon, narrowly missing his head. It was followed by a China plate, then a porcelain bedpan. Stark frowned and ducked, biding his time until the man within showed himself. And very shortly, he did, springing to his feet from behind a crate with another skillet cocked back in one hand and ready to fly. Stark fired, catching him in the chest and pushing him back to collapse with a crash among the family's effects.

He turned. The girl was in the doorway.

"Please! Mister!" she cried, plainly distraught. "My mother!"

That was all Stark needed. He turned and swept across the threshold, pulling the girl after him. "What about your ma?" he asked, looking around the blackened interior. "Where is she?"

"They went out the back door," she moaned, wiping tears from her cheeks. "They took Danny, too! Just grabbed him and dragged them off!"

"It's okay. It's okay." Stark squeezed her shoulder. "Come on."

He steered her into a side room and shut the door behind her with a promise to return. And he would. But meanwhile, she would not present a target for the remaining marauders.

Out of sight, out of mind, he thought.

There was a back door. He sidled toward it, gun up, flattening himself on the wall beside the opening. Silence. He counted to ten and took a quick peek around.

The two men had their backs to the store, having dragged the mother and son outside a short distance from the structure. They had forced them both to their knees. At first, Stark could not fathom the reason. Until it suddenly dawned on him that they intended to kill both.

It was illogical. Insane. And yet . . .

They're going to slaughter them! He shook his head at the realization.

Then he was moving, booted feet crossing the threshold and emerging outdoors. The mother had decided to resist and was trying to struggle to her feet. As one of the men turned to cuff her, Stark shot the other one on the run with studied calm. The bullet tore the man's life from his body. He was slumping to the ground when his partner turned.

There!

Stark swung the barrel of the Colt toward the second man. But he suddenly grabbed the woman by the hair and yanked her upright, dragging her in front of him as a shield. Stark cursed his bad luck.

"Steady on, friend," said the man. He flashed a smile, twisting his fingers in the woman's hair clutched in his fist. He flashed a smile that was as dull as it was malicious. "Surely we can come to some arrangement regarding this little dainty! I'll share if you will."

"You'll let her go," Stark replied woodenly. "You'll do it now and we'll finish this, or else I'll just end you here. Trust me. You don't stand a chance."

"Well! I'd say that's downright unneighborly!" The man yanked the woman's hair brutally, causing her to loose a shriek. "Here I am offering to share, all gentleman-like, and there *you* are, being a rude, condescending so-and-so!"

"It's a hell of a thing to call a man rude when you're dragging a woman around by her hair like that!" Stark thundered. "Let her go!"

The woman chose that moment to rear up like a snake and bite down hard on the gunman's hand. He screamed and released her, stepping back and raising his bleeding hand to examine it. The woman scuttled away and the man turned, leveling his pistol on her.

Stark squeezed the trigger. And nothing happened.

He cursed, tossing the Colt aside. It wasn't the first time in his life a gun had jammed on him, but the event was a rarity. He quickly drew his knife, grasped it by the point, and threw it at the man.

The blade sank into the gunman's shoulder, causing him to drop his iron. By then

Stark had launched himself forward in a cannonball tackle, grasping the varmint around the elbows and waist, and pitching the two of them to the ground. Stark's teeth clinked painfully together as they landed. Then the man beneath him managed to land a punch on Stark's head before the struggle began in earnest.

Both rose to their knees. The knife fell from the man's shoulder and they both grabbed for it, fingers slipping across the blood-moistened handle. The blade evaded both of them, tumbling into a crevice in the ground. They returned to pummeling one another.

Stark blocked an awkward punch, then reared back and brought his forehead down sharply on the bridge of the other man's nose. The man howled and drew away, panting moistly through blood and snot. Stark's hand shot to his neck, finding tendons and squeezing, glorying in the rage and the kill.

The man gagged, hand rising to break the choke hold. Stark gritted his teeth and doubled down, squeezing as hard as he could, his opponent's face widening in a terrifying rictus. It then reddened to a mottled purple until Stark felt something snap between his fingertips and the man sank like a sack full of potatoes.

He was done.

Stark staggered upright and looked around.

The log structure still smoldered moodily. The bodies of dead men lay strewn within and to either side. And huddled together nearby were the woman and her two children. Beyond the wagon lay the body of the dead father and husband, and for that Stark felt terrible sorrow.

"I'm sorry about what happened here," he told the woman. "I'm sorry about what happened to your store. I'm sorry I couldn't get here sooner."

Gratitude welled up in the woman's eyes. She was a plain woman, her face weather-hardened and unadorned with makeup of any kind, yet she was handsome in her way. Strong and kind, Stark suspected. She radiated that kind of light, even amid profound grief.

"We are grateful to you, Mister . . . ?"

"Nathan Stark, ma'am."

"Well, Mr. Stark. My name is Annabelle Reed. And you saved my life and the lives of my children, Steven and Sarah. I can't thank you enough. I know my dear husband would thank you, if he could."

"I'm sorry for your loss, ma'am."

"He was a good man." She fought back

tears. "The least I can do is give him a decent burial."

Chapter 3

They buried Richard Reed a short distance from the store. Stark used Buck to help drag the outlaws' bodies away, then dug Richard's grave while Annabelle gathered her wits and sewed her husband a shroud of burlap. The children fashioned a simple wooden marker — crossed sticks secured by strips of hide. When all this was done, they moved Richard's body and lowered it into the grave.

Stark stood across the mouth of the hole from Annabelle and the two children. At some point in the afternoon, she had produced the family Bible and brought it outside. She flipped it open to a page.

"For none of us liveth to himself, and no man dieth to himself," she read. "For if we live, we live unto the Lord. And if we die, we dieth unto the Lord."

Stark stared out at the horizon, pondering these words. He had seen a great deal of death. The War Between the States had been sufficient to give him a bellyful. But the lawlessness afterward, the skirmishes of the Indian Wars and the endless series of gunfights he had endured both on the plains and upon the unmarked streets of nameless frontier towns, had etched weary lines on his face and on his soul.

Many men had died under the smoke of his gun. Annabelle Reed's words made him wonder how many had lived and died unto the Lord. And if he killed a man who believed, what did that make him? It was a line of reasoning he preferred not to follow too closely. But today the words gave him pause.

"Ashes to ashes," whispered Annabelle, taking up a handful of dirt and scattering it on her husband's shroud. "And dust to dust. From dust we came. And to dust we shall return."

"Amen," said the children.

"Amen," echoed Stark. Then he took up the shovel and proceeded to fill in the grave.

It was always faster to fill one up than dig one out, he thought. But it still took him a good forty minutes to tamp down and smooth out the soil. By the time he was finishing up, the shadows were stretching toward late afternoon. Annabelle Reed appeared in the door of the ruined building wearing an apron.

"Mr. Stark? It's getting on evening and you've been such a help." She smiled. "The least you can do is stay to have supper with us."

Stark didn't particularly want to. But he was moved by the woman's grace and courage. And he figured his continued presence might help the children in this difficult hour. So he took up his hat from where he had left it, put it on his head, and told her yes, ma'am, dinner sounded like a fine idea. He would be only too pleased to sit in, thank ye.

The kitchen was one of the few rooms in the building that had suffered only minimal damage. Although one wall was fire-blackened, the stove and counters gleamed with the care of a woman who took her role as wife and mother seriously. Someone had taken the trouble to gather some wildflowers into a little vase and put it on the table. Places were set at every chair, including the one at the head of the table.

"That was Richard's chair, Mr. Stark," said Annabelle. "We'd be much obliged if you'd take his seat tonight."

Stark was surprised to find himself fighting back a wave of emotion at the prospect.

He swallowed until it was a hard knot in his throat and nodded coolly. "Certainly. I'd be much obliged, ma'am," he said. The boy, Steven, held the chair for him as he sat.

It was a simple meal — rabbit, potatoes, green beans. There was lemonade for the children and a pot of coffee for Annabelle and Stark. Once all this had been brought out and set, Sarah and Annabelle took their places.

"We usually begin our meals by saying grace, Mr. Stark," she said, folding her hands. "I hope you don't object."

"Not at all," he said, pulling his hat from his head and hanging it on the chair back behind him. He wasn't much of a man for religion, but he reckoned words of faith were a comfort to this family just now. He found himself remembering the loss of his own family in Kansas a decade and a half before, how quickly he had forsaken the Gospel words of forgiveness and understanding for vengeance. He wondered how his life might have been had he chosen otherwise.

Annabelle folded her hands, bowed her head, and intoned a simple grace. "For what we are about to receive," she whispered, "may the Lord make us truly thankful."

"Amen," said the children.

"Amen," said Stark. "Let's eat."

Annabelle cracked a bitter smile. "My dear husband used to say the same thing," she chuckled. "Exact same words and all. You'd think men were squeezed out of a mold press."

"I reckon one man's not so different from another," Stark joked back. "And Lord knows, it does a body good to eat."

"That it does," said Annabelle. "Mr. Stark, what brings you out this way? You don't look like a settler or a prospector."

"No, ma'am." Stark accepted the tureen of potatoes from the girl Sarah and spooned a few onto his plate. "I'm employed by the United States Army as a civilian scout. I have been dispatched here at the request of the Indian Agency."

"To help with the war," Annabelle said with a kind of firmness that suggested she did not approve of the strife.

"That's right, ma'am," Stark replied quietly. "To help end it."

"Well . . . I can't say I mind the sound of that." Annabelle's features softened into a sour smile. "Forgive me, Mr. Stark, if I am less than patriotic these days. My family suffered during the War Between the States, and the violence here in Arizona Territory has sometimes been almost as bad. And forgive me — I'm just a woman and all, and don't know much of military matters. But it seems to me that so much of this rage and murder could just as easily have been avoided, if men had put aside their violence and pride for a more humane outcome."

This piqued Stark's interest. "Woman or not, you're entitled to an opinion," he said. "And it sounds like you've given some careful thought to yours. Tell me. How do you see matters?"

Annabelle set down the knife and fork, folded her hands and leaned her chin on them. She sat there for a long moment, studying the children.

"Richard and I came out here from Missouri. We married a few years after the war, but there was still ruin and bad memories all about. We decided to try for a clean slate. We decided to head to the frontier."

"Many folks did."

She nodded. "There was something clean about the promise of the desert. Something pure. It called to us. And many others, I suppose. A great wave of people came out this way. Indians were few and far between in those days. We knew they were out here, but we rarely saw them. And when we did, it was usually the friendly tribes. The Navajo and the Papago. They were good to us.

Some were Christians. We traded and had good relations.

"But then we started hearing about the raids. First the ones in Mexico . . . the missions that were attacked and burned to the ground, the villages that were razed. At first, I thought it was rebels from Mexico. But then we heard the name. *Geronimo.* And we learned his story." She bit her lip. "His family was slaughtered. Like my Richard was slaughtered. I can understand the hate he felt."

Stark, whose family had been killed in a Cheyenne raid on his home in Badger Creek, Kansas, knew a thing or two about nursing hate.

"But the Lord calls on us to forgive." She sighed deeply. "And that's a blessing, Mr. Stark, because hate is a very large load to carry. A very large load, indeed. The burden of Geronimo's hate spilled out onto this land. He and his warriors are like a plague of locusts. They keep to ground until it's time to raid and then they fall like lightning bolts upon the innocent, upon the families living here. His raids are swift and brutal, and his warriors spare no one. Women, children, the old . . . all get slaughtered in an Apache raid."

"But it wasn't the Apache that raided you

here," Stark pointed out. "Who were those men? What brought them here?"

"Them?" To Stark's surprise, Annabelle gave a bitter laugh. "Those are the demon seed, Mr. Stark. They are the children of Geronimo's wrath."

The Apache raids on ranches and villages in the Territory were swift and terrible. And they had unforeseen consequences.

"Some of the settlers began organizing themselves into informal militias to protect against the raids," she went on. "A few were war veterans. Most weren't. And it went about as well as you would expect. Farmers and store-keepers armed with store-bought guns going up against mounted raiding parties of a hundred or more Apaches. It was a slaughter. Farms burned across the Territory.

"Joined together, the surviving militias began marauding across the ruins left by the Apaches. Living off of whatever was left behind. So we call them the marauders. Gangs of dispossessed settlers, raiding and killing each other for the scraps that fall from Geronimo's table. The group that fell on our dry goods store was such a one."

"They come and steal?"

"If it were only theft, that would be fine," she whispered. "But these groups are fueled by whiskey and madness. They're not content to just steal. No, they like to inflict pain. Make people bleed. Destroy their homes and property. The Devil lives in those marauders, Mr. Stark. It's like they're possessed by evil spirits. If you can imagine such a thing."

"I've seen how one candle can light another," Stark admitted. "Doesn't take much. A lit wick touches a dark one. Next thing you know, they're both aflame. Perhaps anger acts the same way."

"Perhaps it does." She took up the tureen of green beans and spooned herself a helping. "So we've got the marauders and the Apache. The two groups feed off of each others' anger and violence. And that's poured fuel on the fires of profit for those who make money from such madness. Gunsmiths. Armorers. Undertakers. Not to mention the bounty hunters."

"You mean freelance law enforcement?"

"There are plenty of them," she admitted. "But no. I'm talking about the bounty set by the U.S. and Mexican governments on Apache scalps."

Stark raised his eyebrows.

"It's true." Her mouth firmed. "You get Mexican soldiers. And American outlaws. Both scouring the Territory for Apaches to waylay and scalp. The government is paying sometimes upward of ten dollars per scalp. Of course, there's no way of proving an individual scalp came from an Apache or a white or Mexican person. So . . ."

"So when the pickings get lean, the scalp hunters will take scalps from whoever is available."

"Yes."

"You enjoying the food, sir?" asked young Steven, looking up at Stark with a shy glance.

"Sure am, sonny." Stark smiled, doing his best to ignore the fact that Steven had black hair. A desperate scalp hunter might get ideas.

He spent the night camped behind the store and saw the family off the next morning, helping to load the wagon, then sitting in the doorway of the ruined store and watching until they vanished into the distance, bound for Tucson.

Incredible, he thought, rising and striding over to where Buck waited, already saddled, by Richard Reed's grave. All the family's effort and passion had ended in this. They had come to the Arizona Territory in search of a clean slate and ended with their father's grave and a burned home.

He looked up. The buzzards were back, circling over this land of death and disappointment.

He took Buck's reins and hoisted himself into the saddle. It was time to ride on.

Chapter 4

By Stark's reckoning, he was within a day's ride of the telegraph station. As he rode, he reflected on the fluid nature of war in the Territory. The tactical situation changed around him daily as raiding parties descended upon helpless settlements, troops were deployed and redeployed, and the massive trains lumbered in and out of their stations, disgorging troops and travelers and supplies for the newly rediscovered frontier. It was, Stark admitted to himself, a very different situation from the War Between the States. Which still haunted him.

He shivered when he thought back on it.

The war against the North had occurred mostly in civilized and populated areas. Cavalry routinely journeyed through cities and towns, bivouacking in farmers' fields, pausing to replenish canteens from public wells, sabotaging railroad tracks in common use by ordinary civilians. That, he reckoned, was what had made the war so terrible — the fact that it was fought in the midst of a settled population. The sight of soldiers had become a workaday reality for the average American. And along with those soldiers had come carnage, murder, and death. Stark had seen his share.

Arizona Territory was different. He could feel it whenever he drew a deep breath of the crisp desert air. There was a newness out here — a virgin quality to the sleeping land, like an infant at rest. It was just waiting for the onrush of civilization. Hell, it was ripe for the plucking!

But that virgin quality was intermixed with a sinister quality. *Like finding a fresh egg in the henhouse and cracking it open to find a snake inside,* he thought.

Annabelle had told him about marauders, gangs of dispossessed settlers, raiding and killing each other over scraps. Stark had seen something similar in the devastated Confederate South. Nothing could grow in those scorched orchards and fields, and brutal gangs of horsemen had ranged across the fire-blackened wasteland. Newly freed blacks were the principal target of these groups, but they would just as readily fall on and lay waste to any homestead or plantation they came across. Fear and hunger did terrible things to people. And war turned them into savages.

One day, Stark reflected, this war would end. Same way the Civil War ended, with the surrender at Appomattox. Stark wondered who would offer that surrender. Because he doubted very much Geronimo ever would. Geronimo would sacrifice everything and never stop fighting until he was either killed or incapacitated. It only remained to be seen how much would burn before then due to the man and his madness.

Stark knew the signs of civilization when he saw them. All those years of riding trail had taught him to pick up on the subtle marks of nearby settlements. Strewn garbage was always the first.

He had visited big cities, of course. Had seen Atlanta before it burned and even visited the Confederate capitol at Richmond. Cities were not for him for many reasons, not least of which was the inevitable congestion of trash choking their perimeters. Something about humans predisposed them to consume and discard everything around them at an alarming pace, all of which spiraled out to the environs. He remembered heaps of garbage piled high on the street corners of Atlanta, and that same impulse lived here on the frontier.

The path he was on widened into an honest-to-God road. At its edges were heaps of discarded newsprint, broken bottles and wagon wheels, rotting apple cores, and empty tins. *Like a road sign saying "civilization ahead,"* he thought bitterly. Around the bend of a curve, a set of railroad tracks appeared, descending toward the cut in which, he was confident, a town awaited him.

And it did. Stark saw the outlines of buildings as he descended into the narrow valley along the road that paralleled the tracks. Chimney smoke sketched the skies, and the streets pulsed with the bustle of humanity. There was no CITY LIMITS sign, nor any indication that the town had a name — and no reason to believe it necessarily had one. Little railroad towns like this popped up all the time alongside the tracks of the various rail carriers. The city dwellers knew well enough to allow the town to succeed or fail before bothering to name it, and this one was no different.

Like any good town, it had a saloon. At this time of day, it wasn't busy. Not by a long shot. Stark tied Buck up at the porch rail, mounted the steps to the batwing doors, and pushed inside.

The large, split-level barroom was empty, the tables clear, the piano in the corner silent. A lone man worked behind the bar. He was a young fellow wearing a white shirt, vest, and string tie. He sported a Vandyke beard and his hair was a little long. The young man looked up, mouth widening in a broad grin as he eyed his first customer of the day.

"Well, lookee here!" His tone, while a bit teasing, contained no malice. "A real live cowboy like you might read about in one of those western dime novels, yes siree."

Stark doffed his hat and set it on the bar. "I don't know about that." He'd seen those tawdry yellow-backed books, the ones that glorified cavalrymen and gunfighters, on the shelves of dry-goods stores and didn't care for the notion. "But I know a thing or two about riding trail. And thirst."

"We have a fine beer on tap," replied the young man, all business now. "It would be my pleasure to offer you a sample."

"Nah. Skip the sample." Stark put a dollar coin on the bar. "Just set me up with a schooner, if you please. And point me toward the outhouse."

"Right through there," the young man said, scooping up the coin and grabbing a mug. "Out the red door. Right behind the building."

"Thanks."

He followed the narrow hallway toward the rear of the saloon. Closed doorways either side: either bedrooms or offices. This didn't look like the sort of place to traffic in soiled doves, but you never knew. Stark didn't aim to stick around long enough to find out. A beer or two, and a meal, and he would be on his way.

The red door opened onto a narrow dirt alley that ran between the rear of the saloon and the wall of a warehouse. Three tired-looking outhouses crouched in the alleyway. Stark was headed toward the middle one when he heard voices.

"*. . . but please don't hurt me!*"

"Shhh!" The sound came out guttural and harsh from a man's throat. "You behave yourself, padre, and there won't be any trouble. You just hand me your coin purse. Nice and easy, now . . ."

Stark stepped around to the rear of the outhouses and saw the source of the noise.

Two men. One, a rotund hombre of late middle age who was dressed in a preacher's cassock, was backed up against the wall of the outhouse, hands high and eyes wide behind his round steel-rimmed glasses, sweat beading on his bald forehead.

Before him stood a long-haired, unshaven pilgrim brandishing a hunting knife. The knife man, too, was sweating, but Stark figured it was the sweat of a man who was long past due for his first drink of the morning. Although the fierce snarl that ringed his face made him look a serious threat, Stark detected a slight tremor in the knife hand.

"Hey," he said.

The man with the knife snapped his gaze around. "Go away," he growled.

Stark ignored this. "You all right there, padre?"

"No!" The preacher's voice was strained with terror. "I'd be much obliged if you'd give me a hand."

"*I said, get lost!*" the man with the knife yelled, whipping around to face Stark, the point of his blade extended. "Get lost, or I'll cut you, too."

In one smooth movement, Stark drew his Colt, cocked it, and aimed right between the man's eyes.

"I'd say if there's anyone getting lost, you're the one to be getting it."

The man's knife point dipped and his shoulders slumped. But a bright edge of defiance glittered in his voice as he snapped, "You'd best be careful, stranger! Ain't no law in this town!"

"So there won't be any consequences if I shoot you dead right here and leave your body for the dogs." Stark smiled coldly. "Nothing would make me happier, pilgrim."

With that, the man backed away, hands raised. When he reached the edge of the buildings, he sheathed his knife, spun around, and sprinted off.

Adams, the preacher, insisted on paying for Stark's drinks and meal.

"Mr. Stark, you are a godsend." Reverend Adams smiled as he watched the barman making Stark's sandwich. "Now be generous with that ham, Mordecai. We got us a godly man here. A friend to the church."

"Dadgummit, padre!" snapped Mordecai. "I been in salooning since I was in knee pants. You stick to preaching and leave the sandwich making to me!"

Stark, who had been called many things in his life but never a godly man, sipped his second beer and looked on with amusement. Soon, Mordecai was lifting a plate heaped with sandwiches and handing it across the bar. Adams took it and led Stark to a table where both sat.

"I can't thank you enough," the preacher said quietly, putting the plate down before Stark. "You saved my bacon. I've been darned lucky the time I've spent in this town. Never came across a cutpurse until today. And I do believe he would have killed me."

"I believe it, too," said Stark, picking up and biting into a ham sandwich. It was good fresh bread, salted ham, and mustard . . . a welcome respite from the blandness of trail food. "He one of those marauders I keep hearing about?"

"One of many." Frustration was plain in Adams's voice. "Murder and misfortune has scattered many a rancher, many a homesteader, to the winds. He's just one."

"In between killer farmers and Apaches, I can't imagine the preaching business is too good in Arizona Territory these days," Stark observed.

"Apaches?" Adams shook his head. "They are a terror, it's true. But we'd be fools if we didn't admit that the white man bears some responsibility for their rage. It was we who came, settled on their land, slaughtered their game, made and then broke promises to them. In a sense, Mr. Stark, the Apache are as much victims of this situation as the marauders."

That kind of talk didn't sit particularly well with Nathan Stark. He hated the redskins with a passion that had only grown since the Cheyenne had slaughtered his own family and taken his little sister Rena. The tribe didn't matter. Cheyenne or Pawnee, Sioux, Kiowa, Apache, or Blackfoot . . . Stark despised them all.

Victims? he thought. *Not likely.* But since the preacher was paying for his lunch, he kept the thought to himself.

"Do you know what's really driving all this?" Adams asked, a serious edge to his voice.

Stark, mouth full of sandwich, shook his head.

"It's commerce." The preacher spread his hands. "Nothing moves faster than the speed of money. That's what's driving this settlement of the West."

Stark couldn't argue with that.

"Love of money makes men do terrible things." Adams gestured toward the outhouses out back. "Whether it's that man with his knife, a railroad tycoon and his empire, or the armies that marched through and laid waste to the South. In the end, it all comes down to greed and money. We're both old enough to have lived through the war and seen terrible things, Mr. Stark. I was at the seminary in Gettysburg when Lee's armies met the Union."

"Did you see any fighting?"

"We stayed inside and prayed," Adams replied. "And when it was over, we came out to help bury the dead. It was the least we could do."

Stark couldn't argue with that, either.

Chapter 5

His sandwiches eaten and his beer swilled down, Stark was glad to mount up and ride out of that town. A quarter mile outside city limits, he paused and turned back to look. The buildings were miniatures from this vantage, and the troubles he had been glad to leave behind now no more than a memory. He thought of Adams, the preacher, and hoped the man with the knife would not return to finish what he had started. As the knife man had noted, there was no law in that town.

Town doesn't even have a name, Stark thought. It occurred to him that you couldn't be sheriff of nowhere. Perhaps, once the town received a name, it would receive the benefit of the law. But until then it would remain a nameless, lawless settlement in the middle of nowhere.

He sighed and turned back to the trail before him. The telegraph station was somewhere up ahead. He had miles to go before he rested.

His trade relied on a combination of skills, knowledge, and applied experience. Luck also played a part. But intuition was the key ingredient.

Stark had always kept a close eye on his feelings. He recognized the value of gut instinct. Out on a trail, miles from the nearest inhabited settlement, a man's ability to sense trouble coming could save his life. Stark's had saved him from scalping, bullets, and once, from being eaten by a bear. He smiled when he remembered the sudden fear and how he had jerked Buck's reins and brought them to a sharp halt just in time to avoid catching the grizzly's eye. Another step and they'd have both become dinner, more than likely.

A similar instinct alerted him now. Something wasn't right. So he reined Buck to a stop, dismounted, and squatted on his haunches, eyes closed, mouth and ears open.

Waiting.

It was the most difficult part of scouting — the need to suddenly pause and do . . . *nothing.* It went against his innermost grain. Stark was a man of action, who faced the world head-on and, when necessary, bent it to his will. To wait and see galled him.

But it was absolutely essential. And, after a half hour or so, it paid off.

It wasn't so much a sound as the suggestion of sound that got him to turn back and examine the trail behind him. The instincts were strong now. There was something . . .

No, some*one*. And after a minute or two of studying the terrain he'd covered, he saw it: for just a moment, the slightest suggestion of rising dust. It stopped abruptly as if some rider were keeping an eye on him and timing his own journey and breaks to coincide with Stark's.

He watched the place where the ghost dust trail had been. When he saw no sign of its return, he mounted and continued on his way. After a stretch, he paused and turned to see it rising again.

So. He had a shadow.

Who could it be?

Stark had enemies. But most of them were back in plains country or down south. It had to be somebody from the town he had just left. Either that or the marauders he'd killed back at the Reeds' place had friends. There was no way to be sure until he learned more about the man following him.

Stark varied his own speed and the tempo

of his breaks, studying the effect on the man behind. Stark tested the man, stopping several times in the course of an hour. The horseman paused swiftly each time, obviously monitoring the plume of dust Buck kicked up and responding to it smartly. Whoever this tracker was, he was good.

Very good, Stark thought. He was now convinced that the man following him was a professional.

The alternative was that his pursuer — and he was now certain there was just one — could be an Apache. It was possible that the Apaches had lone scouts working the areas near town, seeking lone riders and lightly defended wagons for plunder. Maybe there was some signal they could give off, a bird call or some such, that would alert others to the quarry's presence.

Either that or he's watching me as I ride into some ambush that's already been laid.

Although he was not on a formal road, he was following a worn path through the desert. Goat paths, folks sometimes called them. It could be that many a rider had met his doom in an ambush along this road. Stark considered his options.

He saw hills up ahead, perhaps a mile or more away. If an ambush was planned, that would be the place for it. Given the obvious skill and patience of the tracker behind him, Stark had to take some sort of action. *But what?*

Then, with a smile, he remembered Ben.

Ben had been the best hunting dog his father had ever owned. As a youngster, he and Ben had been inseparable. Stark had spent many a pleasant afternoon in the dog's company, rambling all around the woods near Badger Creek. Stark reckoned he had learned a lot from Ben about tracking, having seen the big shaggy mutt with his nose to the ground day after day. Until the day of the rabbit.

Ben had spotted the bunny and lunged after him at a rate of speed that seemed physically impossible for such a large creature. Stark hadn't even bothered trying to chase Ben but had merely stood and watched as the dog disappeared into the underbrush, baying for all he was worth. Stark remembered listening to those barks disappear into the distance as the rabbit reappeared, circling back to the exact spot where he'd been when Ben sighted him.

Rabbit, rabbit, Stark thought with a chuckle, and turned off the trail.

His stalker turned off, too.

Stark knew that if he urged Buck into a

gallop, that would increase the dust cloud raised by his hooves. The man behind him would know immediately and speed up. The best thing was to look for an area of rock across which he and Buck could traverse in their journey. Tracks that suddenly disappeared would only add to the stalker's confusion and buy them valuable time.

Rabbits were not dumb creatures. The ease with which that one snow-white bunny had evaded old Ben back in the day was telling. But Stark supposed that if you were born without teeth, claws, or horns, all you had to fall back on was speed and brains. And that rabbit had led that poor dog on a wild-goose chase that lasted all afternoon. Stark intended to do something similar to whoever was on his trail.

Their travels brought them to an arroyo. Stark slipped down from the saddle and guided Buck by the reins down the shallow, rocky incline to the riverbed. The sand here was cut by scores of rocks and pebbles — not quite enough to hide their tracks completely, but sufficient to obscure them. Once they reached the center of the riverbed, Stark remounted and put the spurs to Buck's sides.

A professional tracker, he thought. And shook his head. Who would go to the expense of hiring a professional tracker to stalk him? The man in town whom he'd stopped from robbing Adams was a low-class thief, hardly the sort with pockets deep enough to pay the fee of a man in Stark's class. No, this was something else.

He halted Buck again. Turned.

The damn plume was still on his trail!

He spurred Buck on and began enumerating enemies. With the exception of one or two men a thousand miles away, none were wealthy enough to hire someone that good. Stark began to wonder if perhaps some fellow army scout might have it in for him. But that seemed even more unlikely. He tended to be on good terms with men of his profession and military men in general. No, this was something different. Unusual!

Very unusual indeed.

The arroyo curved around in an S-shape. At its middle, the shallow banks abutted a field of stone. Judging that to be perfect, Stark dismounted again, grasped Buck's reins, and led him up the bank. Then he mounted again and kept riding, Buck's hooves clippity-clopping across the rock.

Something caught his attention ahead. Narrowing his eyes, he scanned the terrain, sensing that something about the desert ahead wasn't quite right. He tried putting his finger on it . . .

No . . .

But the notion evaded him until he recognized —

It can't be!

A series of furrows split the landscape. Perfect, straight furrows. Someone had tried plowing the soft ground at the edge of the rocks! Stark reined to a full stop, disbelief in his eyes.

Furrows? He squinted at the roughened ground. *Neat and straight ones, too. Someone tried to cultivate this land.*

But who?

In the distance, he spied the skeletal remains of a fence. He nudged Buck forward. The horse's progress through the tilled desert kicked up huge clouds of dust. These died down when they reached the edge of the field, where the ground changed. Now they were on untilled sand and rock. And staring at the edge of what had once been — a sheep pen?

The area had all the hallmarks of a farm. Or more precisely, a *failed* farm. In the middle distance was a busted wagon, the sort used to haul bales of hay.

And beyond it, a house. But Stark could tell, even at this distance, it was more of a ruin than a house. He rode up to it and paused, studying the walls and frame.

Someone had taken the trouble to bring building materials out here. There was a quantity of brick and cut stone that made up the front wall of the place. The rest had been done in wood. Mesquite, from the look of it. Old, dry, rotten mesquite that had proven poor construction material. Part of the wooden wall had fallen down. Stark dismounted and climbed the porch steps to the empty doorway for a look inside.

A rocking chair, facing a tumbledown fireplace, occupied what was left of the front room. Someone had loved that chair. Stark could tell. It bore the weariness and wear of a piece of furniture that had been dragged around for much of someone's life. The fireplace itself was made of adobe and stone. The remains of the last fire lay in the grate, covered by material from the partially collapsed flue. Stark went to examine the rest of the house.

One small bedroom was still intact. A wooden bed frame sat in the middle of the room, a corral for cobwebs. The mattress was gone. The kitchen lay open to the elements, its roof dilapidated. The iron box of the woodstove was still in place but the flue and doors were missing. A worktable and one set of cabinets ran along what was left of one wall. The other lay crumbled on the floor, and the back of the room was a scatter of wood and stone on the desert floor outside. Stark returned to the front room and peered out the front door.

There he is.

The distant plume of a single rider continued to approach. Whoever he was, he had managed to track Stark down the arroyo and across the field of stone to this ruined farm. So be it. Stark would make his stand here.

He went out and grasped Buck's reins, guiding him around the rear of the house and in through the broken back wall of the kitchen. Stark put out some feed for Buck, drew his pistol, and waited.

Chapter 6

Whoever he is, thought Stark, *he's good.*

The tracker was patient. It was the most important element in their particular line of work, and the man on Stark's tail had it in spades. The plume of dust continued to approach until late afternoon, at which point it stopped. How far had he come? Had he reached the stretch of furrowed desert? Stark didn't think so — the plumes weren't yet high and wide enough — but he couldn't be sure. Nevertheless, as shadows lengthened, the plume stopped and with it all traces of the tracker's progress.

Stark sat watching for a full hour before deciding it was time to see to his supper needs. He had water and dried hardtack in his saddlebags. He checked on Buck as he went to retrieve them. The horse had eaten his fill of oats and now snoozed in a standing position, rousing himself to whinny as Stark approached.

"I'd like to unsaddle you, too, Buck." He retrieved the foodstuffs from the saddle and passed a soothing hand along Buck's withers. "But I need you primed and ready, in case we need to make a fast getaway."

Buck sighed, whinnied, and stamped as if he were saying: *Okay, boss. I don't like it, but okay.*

Stark took the hardtack and canteen into the front room and resumed his seat at the observation post by a break in the wall. The dinner hour was approaching and the sun was well advanced in the west. Another hour would bring dusk. He would have to decide what to do once it got dark. Then an uncomfortable thought occurred to him.

What if that rider out there is an Apache?

No particular reason to assume he was. No particular reason to believe he was not.

Stark's dealings with the Apache had been rare and always at a distance. He knew a half dozen savage dialects. His knowledge and understanding of native ways was deep enough that he could easily hold his own among a discussion of learned academics on the topic. He was, after all, a hunter of Indians. And like any hunter, he knew his prey.

The Apache were a different breed. The word itself brought images to mind of blurred riders moving at lightning-fast speeds. Apache were born to the saddle. They were expert horsemen and hunters, and fearless in battle. In their war against the white settlers, the Apache were known to be particularly ruthless and cruel. In the plains wars between cavalry and mounted war parties, there was a tacit understanding that women and children were to be spared slaughter. Not so with the Apache. Under Geronimo's iron fist, they had taken to slaughtering anything and anyone in their path. Accounts of the raids and their aftermath were fearsome, blood-drenched stories indeed. It was as if the tribe delighted in practices that were insane, chilling, and devilish. What men behaved in that way?

Savages in the truest sense of the word, he thought.

He looked up.

Night was coming.

The tracker waited until the last few minutes before sunset to reveal himself.

It had been several hours since the last sign of a dust plume. Stark was still sitting at his post by the ruined wall of the front room, eyes back in the direction from which he had come. He intended to wait until deep dusk, the last few moments of daylight, to slip out with Buck and make off.

That's when he saw it.

The edge of the furrowed field was the visible horizon line from Stark's position. For hour upon fruitless hour, he had watched it, waiting for a streamer of dust. His eyes had begun to water and he had just blinked away the moisture when he saw a dark dot shift on the horizon.

There!

The scout had obviously dismounted and crawled to the edge of the field for a look-see. The shape of his head, just a dark smudge at this distance, appeared briefly and shifted from side to side before dropping back below the horizon line.

He's spotted the fence. And this place, Stark thought. To his mind, there was now no doubt the tracker would come in for a closer look. He scanned the sky to the east. The moon was already starting to climb and it was three-quarters full. It would shed ample light on the plain between the furrows and the front porch. That's when Stark decided to start setting up an ambush of his own.

He slipped away from his post and back to the kitchen where Buck snoozed. He watered and fed the horse and finally unsaddled him. He lay the packs, saddle, and blanket to one side and gave Buck's coat a quick hand brush. Buck whinnied, stamped, and shook himself — an equine expression of gratitude for the unburdening. Stark helped himself to more hardtack and a few more sips of water before returning to the front room.

The most dangerous time would be in the interval between sunset and full night. Then the dark plain between the furrows and the house would be entirely without light. Stark felt sure that was when his mysterious companion would make a move.

But to his surprise, the man stood upright, silhouetted against the dimming sky.

Stark's eyes crept to the Springfield 73 propped in the corner where the wall met the edge of the fireplace. He could easily put a bullet in his pursuer at this range. But if he did, he would be losing out on an opportunity to find out who the tracker was and why he had been sent after Stark.

Shooting him would be the simple solution, he thought. *Harder by far to take him alive, but that would be the wiser choice.*

It wouldn't be easy. But chances were if he did, he would save himself a big peck of trouble in the days ahead.

Now the man was advancing on horseback across the plain to the house.

Stark withdrew into the shadows and waited.

From the tracker's standpoint, the house must have looked deserted. Stark smiled tightly as he watched the man advance across the field, pleased with himself for having pulled off the ruse. The tracker must have first concluded that Stark had taken refuge inside. And then, when prolonged observation failed to verify this assumption, he had likely begun to panic, figuring Stark had slipped away at some point during the afternoon.

He's figuring he'll come here and see for himself, Stark thought. *And if I'm gone, he'll be fixing to bed down in here for the night before traveling on.*

Stark checked the man's progress. He was about halfway across the plain now, just minutes from arrival. Stark took that opportunity to slip into the kitchen and rouse Buck. Gently taking the reins, he guided the horse out behind the structure and tied him to a fencepost before returning indoors. Full dark was coming now. And the tracker was near. Stark took up his Springfield and withdrew into the bedroom.

He could hear the jangle of the man's horse tack, then the slow and steady tread of hooves. At length, the tracker reined in, and his horse sighed and stamped as he dismounted. Stark cocked his ears and heard no answering noise from Buck. He didn't need that kind of bad luck fouling the pitch.

Footsteps. The tracker had come up onto the porch. A shadow loomed in the break in the wall. He had arrived.

Stark watched.

The man moved with preternatural care, pausing at the door to scan the front room. He was a well-built man with a gun on his hip and a rifle in his hand. Beyond that, Stark could not tell much. But he appreciated the man's patience. For he remained in the doorway for a full minute. Two. Then he moved stealthily across the threshold, taking in the room from a closer vantage. For a full minute. Two.

This hombre is cautious, Stark thought. *Almost as cautious as an Indian.*

The tracker advanced into the front room, pausing by the rocking chair before the fireplace. He knelt, reached out, and placed his hand on the seat.

Checking for warmth, Stark thought. He would have done likewise.

Now he was coming toward the bedroom. Stark breathed in and rotated his body a few degrees to the left, bringing him out of the man's line of sight and just to one side of the doorway.

The footsteps came closer. Then stopped.

He was only a few feet away now.

Stark heard clothes rustle, a strange rattling, and then the familiar scratch of a wooden match against a striking pad. A glow blossomed in the front room. The stranger was approaching the open doorway. As he had with the front door, he paused on the threshold. And waited.

Stark held his breath.

A full minute. Two . . .

The man stepped forward, his arms extended, a lit match cupped in one hand and shielded by the other.

Stark moved.

He body-slammed the man the second he walked through the door. Stark's shoulder caught him just below the left armpit, driving him back against the wall. The man slammed into the mesquite there with a roar of pain. As he turned to fight back, Stark raised the Springfield to deal a blow to the side of his head, but the tracker anticipated him.

Ducking low, he charged Stark, catching him about the waist and tackling him to the floor. The Springfield clattered away. Blows rained down from the tracker, fast, hard punches to Stark's head and neck. He covered up, kicked free, then kicked out.

His bootheel caught the stranger in the stomach, stunning and driving him backward through the door into the front room. Then Stark was on his feet, surging forward, reaching out and grasping the man by the lapels of his jacket just as the moon slid into place, beaming a shaft of silver into the room through the ruined roof.

Stark stopped.

"Red Buffalo?"

"Well, who did you think it was?"

Stark immediately let go and stepped back. "You shouldn't sneak up on me like that, you dumb Indian!"

"And you should be a little more hospitable to your guests." The Crow scout retrieved his old high-crowned hat where it had fallen. Taking care to ensure its eagle feather plume was unhurt, he clapped it back on his head and looked around. "Nice place you got here."

Stark's lips flattened in embarrassed amusement as the moon's brightness grew, banishing shadows from the room. He had first met Moses Red Buffalo at Fort Randall, under Colonel Ledbetter. With his loincloth and leggings, creased hat and two long braids, he was every inch the savage Indian. The two men had hated each other on sight but, over the course of numerous postings together, had learned to get along. Stark had cultivated a grudging admiration for Red Buffalo's instincts, skills as a tracker, tenacity, and courage. He was a scout of rare skill and a valuable asset to the U.S. Army.

"Why are you following me?" Stark stood back to give Red Buffalo some room.

"Wasn't sure it was you." The Crow scout dusted himself off. "I thought I saw you in that town back there. I have orders to get to a telegraph station near Tubac and I thought perhaps you were doing the same thing. Either that . . . or you were someone else tracking Nathan Stark and meant him harm."

"So you kept an eye on me." Despite himself, Stark was moved by Red Buffalo's gesture. "You closed in to make sure I wasn't a hostile bent on harming the famous Indian killer."

"Pretty much."

"You were aiming to save my life."

Red Buffalo winced and flexed his shoulder where Stark had struck him. "Which may turn out to be one of my bigger mistakes," he said.

Chapter 7

"What are you doing out here?" Stark asked.

Beans bubbled in a cook pot on the small fire Red Buffalo had built out in front of the cabin. The two men sat on nearby stumps, sipping coffee. Buck and the Indian's horse grazed nearby. The moon washed the desert in silver.

Red Buffalo seemed to hesitate before speaking, which was uncharacteristic. And the words, when they came, were even more so. "It's . . . complicated."

"Think I'm too simple to understand?" Stark smirked as he needled his old partner.

"Most white men are."

"Very funny." Stark shook his head and studied the stars. "I know you're not too fond of non-Indians. But we've known each other for a long while now. Try me."

Red Buffalo heaved a huge sigh.

"I came here . . . on a spiritual quest." He

seemed to be groping for the right words, anxious to not be misunderstood. "Things are happening in the red man's world right now that you don't know about. That *no* white man knows about. Very serious things."

"So tell me."

"I will try, Nathan Stark." Red Buffalo poured himself another cup of coffee and studied its rippling surface where it sloshed in his mug. "Some of what I say may sound strange. But it is relevant to the war against the Apache. And our shared journey to the telegraph station."

Stark shrugged. "I've heard plenty of strange yarns in my day."

Red Buffalo's eyes pierced him. "These are serious matters," he said in a warning tone Stark had rarely heard him use before. "Very serious to Indian people."

And while he told his story, Stark listened and did not say a word.

Red Buffalo first heard of the Prophet not long after he and Stark last parted ways.

"I made the decision to leave the white man's world for a spell," he began. "The world of towns and forts and cavalrymen. It has been a generous world to me. The money has been good. And I have made some . . . interesting friends." He smiled at Stark. "But it's probably hard for you to understand that for an Indian person, spending lots of time around whites can be draining. We sometimes need to go and refresh ourselves among our own kind. And that's what I decided to do last time we waved good-bye and rode in separate directions."

Red Buffalo had ridden deep into the plains, far away from the nearest settlements and towns. He had pitched camp in the middle of nowhere and simply spent a week by himself.

"I reacquainted myself with the spirits of the land," he explained. "To the Crow — to most Indian people — the land and the creatures that dwell on it are our relations. Man was put here amongst the splendor. Becoming a Christian did not change this relationship for me. It made it stronger."

Stark remembered that Red Buffalo had converted to Christianity in his youth, as a result of time spent at a mission. The priests there had tagged the "Moses" moniker onto his Indian name. Stark had to admit the Crow cleaved harder to the Good Book and its instructions than most white men he knew. But Red Buffalo remained Indian to the core.

"Those days I spent under the sky, praying and fasting. They helped me reconnect to my spirit. And to the good Lord above. I was alone in my camp for seven days. When visitors finally came, I took it as a sign. Two brothers rode into my camp. Lakota men. Sioux from the Plains. I shared my coffee and tobacco with them, and they told me about the Prophet. They said they were going to see him. I was curious, so they told me about him."

The frontier was changing. Everybody knew it. From the settlers and townsmen out west to the native people and immigrants, it was obvious that the forces of civilization were redefining everything they touched. The world of yesterday was slipping away, becoming more modern and mechanized. The old ways were vanishing.

For the native tribes, it meant being forced onto reservations. It meant the restriction of hunting and fishing, and the depletion of their usual sources of sustenance. It meant an end to their way of life.

Indians had fought the whites since their arrival. Wars, small and large, had raged across the continent but had done nothing to slow the march of "progress." It seemed that no matter what path of resistance Indian people took, it proved fruitless in protecting their traditional ways.

The Prophet had arisen among the Paiute — people of the desert land. The Paiute, like the Hopi and Yaqui, were recognized among the other tribes as having a special connection to the world of spirit, to the mystical world. So it was unsurprising that the Prophet would be of those people.

"What *was* surprising to me was that he spoke of Jesus," Red Buffalo said. "The Prophet claimed that a Day of Judgment was coming for the white man. That our prayers and dances would cause the dead to rise and lead a war against the Great White Father in Washington. The buffalo would return to the Plains. All would be as it had been before. These words were powerful. I had to learn more."

Red Buffalo had broken camp to ride with the Sioux brothers into the desert territories to the west. The journey had taken several weeks during which they occasionally paused in the villages of other tribesmen.

There, Red Buffalo learned the extent to which the Prophet's words were influencing the lives of the Indian people. The Prophet's words had extended far beyond the borders of the desert and struck a chord among all those dissatisfied with the world the white man was bringing to the frontier.

It was in one such village that Red Buffalo had been invited to a very unusual church service. To his surprise, the people of that tribe were Christian. But once the service began, he could tell there were important differences between the religion they practiced and the Christianity he had been taught at the mission.

"The Prophet's teachings about Jesus had found a home among these people," he said. "I was told before going in that we would have Communion. But it was going to be different from ordinary Communion. And it was. Instead of bread and wine, we were given peyote . . . the flesh of the gods, as it's traditionally known. But here it was blessed by the priest and given as the body and blood of Jesus. Peyote is a powerful drug, one that takes you out of your body and makes you see visions. It was a very powerful experience for me. The two Lakota brothers and I spoke about it at length afterward. For many days, during our journey west, we spoke about what we had seen and what it might mean. They were not Christian, but I taught them about the Gospel and explained what the peyote experience had meant for me."

At length, they entered the Arizona Territory. The results of the Apache Wars were immediately apparent. The misery that had been inflicted upon the people, both white and Indian, was massive.

More signs of "progress."

"We came across Apaches. Not in great numbers. But here and there on the trail, we would cross paths. I heard a great deal about Geronimo, much more about him than about the Prophet. He is like a god to some of the Apache. As it turns out, he does not believe in the Prophet. He rejects the peyote teachings, because they are mixed with Christianity, and Geronimo hates the religion of the white man.

"My last night with the two brothers was at a gathering of the Prophet's followers. The Prophet was not there himself. He had gone on a mission to visit the tribes in the White Mountains. But his people made their observances. The peyote was shared and we danced the Ghost Dance, which is the Prophet's gift to the people. The Prophet claims that the dance will bring back the buffalo and the ancestors. I danced, too. But for the glory of the Lord. Said my goodbyes and journeyed to Tucson."

"So Geronimo opposes the Prophet," said Stark at last.

"And he is an enemy of Jesus," Red Buffalo said gravely. "Which makes him my enemy."

They saddled up and lit out at dawn, opting to ride together toward their common destination. It was both odd and comforting for Stark to have his old partner by his side here in Arizona Territory. Their previous scouting assignments had been for commands further north and east. In that, Red Buffalo had provided useful knowledge and contacts. But out here he was as much an alien as Stark himself.

The road to Tubac was really just a sketch in the desert sand. Rough going, even on horseback. But just how rough it could be was soon obvious. An hour out, they spotted a shape by the roadside ahead. From a distance, Stark recognized the wheels and canopy of a covered wagon. As they drew closer, he could see the wheels were broken and the canopy torn. Arrows pockmarked the side of the box.

"Apaches," said Red Buffalo gravely. He drew up beside the wagon and dismounted. Stark watched him touch the arrows gently, leaning in to examine their feathers and decorative markings. "These are hunting arrows," he added. "The braves must have been out chasing down something to eat when they came across this family."

Stark followed Red Buffalo's gaze to the bodies of three people about a hundred yards off. Judging from the appearance and smell, they had been dead about a month — a man, woman, and little girl. An arrow protruded from the woman's neck.

"Seems these Apache wage war a little differently from Indians back east," Stark said dryly, tilting his chin at the dead family. "Dead women? Children? That's not something I've seen terribly often. They're usually taken." He swallowed, forcing down a feeling of despair when he thought of his little sister, Rena, who was three when she was taken by the Cheyenne.

Red Buffalo stepped around the edge of the wagon to study the bodies. "Not all Apaches are like this," he said. "But the ones who run with Geronimo? They kill everything they come across. Men. Women. Children. Livestock. And anything they can't kill, they burn to the ground."

Stark's jaw firmed. "Butchers," he whispered. "Filthy damn butchers. They're insane."

"They are possessed," Red Buffalo said, correcting him. "You know Geronimo isn't just a war chief."

"Oh?"

"He is also a medicine man. A sorcerer of great power." The Crow scout removed his hat and studied it. "They tell stories about his powers. How he can change shape. Summon rain. One story is that he and his people were crossing a valley in the darkness, using the shadows to hide from cavalry. They were only halfway across when the sun started to rise. Geronimo sang a spell that held the dawn back. Allowed his people to escape."

"That's a hell of a story."

"Hell is exactly the right word." Red Buffalo mounted his horse. "For a man to have that kind of power, he has to make a deal with the Devil. These men we will be fighting are in his thrall. You would do well to remember that when we face them in battle."

Chapter 8

They left the family's bodies as they found them. Stark was loathe to do so, but Red Buffalo reminded him that any disturbance of the scene would be a signal to passing Apaches that intruders had entered their territory. Downright uncivilized though it was, they rode on and did not give the dead so much as a glance back.

They did not notice the war party shadowing them until an hour later.

It was Red Buffalo who sensed them first.

The path had narrowed and Stark had pulled slightly ahead to go in single file. Then he noticed a change in the cadence of the horses' hooves and glanced back. Red Buffalo had reined to a stop and was sitting, eyes closed and head cocked, in the middle of the trail.

He was noticing something. Stark knew the signs.

The Crow scout dismounted swiftly, knelt, and flattened his palm against the ground. He drew three deep breaths, exhaled, and pressed his ear to the dirt where his hand had been. A few moments later, he raised his head.

"We are being followed. I am sure of it." He rose to his feet, brushed off his leggings, and remounted the saddle. "A small group. Maybe five, six."

Stark knew better than to be dismissive of Red Buffalo's warnings. The man could scout and track game like there was no tomorrow. And his tricks and sixth sense were rarely wrong.

Stark looked around.

"This way," he said, nudging Buck forward.

He had suspected something was up for the past quarter mile or so. He couldn't put his finger on it, but if he thought hard he could recall shapes in the landscape — scars that he recognized from his days serving the Confederacy. Rail tracks of various gauges were critical to the war effort. The laying down and tearing up of same was a strategic game played by both sides. There were tracks for commercial rail and those for —

His eyes narrowed.

"You see that?" He reined Buck in and

pointed, turning back over his shoulder to Red Buffalo. "You see that thin path? The one that starts partway up the hill?"

Red Buffalo followed Stark's finger to the stony hillock before them. "Yes," he said after a time. "Looks . . . old."

"I'd say so." Stark narrowed his eyes, mouth firming. "I've got a hunch. And it might serve us well under present circumstances."

"I hope so." Red Buffalo pointed back over his shoulder. "Look."

Stark did. And saw dust plumes rising from the desert hills behind them. The Crow's warning had been accurate. There were riders coming, closing in fast.

Stark urged Buck to circle around the base of the hill. Just as the trail behind them fell out of sight, the sound of the approaching riders could be heard in the distance. Stark's gut instinct had kicked in, and not a moment too soon.

If I'm right about this, we should see signs of excavation somewhere around . . .

There.

Two piles of rock lay partially buried in stony sand. To the untrained eye, it was just an outcropping. But climbing over it and descending a short distance down the gully beyond revealed what Stark had suspected all along.

"Now that's a neat trick," Red Buffalo said. "Hiding tiny little railroad tracks like that in plain sight. Even I didn't see them."

The clatter of hooves was filling the air behind and below them, strong in the heated air and getting louder with each passing minute.

Stark guided his horse down to the narrow-gauge tracks used for rolling ore cars in and out of mines. These had been disused, allowed to rust over for two decades, at least. But they curved around the base of the hillock and disappeared into a low tunnel cut into the side of some cliffs. They had left no hoofprints getting up here. And likewise left none traveling along the tracks.

"Come on," Stark said.

They went single file into the tunnel, which rose to a comfortable ceiling just beyond the entrance. They dismounted and secured their mounts to a rusty ore car near the tunnel mouth. Then they stepped to the edge of the tunnel mouth and listened.

The Apache scouts were coming hard now. A young group. Stark could tell by the fury of their movements, the high-pitched *yips* and arguing voices. Red Buffalo recognized this at the same moment his eyes met

Stark's, and they shared a rueful smile. Both shook their heads as if to say, *Yeah, that was us once, too.*

The group of Apaches came to a sudden stop somewhere along the trail. From the other side of the hill, the sounds of their voices rose. And rose even more as they recognized their quarry had suddenly vanished. They began to disagree heatedly about how to proceed.

"You speak any Apache?" Stark asked.

"A little." Red Buffalo shrugged. "Not enough to really carry on a conversation. But I recognize some of the words. One they keep repeating means *stupid.* And the other is a nasty swear word that I bet those boys never use around their grandmothers."

The commotion just out of sight continued, grew — and then abruptly subsided. Someone with an authoritative voice was talking now. When he was finished, Stark heard horses break off in different directions. One group forged ahead, while the other headed back down the trail the way they had come.

"Splitting up," Red Buffalo observed.

"And no sign they ever spotted the tracks." Stark sighed and removed his Stetson, running fingers through thick black hair. "We should be okay in here for now. Let's stay until nightfall. If they're not back by then, we'll light a shuck."

Red Buffalo agreed. They watered the horses, ate some rations, and settled down to rest a while before pressing on.

Red Buffalo found a rusty oil lantern with some fluid still inside and set a wooden match to the lantern's wick. He reset the glass shield and tapered the flame with a twist of the wick wheel. "What do you suppose they mined in here?"

"I think they did a lot of copper out this way," Stark replied, looking around. Abandoned ore cars and mining equipment lay scattered about. Whoever had been working the claim had left in an awful hurry.

"You know, it's worth considering whether or not we're the only ones in here," Red Buffalo pointed out. "Obviously, humans haven't been here in a while."

"So you're thinking . . . ?"

"Could be someone moved in." The Crow shrugged. "We should check."

"That's not a bad idea, actually."

They rose and moved deeper into the tunnel, Red Buffalo in the lead, with the lantern held aloft in one hand, his Henry rifle in the other. Stark brought up the rear, his Colt drawn, thumb caressing the hammer as he crept along behind the Crow.

Slowly, they inched inward and downward as the angle of the ground tilted, angling more steeply now. Red Buffalo paused and held his lantern high.

"I can't see anything for dozens of yards. Any animal that would use the shaft as a home would remain closer to the entrance. It's an instinct. We can probably turn back now."

"Fine by me." Stark's hand fell to the lip of an ore car's bucket. "Wouldn't mind being able to take one of these back."

"Lazy white man. We Indians walk all the time."

"And you still would if we hadn't taught you how to ride."

Red Buffalo laughed aloud as he stepped past Stark, heading back toward the surface. "Who taught who to ride? That's a ridiculous claim you make, Nathan Stark. If it wasn't for we Indian people, you would have all starved to death that first winter on Plymouth Rock."

"I suppose that's true," Stark allowed. "But the hospitality sure didn't last long."

Red Buffalo answered with a surly grunt, marching on toward the place where they'd tied the horses. When they stepped back up to level ground and Buck's flank appeared in the lantern's glow, he doused the wick and walked on in the half light of the tunnel's entrance. Then he came to an abrupt stop.

"What — ?"

"Shhh . . ."

Stark kept his eye on the distant entrance. It was an arch of light against the interminable black of the hill's interior. But it was flickering. Wavering. As if someone were passing a hand in front of it. He heard the echoed crunch of distant footsteps.

Red Buffalo reached out, grasping Stark's sleeve and guiding them through the dark toward the entrance. The steps outside were louder now, the light from outdoors more distinct. Red Buffalo drew them to within one hundred feet of the entrance and paused, hunkering down and drawing Stark with him. They knelt, shrouded in shadows, as a man entered the tunnel.

In the brief glimpse they had of him in sunlight, Stark saw the details of their visitor. His face was blackened to a coal darkness by war paint, the only brightness a ribbon of white encircling each eye and the mouth. He was sinewy and muscled, his chest and belly covered with a bone breastplate, a war fetish girdling his neck. He held a bow taut with a nocked arrow as he advanced into the cave.

He took two steps inside, then stopped abruptly.

He smells the horses, Stark thought.

As if on cue, Buck stamped and whinnied. The Apache put up his bow and spoke tentatively into the dark. Both horses shifted. The man advanced down the tracks until he was swallowed by shadows.

Stark felt Red Buffalo tug on his sleeve. They crept forward, keeping to the ore car tracks, careful to avoid crunching gravel or sand. The Apache scout, meanwhile, had reached the horses and was examining them by touch. Stark could see his outline against the tunnel mouth, which loomed large in the middle distance.

All at once, Red Buffalo sprang.

The Apache youth was taken completely by surprise. He cried out in fear and rage the second before Red Buffalo tackled him to the ground. Stark grabbed up the lantern, struggling with a match. A moment later, he was able to light the wick and a globe of gold filled the tunnel.

Red Buffalo and the Apache kid were rolling together on the ground, grunting and punching at each other. The kid rolled on top and tried to untangle himself, but the old Crow scout kept a hold of the boy, who spat and cursed in Apache. Red Buffalo would not let go. He finally managed to get the kid facedown and mounted him from behind, twisting his arm up until he cried out.

"You speak English?" Red Buffalo asked.

The kid replied with an indignant stream of Apache. Stark thought he might recognize some of those words Red Buffalo said were not to be used before the grandmothers.

"He no speakee English," sighed Red Buffalo.

"He's probably got a horse." Stark tipped his chin back at the tunnel entrance. "Out there."

"Probably." The Crow began tying the Apache kid's wrists together with a length of twine. "Why don't you go fetch it in while I make our guest comfortable?"

Stark did. The Apache war pony grazed by the side of the road where Stark and Red Buffalo had first heard the oncoming warriors. Stark took the reins and guided the obedient little mount over and around the pile of tailings, and along the track into the tunnel's mouth. He returned to find Red Buffalo standing guard over a trussed-up, sulking Apache warrior.

"Nice little pony," Stark said. "And he's got two panniers loaded with fresh food." He nodded at the kid. "His misfortune is our good luck."

"Two panniers full?" Red Buffalo smiled. "We'll make sure none of it goes to waste."

Chapter 9

"Strange trees," said Red Buffalo.

"What's that?" Stark, riding a dozen yards ahead on the trail, was scanning the road ahead.

"Those are some strange trees." Red Buffalo's voice had taken on a teasing tone. "They have no branches. And spin webs like spiders."

"What kind of nonsense — ?" Stark raised his eyes then laughed. "Oh, I see."

They had left the kid trussed up in the tunnel, his horse tied to an ore car. That was yesterday. Now just dimly visible in the distance, a line of telegraph poles sketched the horizon. Stark studied them. He recognized the telegraph wires as the gossamer black threads connecting the Arizona Territory to civilization. Their presence was a sign that Man was coming, and decisively.

"There it is," he chuckled. "The modern Pony Express."

"Pony Express wasn't so bad." Red Buffalo shrugged. "They were useful, in their way. They often brought news from other territories. And they kept us in touch with others who resist the strange trees. Not everybody appreciates the Black Wire."

"Aw, give it time, Red Buffalo." Stark nudged Buck back into motion. "You savages will eventually adapt to the wonders of the modern world."

"We already have." It was Red Buffalo's turn to chuckle. "The last two hundred years have been an education in adapting to white men and their ways. No, I have no problems with the Black Wire. But the Amish do."

"Eh?" Stark frowned. "You mean those German Anabaptists? The ones settled back east?"

"Yes." Red Buffalo sounded surprised. "You've never spoken with them?"

"Can't say as I have." Stark frowned. The telegraph poles were now sharply visible against the landscape. "They keep to themselves."

"That's why we like them."

"You mean the Crow?"

"Most of their native neighbors like them fine," Red Buffalo replied. "They have always refused to fight against us. They would rather negotiate and forgive. Amish farmers cultivate side-by-side with Indians in some areas of the country."

Stark raised his eyebrows, surprised. He had not known this.

"They resist new things," Red Buffalo was saying. "They distrust steam machines. And telegraph machines. They believe the simple ways of farming and logging and building community on the land are God's way. They're sort of like us Indians, in that sense."

"Well, America is a free country," Stark replied. "Reckon people can choose to forgo modern conveniences if that's to their liking. In a free country, people can live however they like."

"Unless they're Indians."

Stark drew in a breath to argue, then thought better of it. Red Buffalo did seem to have a point.

They rode on in silence.

The poles were spaced at roughly sixty yards' distance from one another. Following them over and around the soft round hillocks in this portion of the desert was an easy matter. After a while, Stark spotted a small shack some way off. Wires ran from the top of the shack up to one of the telegraph lines on a pole above. A covered wagon was pulled up beside the shack, with a couple of horses tied to the back. Figures were ranged around the wagon and the shack. It didn't take long to recognize them as cavalrymen.

"Looks like they're expecting company," Stark noted.

They finished their journey at a light trot, turning onto the road that ran parallel to that section of the telegraph line, making their arrival plain and noticeable well in advance. They were met by two cavalrymen, who intercepted them and then turned to accompany them to the others. A stout man, his belly stretching the front of his uniform, stepped forward, hand outstretched, a smile widening below the gray walrus mustache he sported.

"Mr. Stark? I'm Corporal Buell of the United States Military Telegraph Corps. Nice to meet you!" He gave Stark's hand a vigorous shake before turning to his Crow companion. "Reckon you'd be Mr. Red Buffalo. We're expecting you, too!" He stuck out a hand. "Welcome to our little substation."

Red Buffalo shook the man's hand. "I thought the army had disbanded the telegraph corps after the war," he said. Nodding toward the covered wagon, he added, "I have not seen a telegraph battery wagon like that since the war."

"They did!" Buell chuckled as the men dismounted and brushed trail dust from their clothes. "Disbanded us in 1866. The government returned control of the national telegraph system to private carriers like the Western Union company."

"You served with them during the war?" Stark asked.

"Sure did. Back when I still fit into this jacket." Buell laughed and thumped his tummy. "A decade or more of soft living with a generous wife who likes to cook will do that to a man! But I got the call six months ago. Reactivated to temporary duty. They even rolled a few of these old battery wagons out of storage. General Crook's order. He wants insurance in case the Apache start sabotaging the lines." He narrowed his eyes, his customary good humor fading. "We all remember Sweetwater Station," he said gravely.

Stark found himself remembering the story. It was one of those incidental bits of news you heard, mused over, and forgot. But now that Buell had mentioned it, he did recall the story of the Sioux attacking a station in South Pass, in an action that lasted several days. The station operator had immediately cabled the nearest fort for reinforcements and then started returning fire. During the action, the Sioux cut the lines to prevent further communication. Casualties on both sides had piled up over successive days.

"I've got a squad of boys out here keeping an eye on things." Buell gestured toward the cavalrymen ranged around the shack. Several loafed, while three riflemen kept the watch on high ground. "So far, it's been quiet."

"Let's hope it stays that way," Stark said. "We've gotten a taste of how the Apache operate. They're damned brutal."

"You can say that again. Savage, even by Indian standards . . . no offense meant, Mr. Red Buffalo." Buell seemed genuinely eager to avoid insult. "Let's say rather, you Indians are fierce in battle. These Apache are similarly fierce. But entirely without honor."

"No offense taken," Red Buffalo replied softly. "There are as many definitions of honor as there are men in the world. And it is between men that wars are best kept."

"Can't say I disagree," Buell replied, with a sad smile. They had all seen their fair share of innocence sacrificed to carnage.

■ ■ ■ ■

"This substation belonged to Western Union," Buell said, dragging the chair out from the telegraph bench. "They closed it a year ago, due to the Apache raids. But we were ordered out here from Fort Lowell last month. Took some doing to get her up and running again, let me tell you!"

Stark and Red Buffalo entered the small, stuffy office space and found places to sit. Stark took the windowsill opposite the bench, and Red Buffalo seated himself in the one remaining chair. Stark removed his hat and swabbed at his neck with a kerchief. It was warm as the blazes out here in the Territory.

Buell bent forward and activated the telegraph key. He sent out a brief alert signal, then applied himself to tapping out a message. The machine relayed the signal, after which Buell sat back and dragged a notepad and pencil across the bench to himself. He wrote down the reply which clattered in a moment later.

"Okay. Army telegraph office has received our signal." He took out a pocket watch and noted the time. "Says the orders will be relayed once they receive them. Meantime, we should get you fellows something to eat."

"Works for me," said Red Buffalo. Stark couldn't disagree.

Buell told one of the junior cavalrymen to watch the telegraph bench and note any incoming messages. Then he led Stark and the Crow around back of the shack. In the meager shade there, the men had set up a small field kitchen. A large iron pot bubbled over an open fire tended by a cavalryman, who had doffed his hat and jacket to work in his shirtsleeves.

"How's it coming, Josiah?" asked Buell.

"Doing good, corporal." The young man straightened, flashing Buell a grin. "Think I've outdone myself today."

At this Buell uttered a hearty laugh. "Gentlemen, allow me to introduce Private Josiah Lampkins of Tucson. This young man worked as a chef's assistant at a fancy hotel before joining the cavalry." He winked. "I managed to pull some strings and get him assigned to our little unit out here."

"Good thinking," said Stark. It was already plain the young man was making meals a cut above the usual army fare. A delicious smell wafted from the chili bubbling in the pot, and steam rose from two pans of cornbread Lampkins had just pulled from the coals. Stark suspected he was in for a real treat.

Lampkins did not disappoint. Quick as a whip, he had dished up three servings of chili. Stark noted that Buell's was slightly larger than the others. He suspected such generosities accounted for the corporal's slack enforcement of uniform discipline where the young cook was concerned.

"Lampkins, pour yourself some of that coffee and come sit yourself down for a minute," said Buell between bites of cornbread. Turning to Stark and Red Buffalo, he went on, "Josiah's lived out here his whole life. Knows more about the Apache than any man here. Figured you might want to pick his brains a bit."

"Don't mind if I do." Stark stirred his chili as the young cook took a seat. "How active is Geronimo around Tucson and Fort Lowell?"

Lampkins acknowledged the question with a nod, took a sip of coffee, and pulled out the makings to roll himself a cigarette.

"Geronimo and his people are living on the San Carlos Indian Reservation," he said. "That's up-Territory." He pointed. "Thataway. Maybe a week's ride or more. Problem is that he keeps to that reservation until there's a problem, usually with the authorities administering the reservation on behalf of Washington. Then he'll whoop and holler and gather up a bunch of followers and light out. They're breakout raids. He used to keep these raids short, returning to San Carlos after a few days. But lately, he's taken to bringing women and children along, and establishing rebel strongholds in the mountains."

"Which mountains?"

"He likes the Sierra Madres. Also, the Chiricahuas." Lampkins struck a match and touched it to the point of his quirly. "He raids. He runs. And when he has a mind to, he crosses the border into Mexico. The cavalry ain't allowed to cross, so it's like a fresh start for Geronimo and his band. And by the way, it's more than just one band. He's got generals under him. Guys like Nana, Naiche, and Chatto. Just as bad as him, and they each have their own little force.

"About them attacking Fort Lowell? No, they haven't. And Tucson is too big a target for them. Mostly he raids farms, ranches, missions. Small towns and villages."

"Is it true what they say about him killing women and children?" asked Red Buffalo.

"It's true." Lampkins took a deep puff of his cigarette and then held it out, examining it as he spoke. "They figure white men have killed their women and children, so why not repay the favor? And that's what happens. They come and it's a blizzard, a blur of violence. I was once at San Carlos when they hit. I was just a boy, but even my mom and dad were terrified. The adults closed and barricaded the mission gates, every window. We could hear the sound of hooves thundering down on us, then the screams of the warriors. The shutters on a few windows started to burn where the Apache had fired flaming arrows into them. They threw lit torches over the wall. Killed our sharpshooters whenever they could. It was a blur. Just an ocean of fire and rage breaking against the mission walls. The Apache are a terrible enemy to face. Like the very hounds of hell itself."

Chapter 10

Their meal finished, Stark mulled over Lampkins's story at length.

It's pretty clear this damned war has been going on for a long time, he thought. *Long enough to scar up plenty of young lives.*

War. The country was sick of it. You couldn't ride more than a dozen miles in any direction without finding traces of its wreckage. Burned crops, ruined houses, twisted railroad tracks . . . the evidence was everywhere.

The difference is the folks back east are making a go of healing from it, he thought. *Out here, they've just traded one war for another.*

"You're awfully quiet," Red Buffalo muttered as he wandered past Stark and bent to root around in his saddlebags.

"I'm just thinking about what Lampkins said. And everything we've seen so far here in the Territory."

"Come to any conclusions?"

"Yeah." Stark laughed. "This place would be a whole lot better off if somebody were to put a bullet in Geronimo."

"The trick would be finding him first."

Stark nodded. "True enough."

Just then, a young private jogged over. "Corporal Buell needs you in the telegraph office right away," he panted.

Stark and Red Buffalo hurried inside.

Buell was hunched over the bench, fingers flying between the telegraph key and the notepad he was using for reference. Messages were flying back and forth between Buell and General Crook, wherever he was.

"Come on in," Buell said, not taking his eyes from the key. "We got some signals traffic coming thick and fast, now."

"Orders for us?" Red Buffalo asked, taking the windowsill this time so that Stark could have the chair.

"For all of us!" Buell exclaimed, then snatched up a pencil and began noting down the reply he was receiving, in dots and dashes, on the telegraph sounder. After a spell, he finished writing, and then he sat back and rubbed his face.

"There's a lot here," he admitted, peering down at what he'd written. "General Crook had General Miles send a report. And we have news from some units down south. The short version of the news is that the fighting has moved north."

"How far north?" Stark felt a knot tighten in his stomach.

"Far enough north that this post is now considered to be at risk." Buell stood. "Your orders are to proceed to Fort Apache to meet with General Crook."

"And yours?" Red Buffalo asked.

"We're to ride with you." Buell's expression turned grim. "We're to provide an escort, pending our reassignment, in light of Geronimo's latest offensive. But basically, we'll be attached at the hip for the foreseeable future."

"At least we'll get to enjoy more of Lampkins's cooking," sighed Stark.

Buell let out a hearty laugh. "There's always a silver lining, ain't there?" He made for the door. "Time to saddle up, gents. We're burning daylight."

It didn't take Lampkins long to tear down and pack up his field kitchen, or for the cavalrymen to gather up their supplies and make ready to light out. Buell's orders contained instructions to render the station "unattractive" as a target to enemy combatants, so he sent one of the young troopers up to unfasten the wire connecting the substation to the telegraph lines. Within minutes, the wire had been unfastened and left dangling from the pole, ready to be reconnected as necessary.

While that was going on, the team was hitched up to the battery wagon. They would abandon the vehicle if they had to, such as galloping for their lives away from an Apache war party, but they would save the wagon, if it was possible.

Buell mounted up and came forward to join Stark and Red Buffalo where they sat at the front of the group, already mounted and ready to ride.

"We're in for a couple days' ride," Buell confessed. "Near as I can make out, General Crook is consolidating his forces in the north, in preparation for a major counteroffensive against Geronimo's troops. I reckon that's where you two fit in with his plans."

"Before he can attack Geronimo, Crook has to know where he is." Red Buffalo frowned.

"We may find him much sooner than later," Buell offered. "Like I said, the fighting has moved north. That's why we were instructed to disconnect the lines here. This is a target. And from the look of things, we are, too. Look yonder."

Stark and Red Buffalo looked in the direction Buell indicated. The corporal had sharp eyes. What Stark had initially taken to be a dust cloud on the horizon thickened into a wisp, then a streamer, of black smoke climbing into the clouds.

"Someone set a house on fire," Buell noted.

"Could be a fire that started by mistake," said Stark.

"Not likely. Look again."

Stark did. A second streamer darkened and began lifting its smoke toward the sky.

"Geronimo's on the move." Buell grimaced. "He's given us a wide berth. Several miles, at least. I say we take advantage of that while we can."

"Lead on, corporal." Stark waved a hand.

Buell got the men in marching order. Then he and the two scouts took the front positions and lit out for Fort Apache.

Stark felt the change in the desert immediately. It was a strange, although not entirely unfamiliar, sensation — as if the entire region had suddenly come to a stop and held its breath. The wilderness had the feeling of a forest sensing an impending wildfire, with everyone seeking refuge and keeping their heads down.

"I want to get a look at things from a higher vantage point," Stark told Buell. He pointed. "There's a ridge about a mile up ahead. If me and Red Buffalo light a shuck, we can get there fast and then rejoin you on the downslope."

"Sounds like a fine idea," said Buell. "You two take care, now."

"Thanks." Stark spurred Buck ahead and his Crow partner followed. They made good speed, arriving at the foot of the ridge quickly. Within a few minutes, they were scaling the heights and pausing on the summit to survey the desert below. After a minute spent in silent contemplation, Red Buffalo spoke up. As usual, he didn't waste time beating around the bush.

"General Crook is making a big mistake," the Crow said quietly.

"How's that?" Stark was digging through one of his saddlebags for a field telescope he kept there.

"Corporal Buell mentioned the general was preparing for a counteroffensive." Red Buffalo shook his head. "But that's white man's thinking. He's treating Geronimo's forces like a conventional army. But Geronimo is not going to line up his men in neat, orderly rows like General Grant or General

Beauregard used to do. No, they'll skulk and sneak, raid and run."

"So this movement north — it's not part of some broader campaign? That what you're saying?" Stark produced the field telescope, snapped it open, and set his face to the eyepiece.

"I'm saying Geronimo's move is a distraction." Red Buffalo thought for a moment. "He's distracting the army to focus on one place. But his real attack will be somewhere different."

"I tend to agree." Stark found the silhouette of two buildings burning in the distance. "Putting us close to the army will be a good way for us to read the signs as they come. Because we'll know those signs have been left for a specific purpose."

"Once we rendezvous with General Crook's troops, we can do that," Red Buffalo allowed. "But what if we would do more good staying right here?"

"Do you think we can?" He handed the field telescope to the Indian. "In the face of that?"

Red Buffalo scanned the burning buildings in the distance. "I can just make out the raiding party," he said. "It's a small group. I am guessing no more than a dozen or so. Perfect size for hit-and-run raids of this type."

"So, you're saying you don't see Geronimo as having some strategic objective in mind? Like, say, the capture of Tucson?"

"I think his tactics and motives are much simpler than that. Besides — what would he do with Tucson but burn it to the ground? No" — Red Buffalo chuckled and handed the telescope back to Stark — "his goal is to sow fear in people's minds."

Stark considered those words carefully. He tended to agree with Red Buffalo's assessment of the situation. Geronimo was trying to needle the army into motion. But to what end? One thing, though, was certain.

"If Geronimo is attacking here, then his real objective is elsewhere," he said.

"Yes," intoned Red Buffalo.

It was a lot to think about. Stark chewed it over in his mind as they rode down to meet up with Buell and his men. The column of cavalry, with the battery wagon trundling along behind it, was just now reaching the rendezvous point. Stark waited until they were underway again, one riding to either side of Buell, to take up the thread of his discussion with the man.

"What do you think Geronimo's overall goal is?" he asked.

Buell thought for a moment. "To make it so costly for us to remain in Arizona Territory that we eventually abandon it," he said. "It's a war of attrition. He figures he has all the resources he needs to live off the land while we have to wagon-train everything out here from forts back east. Our success will depend on cutting the numbers out from under him."

Red Buffalo remarked, "He probably has the same plan for you."

They saw more smoke plumes on the trail — more narrow streamers of black smoke. Geronimo's campaign was in full swing, and he was targeting every ranch, every rancher and his family, that he came across. At one point, they saw three such plumes, and their width and darkness suggested that the structures in question had been on fire long enough to get up a good head of steam.

By now they were riding between two long hills, the tops of which were high enough to cut off the view of the horizon. At points, it felt to Stark as if they were traversing a canyon.

Red Buffalo reined to a stop. Buell and Stark paused beside him.

"What is it?" Stark asked.

"That . . . *cloud.*" Red Buffalo was frowning, clearly puzzled. "Is that a storm?"

"At this time of year?" Buell shot a look skyward. "No. Rains don't come until summer, out in this part of the Territory. That's . . ."

He trailed off. When he spoke again, his voice was loud and sharp enough to cause Stark to twitch.

"Lampkins!"

The young cook broke ranks and galloped up to Buell. "Here, Corporal," he said, coming to a stop.

Buell pointed at the cloud. "What do you make of that?"

"It ain't a dust storm." Lampkins squinted. "And it isn't rain."

"Lampkins, take that pony of yours, get up that rise and go take a look-see. If I'm right, we're in a peck of trouble!"

Lampkins didn't wait to be told twice. He spurred his mount and tore up the hillside, moving with the swift confidence of a man born to the saddle. It was only when he was a hundred yards off that Stark noted the frying pan clanking where it was tied to the outside of a saddlebag. When Lampkins stopped, he had shrunk to a tiny figure at the top of the rise. Stark watched him sit there, motionless, for a full thirty seconds before he turned and tore down the hill at full gallop. He hauled the reins and skidded to a stop scant feet before Buell.

"You were right, Corporal. It's a peck of trouble, all right. A damned *big* peck, too!"

"How big?" Buell demanded.

Lampkins just shook his head. "Massive, sir. Maybe . . . two hundred or more."

"That would be Chatto's band." Buell's lips firmed. "He's been harassing the settlers out this way for a month now. Only — we thought he was further south. Damn!" He struck the pommel. "Gents," he said, "we've got company. About two hundred Apache warriors. And they're headed this way!"

Chapter 11

They had three options. They could run. They could hide. Or they could fight.

No matter which we pick, Stark thought, *the high ground is the place to be.* He started scanning the slopes of the hills around them, until he found a promising site.

"There!" He jabbed a finger at a stand of boulders roughly three hundred yards up the hill to their left. "Lampkins, how far off were they?"

"Reckon they'll be here in ten, fifteen minutes, Mr. Stark."

Stark turned to Buell. "If your men can harrow out a trench two or three feet deep behind those boulders, we can post up there, the entire group of us, with the horses. Keep our heads down until they pass."

"Worth a try!" Buell agreed quickly. He turned in the saddle. "Come on!" he yelled to his men. "Move sharp!" Then he spun to face front, grasped the reins, and spurred his mount up the hillside, followed by his troops.

Stark and Red Buffalo spurred their horses up the opposite hill to the vantage point from which Lampkins had first spotted the approaching horde. Upon arrival, Stark almost wished they hadn't.

The Apaches presented a massive formation. Unlike regular soldiers who rode in columns, the Indians rode all together, with a dozen pickets out in front of the main body to scout the way. When adjustments in direction were indicated, the whole body shifted.

Even at a distance, it was obvious the men were armed and riding with deadly purpose. The energy that boiled up from the group was aggressive. The yipping cries of the excited warriors carried across the distance and dust rose from the hooves to form what had looked like an ominous gray storm cloud they'd spotted earlier.

"Hell on horseback," muttered Stark. "And headed straight for us."

"If we're taken," Red Buffalo noted, "it won't be pretty."

"I don't intend to be." Stark checked the load in his Colt and stroked a fingertip over the rounds packed on his belt to count them. "I'll save the last bullet for myself."

Red Buffalo seemed surprised. "You'd kill yourself?"

"Rather than be caught by Geronimo's men?" Stark shook his head. "Unlikely, but I wouldn't dismiss the idea out of hand."

"Look, there!" Red Buffalo pointed to a small group of riders galloping a good distance ahead of the main body. "I don't think those are pickets."

"You may be right." Stark reholstered his Colt. "Time to go see how well Buell and his men can dig."

The sound of the approaching war party rang in the air as they descended one hill and began scaling the other to where the small cavalry troop had hidden itself behind fat rocks on the high ground. To Stark's relief, Buell's men had outdone themselves. They had managed to excavate a low wide trench almost two feet deep. Standing in this trench, both horses and cavalrymen were invisible from below.

"Hurry!" Buell cried. "They're damn well almost here!" He turned to a private holding a makeshift broom of cactus fronds. "Demer! Get out there and scrub off those tracks! Sharp, now!"

The private scrambled off. Stark and Red Buffalo dismounted and led their horses behind the boulders to join the cavalrymen hunkered in the trench. The horses had been given trail feed. This served the combined purposes of keeping them quiet and their heads down. The squad had no sooner finished concealing itself behind the boulders than a streamer of dust appeared at the mouth of the pass. The outriders were coming.

"Apache scouts!" cried Buell, peering out through a break in the boulders.

"No," said Red Buffalo, standing beside him. "I don't think so. Look!"

Stark removed the field telescope from his saddlebag and trained it on the approaching rider.

This was no Apache. The rider was definitely a white man. And from the look of him, grubby and trail hardened. That's when Stark knew he was looking at the first of a band of marauders. Because following him came a group of similarly dressed and trail-dusted desperadoes. All had the hunted look of men engaged in desperate flight. For rising behind them loomed the black cloud of the oncoming Apaches.

"Corporal!" cried Lampkins. "Should we offer assistance? What are your orders?"

"Hold fast," Buell said harshly, keeping watch on the unfolding situation from behind the iron sights of his Winchester rifle. "Those men are outlaws. And where the Apache are concerned, they made their own bed. They have to lie in it."

Stark had to wonder what those marauders had done to upset the Apache. Truth was, that usually didn't take much effort. Perhaps they had raided an Apache settlement. More likely, they had simply been spotted by a passing war party, who had set off in pursuit. Thus far, the marauders appeared to have evaded death or capture. But that was about to change.

As he watched, the lead rider dragged up on the reins and brought his horse to a sudden stop in the middle of the pass. Stark followed his line of sight.

There. At the far end of the pass . . .

Apaches!

The war party had split up and managed to encircle their quarry, trapping them in the pass. The marauders, all five of them, now found themselves in a situation where mounted Indians were bearing down on them from both behind and in front.

"Nobody move!" Buell cautioned. "Keep down. Stay still. Await my order."

Stark had to hand it to the portly corporal. Although long retired, he had recovered all the skills of command when it mattered most. And right now, it was a matter of life and death.

Two groups of Apaches thundered down on the marauders, each one containing maybe twenty-five riders. To their credit, the white men didn't lose their nerve but drew their horses up in a tight circle, facing outward, and grabbed up their guns.

The Apaches were sweeping closer now. Arrows flew, hissing past the circled riders, the first cracks of gunfire filling the pass. The Apaches stopped short of the marauders, aiming rifles and arrows. A few broke from the main group and began climbing the hills on either side of their quarry to obtain a clear shot.

Stark looked down. Some of the warriors had begun climbing toward their position, obviously unaware of the cavalry's presence.

"Corporal!" whispered Lampkins. "Surely, we should break cover and provide support for —"

"Stand fast, Lampkins," snapped Buell. He eyed the rest of his small squad. "We gain nothing by imitating General Custer! We stay put!"

The cavalrymen seemed divided on this point, and Stark couldn't blame them. As serving members of the armed forces, protecting Americans against hostiles was second nature. But Buell had made a call and Stark agreed it was the right one. The men below were very obviously marauders — murderous outlaws who preyed on the misfortune of those left destitute by Apache raids. If such men fell victim to the Apache, then so be it. Their deaths would leave the world a better place.

Two of the five marauders had fallen. The Apaches were coming in for the kill now. Stark glanced at the far end of the pass. A lone Apache rider had scaled the hill to a vantage point from which he could watch the action.

Stark could tell this one was a leader. He was of middle age, adorned with the colorful shirt and smart leggings of a chief. A single feather stuck up from his head, pinned in his hair. He had a dark brooding face, and penetrating eyes that watched the destruction of the marauders hungrily.

I wonder if that's him, Stark thought. *I wonder if maybe that's Geronimo.*

By now, the final blow was being struck against the outlaws. By arrow and gunfire, the marauders were cut down until only a single man remained. His horse reared as the Apaches closed in, twisting around and around in a full circle, eyes wide, nostrils flaring, mouth foaming. The rider's eyes were wide, too, as he struggled to remain balanced in the saddle, snapping off shots from his revolver. The Apache braves were yipping excitedly, grinning as they encircled him and began pressing inward.

They're playing with him, Stark thought, disgusted by the cruelty. In all the years he had fought Indians, his hate for them had been leavened by the numerous feats of valorous, even honorable, conduct he had witnessed them performing.

He saw no trace of this in the carnage below. Only savage cruelty and a blood lust that would not be satisfied until the quarry had drawn its final breath. When an arrow zipped in from the melee to end the last rider, piercing his neck straight through from side to side, he fell.

One of the braves launched himself from his horse to descend upon the dying man. He dragged the gagging marauder upright by his hair, drew a knife, and took the scalp with a single fierce swipe of the blade. Then, holding it aloft, he screamed in triumph. The other braves cheered and yipped, delighting in the action while, below their feet, the marauder pulsed and squirmed through his final moments of life.

Sickened, Stark looked away.

■ ■ ■ ■

The Apaches took scalps from the remaining dead. Stark, Red Buffalo, Buell, and the cavalrymen crouched behind the rocks, waiting. After a time, the hubbub of talk and celebration died down. Then a great din arose as the main body thundered through the pass. When silence finally fell, Stark took a chance and peered around the rocks. The last of the Apaches was just disappearing out the far end, his single dust plume the only indication of the group's passage.

"Damned shame," Buell said, guiding his horse down the draw toward the floor of the pass behind Stark. He paused to examine what was left of the outlaws' bodies.

"Want we should bury them, corporal?" asked Lampkins. But Buell shook his head.

"Leave them," he said. "Any change will be an indication to the Apaches that we've been through here. We don't want that. We just want to melt away into the desert. And make it to Fort Apache."

"The sooner the better," said Stark.

Buell gave no argument. The group saddled up and resumed their journey north.

■ ■ ■ ■

They made a fair bit of distance on their first day's ride. When they stopped to bivouac for the night, Stark spoke to Buell. By the corporal's reckoning, they had less than another day's ride ahead of them provided the trail was clear and they didn't run into another raiding party. By now they were deep in the desert, far from any ranches or settlements. The night air was cool and the stars shone brightly against the night sky.

After chatting with Buell, Stark made his way back to the tent he and Red Buffalo would be sharing for the night. They had built a small fire out front, and it was before this that Stark found the Crow scout, kneeling, his hat off and head bowed. Stark paused at a respectful distance, waiting until the man finished his prayers, crossed himself, and replaced the hat on his head. He spoke to Stark without turning.

"You caught me," he said.

"I didn't want to interrupt your conversation," Stark said.

"Conversation." Red Buffalo savored the word as he spoke it, turning the concept over in his mind. "Isn't that usually when one person speaks, then listens as another speaks back? I know I'm speaking. But I don't always hear an answer."

"I guess that's how prayer works," Stark offered. He was no theologian and had only a rudimentary interest in such matters. He was more interested in living this life than focusing on the one to come.

"I was praying for those men. The ones the Apaches killed. And for forgiveness."

"Why?"

Red Buffalo shrugged. "For not burying them. I understand we couldn't under the circumstances. But still. That doesn't make it right."

Stark, agreeing, merely nodded.

"A place like this Territory forces men to make hard choices. Choices they wouldn't otherwise make." The Crow sighed. "And those choices change men, I think."

Stark wondered if that was Geronimo's story.

Chapter 12

Their trail took them from the lower Sonoran region into the White Mountains. Neither Stark nor Red Buffalo had ever visited the area before. What struck them was the dramatic change in their surroundings as they left the desert floor and climbed into the hills. Within a matter of a quarter hour or less, they were moving into a forest of chaparral, mesquite, and pine. The ground was soft here, and Stark saw indications of plentiful game. As if sensing his curiosity, Buell took the liberty of introducing both scouts to their new environment.

"Gorgeous, isn't it?" The portly corporal's walrus mustache widened with a smile. "Used to hunt here when I was a young private stationed out thisaway. These hills are thick with deer, rabbit — all manner of game. Back then, it was called Camp Ord, after the old brigadier commanding the place. The man had a hell of a mustache."

Buell fingered his own with a rueful grin. "I think I might have started this one in imitation. Maybe also to keep warm through that first winter.

"It was primitive back in those days. There were still no walls to speak of and, back then, nothing resembling a decent military facility. Just log huts and tents. And a parade ground. Wore the skin off the soles of my feet on that ground, I swear."

"It's a good place for a fort," said Red Buffalo. "High in the hills. Lots of game." He looked around. "What about native people? Is this traditional Apache land?"

"It is," said Buell. "Home to the White Mountain Apache. They're friendlies. So are the Cibicue. They don't much cotton to Geronimo or his way of doing things. In fact, when the army arrived, they welcomed us. Maintaining cordial relations with them is the priority of any commanding officer in these parts. They serve as both scouts and an auxiliary force for the folks at Fort Apache."

"How large a force?" asked Stark.

"See for yourself," replied Buell with a grin.

They topped a rise and looked down into the valley that was home to Fort Apache. As Buell had noted, there was no stockade wall as was customary in hostile territory. Instead, a series of long, low buildings surrounded a parade square. And encircling the buildings was a sea of tepees.

"It's not just a fort. As you can see." Buell chuckled. "This is also the home of the Fort Apache Indian Reservation. So they've got plenty of neighbors."

"That's got to come in handy," Stark noted, suppressing a shudder at the prospect of traversing all those tents. Being among so many natives was uncomfortable to him in the extreme. He was grateful that his reputation as the "Indian killer," while something known back east, was less so out here in the Arizona Territory.

Buell guided the little squad down the slope into the valley. As they approached the fort, a group of riders burst out of the sea of tepees to meet them. Stark felt his heart fill his throat for a moment before the riders became visible as a group of high-spirited Apache youth that had scrambled onto horseback, excited to rush out and welcome the arriving cavalrymen. Stark watched as they approached.

Those kids are really at home in the saddle, he thought. The Apache youth rode bareback, their young brown bodies lithe, their movements effortless. They swarmed around

Buell and the oncoming troopers, pressing in close, but never quite close enough to impede or delay the men. The boys were smiling, and the whole affair had the feel of raucous, welcoming good humor.

"Welcome!" cried one kid, falling in beside the lead riders. "Where have you come from? Was your journey a good one? Did you bring any tobacco?"

Buell shook his head and emitted a fatherly chuckle. "We're up from Fort Lowell," he said. "And these two gentlemen are scouts from back east."

"You're an Indian!" exclaimed the kid, staring at Red Buffalo.

"Last time I checked, yep," replied the Crow, with deadpan humor.

The kid fired off a statement in Apache.

"I'm sorry. I don't know your language," Red Buffalo replied.

"We'll teach you some while you're here!" offered the young man. "Come and visit if you can. And bring an appetite. The grandmothers will stuff you full of food!"

With that, the boy wheeled his horse and took off back in the direction of the tents, yipping and hollering, and drawing the others back with him as he went. Soon it was just Buell, the two scouts, and the cavalrymen again. Buell led them along a path that wound through the Apache settlement. Their arrival generated a certain amount of attention. But mostly, the tribesmen who were outside their tents, tending fires or horses, or knapping flint for arrowheads, just glanced at them and went back to their business. Here was a place where white and red men had grown accustomed to living side by side with one another.

Buell, as though sensing Stark's curiosity, spoke.

"They're quiet people. Respectful. But they're fierce in battle. Best damn horsemen I've ever seen. And they fight like demons." Buell nodded to him. "You're among friends here, Mr. Stark. You can relax."

Is my discomfort that obvious? Stark wondered. But in reply to Buell, he smiled and nodded, and said nothing more.

The tents gave way to the wooden structures. As they approached, the door to one opened and a man emerged wearing sergeant's stripes. Seeing the approaching squad, he stepped out to intercept them. Buell reined to a halt, sat upright in the saddle, and saluted. The sergeant returned the courtesy before speaking.

"You'd be our friends from Fort Lowell," he said.

"Yes, sergeant. Corporal Erwin C. Buell, Army Telegraph Corps. Allow me to present Mr. Nathan Stark and Mr. Moses Red Buffalo. They're civilian scouts with the Department of the Army."

"Gentlemen, welcome." The sergeant, a hatchet-faced, intense man with dark hair and eyes offered Stark and Red Buffalo a curt nod. "I'm Sergeant Meyers. We've been expecting you."

"Sergeant, we have orders to present ourselves to General Crook," said Stark. "Apparently, he needs scouts."

"Truer words were never spoken," said Meyers. "Our situation with regard to scouts is at sixes and sevens, but I'll let the good general explain that. Meantime, I have some bad news for you."

"What's that?"

"The general's not here." Meyers spread his hands. "Left day before yesterday. You've no doubt heard. Geronimo is on the move."

"We saw evidence of it on the way here," Stark replied. "Almost got smoked by a raiding party in that pass about a day's ride back."

"They're burning ranches all the way from here to the border, sergeant," offered Corporal Buell. "He's coming, all right. And he's coming heavy."

Meyers absorbed this news with an effort to seem impassive. But the twitch around his mouth and eyes betrayed him.

He's worried, Stark thought. And it was a thought that left him distinctly uneasy.

Meyers, meanwhile, was speaking. "General Crook left word that upon arrival, you are to rendezvous with him in his private railcar at Diablo Gap." He produced a pocket watch and checked the time. "We'll telegraph him that you're here. But you might as well wait until morning to set out. Not much daylight left. And you don't want to be caught outdoors in the dark. Not with Geronimo on the move. No, sir."

"With your permission, sergeant, I'll get over to the telegraph office," said Buell. "I'll see that message is sent to General Crook and take the opportunity to request orders for me and my squad."

"Much obliged, corporal," said Meyers. "See to it. You and your men can bunk down in the blockhouse. Over there" — he pointed, then turned to Stark and Red Buffalo. "You men can, too, if you like. Unless you prefer other arrangements."

"I'll stay with the Apache tonight," Red Buffalo told Stark. "Get some information before our ride tomorrow."

"Sounds good," said Stark. "I think I'll

grab a cup of coffee and then go bed down early. I'm trail whupped."

Red Buffalo guided his horse out toward the tepees scattering the plain. As before, his passage went generally unremarked and elicited no special notice. This was just as well. He knew who he was looking for, even though he had never been here before.

He found the group of boys that had ridden out to meet them in the field beyond the last row of tents. Their horses grazed as the group of them loafed in the grass, shouting encouragement as two of their number competed in a fierce wrestling match. Red Buffalo wandered over and hunkered down to watch. The boy who had been the spokesman for the welcome wagon was fighting another, slightly bigger kid. Despite the height advantage, the bigger kid was having a rough go of it.

At length, the match ended with a twisted arm and a shouted surrender. The bigger kid limped off, favoring his arm, while the victor sat back on his haunches and blew the hair from his eyes.

"Not bad," said Red Buffalo. "You showed him."

"You wanna try me, old man?" the kid taunted in English, as Red Buffalo had no

Apache. Despite the brazen words, there was an undercurrent of respectful teasing. For although the Crow was not of the same tribe as he, the boy recognized Red Buffalo as an elder. And there were limits to sassing elders, even in fun.

"I'm too old for that," Red Buffalo replied with a chuckle. "Too many years of riding in the white man's saddle and living in his world have made my bones ache. But I remember who I am."

The other boys crept closer and sat, listening.

"White man's coming. One way or the other," Red Buffalo said sadly. "It will mean trouble. Especially for the Apache."

"Only for the Mescalero!" hooted one boy and spat.

The kid who had been wrestling threw the heckler a sharp look before settling his eyes on Red Buffalo. "You are a long way from home," he said, his tone kinder this time.

"I am. And I could use some help." Red Buffalo picked up a twig and began fiddling with it. "We have to go to a place called Diablo Gap. You know it?"

"Yes." Although the boy was careful to keep his voice calm, Red Buffalo could see excitement dancing in his eyes. "It's rough country out that way. It's Geronimo's land."

"My friend, the white scout, and I. We need to get there." Red Buffalo studied the twig he'd stripped of bark. "We need a path that will keep us safe and out of trouble."

"I can show you," the boy said confidently. "My friend Makata and I rode out there once. I know we could find our way back."

"You would be riding into trouble," Red Buffalo pointed out. "It might be safer for you just to describe the route for us."

"Safer?" The boy spat. "Safe is for grandmothers and little kids. You're a visitor. Good manners demand that we show respect for you as an elder. And your friend, too, even if he's a white man. You are our responsibility."

The trace of a smile twitched at the edge of Red Buffalo's mouth. This kid was growing up to be the sort of man his parents and his people could be proud of.

"I will talk to Makata." The boy rose and brushed grass from his leggings. "We can be ready tomorrow at dawn. We'll take you and your friend to Diablo Gap. Make sure you get there safely."

"Much appreciated," said Red Buffalo. "What is your name?"

"Delshay," the boy said. "Makata and I will see you in the morning."

Chapter 13

Stark was less than enthusiastic when Red Buffalo informed him of the guides he had secured for their trip to Diablo Gap.

"They're *kids*," he exclaimed, examining the two Apache youths as they checked over their horses near the edge of the parade ground. "Are you sure we can rely on them?"

"They know the area," replied the Crow, grasping the reins of his horse and mounting. "And they're young men who are ready to take the next step into manhood."

"That's hardly reassuring," replied Stark, mounting up himself. "But if they know the area . . . They've been to Diablo Gap?"

"They tell me so." Red Buffalo nudged his horse forward, Stark following. The sun was just peeking up over the horizon as Buell emerged from the military telegraph office and intercepted them halfway across the parade ground.

"Morning, gents!" Although plainly tired, the portly corporal mustered a weary smile. "Just got confirmation from General Crook. He's going to rendezvous with you at Diablo Gap the day after tomorrow. That gives you plenty of time along with a margin of error for unforeseen circumstances."

"Thanks for all your help," Stark told him.

"A pleasure, Mr. Stark." Buell stuck out a hand and they shook. He shot a glance at the two Apache boys waiting across the parade ground. "I see you've got company."

"Those two braves will be our guides," Red Buffalo said, a little defensively.

"They know the country," Buell said firmly, relieving some of Stark's doubts. "But good luck keeping up with them! Those two are hell in the saddle."

"Indians don't use saddles," replied Red Buffalo.

"Exactly." Buell smiled. And that seemed to settle it.

Diablo Gap, a low-lying area where two mesas intersected, had long been a landmark for locals in the Territory. The builders of the first rail lines through the area had taken note and laid their tracks to take advantage of both geography and convention. There was no station at Diablo Gap but that posed no great difficulty. General Crook's command train came with its own engine and conductor. It stopped wherever necessary, regardless of convention, and was given right-of-way as a matter of national security.

Delshay and Makata rode sedately for the first two hours of the journey, heads down, plodding along. One could mistake them for elderly travelers, given the pace at which they rode. Stark understood the two braves took their task as guides seriously and viewed it as confirmation of their maturity. They were anxious not to appear childish before him and Red Buffalo.

But they were still boys at heart. When a jackrabbit exploded from behind a nearby cholla, the two were off like greased lightning, yipping and hollering, drawing out their bows and competing to be the first to get it. They streaked back and forth across the desert as Stark and Red Buffalo continued on the trail, finally returning after Delshay pierced the hare with an arrow. He rode up alongside Stark, holding the dead beast by the ears.

"Some fat on this one," the Apache boy said. "Should be tasty later!"

Stark examined the hare and had to admit

it looked good. He was looking forward to dinner.

An hour after the incident with the hare, the two boys, just ahead of the two scouts, abruptly stopped. Delshay held up a hand. Stark and Red Buffalo halted in their tracks.

There was something — or someone — not far from their present position.

Suddenly, Makata launched himself forward on his horse, going all out. Delshay watched him for a full minute before wheeling around to Stark.

"Apache trail sign," he said quietly. "Makata is going to take a look. We should stay here until he returns."

"Apache have been through here?" asked Red Buffalo.

Delshay nodded. "They're not too far ahead of us," he reported. "A small group. Maybe ten horses."

"Could be a raiding party," said Red Buffalo. "But if it is, why aren't they with the main body?"

"We'll find out shortly," said Stark, pointing. Bare minutes had passed but already Makata was on the return trip, a dust plume boiling up from the tiny form on the horizon. He zipped toward them full speed, reining to a clattering halt just a few feet from his friend. He spoke to Delshay in rapid fire Apache. The boy turned and translated Makata's message.

"He says there's a group of about a dozen Apaches up ahead. They're White Mountain tribe. Allies to the white men." He turned and chattered with Makata for a moment before adding, "He says they're refugees, fleeing Geronimo's armies. He spoke with them." He paused. "Some of their party are wounded."

"Let's go see them," Red Buffalo said to Stark.

"Yes." Stark nodded. "Could be they know something that might be useful to us or General Crook." He turned to Delshay. "Lead on," he said with a wave of the hand.

They rode at a sedate gallop, Makata in the lead. After a time, they reached the edge of a narrow arroyo that cut through the rock and sand like a wrinkle. Areas of the dry river's edge leaned out over the bed's sluiceway, creating natural cover from the elements. Perched on the edge of the river was a skinny elderly Apache cradling a Winchester. He nodded and waved to Makata, recognizing him as the riders approached. The two spoke briefly in Apache before Makata dismounted.

"This elder will watch our horses," Delshay explained. "He says their chief wants to speak to us. He's down below with what's left of his people."

Stark's heart clutched at this. "What's left?" he asked. "Their tribe suffered some sort of calamity?"

"What happened?" asked Red Buffalo.

Delshay questioned Makata, who shot back a quick report as they gained the lip of the arroyo and began edging their way down to the riverbed.

"Geronimo," Delshay said. Stark left it at that.

There was a particularly large area in the bank that had been hollowed out by a previous season's floods, and it was below the resulting overhang that the Apaches had taken refuge. One man, an elder like the sentinel on the bank, strode out to meet them. Although his back was straight and his gaze exuded strength of command, attitude alone could not conceal the weariness on his lined face or the limp he did his best to conceal. He stopped a few feet from Stark and his crew and raised a hand in greeting, then spoke.

"He says his name is Kuruk," translated Delshay. "He and his people were driven from their traditional land near Dził Łigai Sí'án — the White Mountain. They are going south into Mexico. He says they have relations there who will take them in."

Stark turned to Red Buffalo and gave him a slight nod, inviting him to take the lead.

"I am called Red Buffalo. My people are Crow," he said, stepping forward as he spoke. He waited for Delshay to finish translating before he continued. "This is my friend Nathan, who is a good man and a friend to me and my people. I vouch for him."

Stark watched Kuruk's face as Delshay conveyed these words. The Apache leader listened without objection and nodded before speaking in reply.

"Kuruk says he and his people enjoyed cordial relations with the white settlers near their homeland. He says you are welcome along with Red Buffalo. The settlers and the bluecoats had nothing to do with the affliction he and his people have suffered."

Kuruk spat before continuing.

"Kuruk says it was Juh and Victorio, two of Geronimo's generals, who attacked them. He says these men had been as friends to their people before turning and betraying them. He says Geronimo intends to retake the entire Arizona Territory." Delshay paused, listening before adding: "He says that Geronimo is evil. He says Geronimo is a skin-walker. Geronimo is a witch."

Stark heard Red Buffalo do a sharp intake of breath and stiffen at these words.

Kuruk invited them to come and sit with his people. Stark studied them. They were a sorry lot, old men, women, and children, obviously hungry and trail weary. The remains of a once proud tribe. As one woman set about digging a hole for a stealth fire, Stark spoke quietly to Red Buffalo.

"He called Geronimo a witch," he said in a hushed tone. "Didn't you say he was a shaman?"

"Different things," muttered Red Buffalo. "A medicine man uses his power for the benefit of the people. Witches seek power for its own sake."

"What is a 'skin-walker'?"

"The most evil damned thing you've ever seen," Red Buffalo replied, his voice gravelly. "A powerful sorcerer who can transform himself into animals. I have heard the word before. It is a Navajo word. If it is true, then Geronimo is a creature to be feared, indeed."

"You don't really believe that about him, do you?" Stark was incredulous.

"What matters," said Red Buffalo, "is that others believe it. And that is destructive."

■ ■ ■ ■

An hour passed in the company of the wandering Apaches. Stark and Red Buffalo were pleased to share some of their coffee with the group. Once the stealth fire had been built, they put on a pot and shared out servings among the Indians, pouring the good black brew into cups and bowls as were offered. Coffee was new to the tribes but it was as popular among the Apache as it was among the Plains tribes with whom Stark had imbibed. They were just finishing up their second cup when he noticed that Delshay and Makata had vanished.

He drained the last of his cup, tossed away the grounds, and stepped over to where Red Buffalo sat on a log.

"Have you seen our guides?" he asked.

"They left. An hour ago." The Crow seemed nonplussed as he blew on his steaming beverage.

"They *left*?" Stark squatted down on his haunches, shook his head, and laughed. "Well, how do you like that?"

"You think they're irresponsible." Red Buffalo's words were not a question.

"Well . . . yes." Stark shrugged.

"They're not."

An hour later, Stark understood.

The two boys appeared astride their horses. They were tired, sweaty, and trail-worn. But slung over the backs of their horses were the fruits of their journey. Stark saw three rabbits on Delshay's horse and two on Makata's along with a long brown cord that it took him a moment to recognize as a dead rattlesnake. The boys guided their horses down the draw to the riverbed and brought them to a halt before the group of White Mountain Apaches.

As Stark watched, the two young men dismounted and brought the game to the tribal elder. Delshay spoke to the man at length, very seriously and solemnly. The man listened, as did everyone in the group. When Delshay was done speaking, he handed over the game. Makata followed suit. Then it was the old man's turn to speak.

Red Buffalo had no Apache, but he seemed to understand what was going on. Stark had rarely seen the Crow smile. But when the old man was finished, he was beaming. And . . . *was that a tear in his eye?*

Delshay turned to him.

"We had better go now," he said. "It's getting late."

Stark and Red Buffalo retrieved their pot

and coffee fixings, and stowed them in their saddlebags. Then they mounted up and, with a wave, followed the two boys as they resumed the journey.

"You were right," Stark said quietly. "They're not irresponsible. In fact, they're the exact opposite."

Red Buffalo nodded. "I cannot speak their language," he said quietly. "But I am fairly sure those two boys will always have a home among the White Mountain Apache if they desire it."

Watching the two young braves plodding along ahead, Stark understood. Indian ways were different from his own, but respecting and serving elders and those in need was something he could understand. And so he plodded along, puzzled by the sudden lump in his throat.

Chapter 14

Stark caught the first glimpse of railroad tracks at a distance the next morning. The steel rails flashed in the sunlight, and the brown line of railroad ties cut a swath through the empty desert like fine stitching. In the barren wasteland, the tracks were impossible to miss, even from afar. Stark wondered which railroad company or military unit had laid down these tracks. There had been so much reorganization and change among the railroad companies since the War Between the States that it was nearly impossible to keep account of them all.

"Diablo Gap is there" — Delshay pointed. "Another few hours and we'll be there. Does your general travel on the iron horse?"

"He does." Stark favored the boy with a grin. "He's important enough to have one of his own."

Expecting the Apache to be impressed

with this, Stark was amused by the boy's response. "Who would want an iron horse?" he asked, a tremor of contempt audible in his voice. "A real horse of flesh and blood is better. In fact, *nothing* is better than a horse of real flesh and blood!" He ran a loving hand across the neck of his mount. Then he paused, thinking. "Unless the general is an elder. Then maybe I can understand why he would prefer an iron horse."

"He is an elder," Stark said. "He's a great and wise leader. He has much respect among the soldiers and the politicians in Washington."

"I don't know that word. Politician. What does it mean?"

"Good question." Stark frowned. "A politician is a man who represents people. The voters elect and send politicians to Washington to speak on their behalf."

"Why don't they just speak for themselves?"

"Uh . . . that's actually another good question. It's just our system of government."

"I like our system better," said Delshay. "A man speaks for himself and his family. If there's a problem, he can go directly to the chief. If your chief lives far away and you have to send other men to speak on your behalf, they could twist your words and lie.

Does that ever happen? Do politicians ever lie?"

"They do it all the time," muttered Red Buffalo.

"Our system is better," affirmed Delshay. And that put an end to the matter in his mind.

As they approached Diablo Gap, Stark studied the rail tracks. Trains had played such an important role in warfare that they were now indispensable to any modern military campaign. He reckoned the armies in Europe probably had a jump on them in that department, but the War Between the States had accelerated the development of both tactics and equipment. Stark doubted the Europeans had anything approaching the power and functionality of the equipment used by the military rail operators of the United States.

Controlling the railroads meant controlling territory. Both the Union and Confederate armies had learned this during the war. Railcars had been used to ferry men, materiel, and horses all over the theater. They were so crucial to the war effort that units were dispatched to both guard and disrupt rail operations. General Stoneman had made a name for himself doing just that in the wake of Lee's army, until hemorrhoids had sidelined him. Later in the war, special engines had been developed to travel enemy rail lines and tear them up as they went, splintering ties and curling steel rails into elaborate knots the boys had called "Sherman bowties."

The same thinking had gone into the campaigns here out west. Once matters had been settled between North and South, attention was returned to conquering and settling the territories. Trains were absolutely vital to the smooth running of that effort. The rail lines were used to transport and resupply the various forts and government installations in the desert. And General Crook used them to get around the area in a swift and safe manner. A general traveling by train was at significantly less risk than one going by coach or horseback.

It was late afternoon by the time they reached the Gap. The mesas rose from the desert floor to tower over them on either side. The tracks ran through the clear section between the mesas. As yet, the general's train had not arrived.

"This is it," said Delshay. "This is Diablo Gap."

Stark looked around, nodded, and dismounted. "We appreciate your help, Delshay," he said. "The general is going to meet us here. You are welcome to wait with us if you like, but it's not necessary. We'll understand if you want to head home."

"We'll go," replied Delshay. He took a hare they had killed that morning and handed it down to Stark. "You go ahead and have this tonight for your supper. We'll hunt something for ourselves on the trail heading back."

Red Buffalo nudged his horse forward to Delshay's. "Thank you," he said quietly.

"You're welcome," replied Delshay.

And with that, he and Makata turned and started back toward Fort Apache.

The two scouts found some shade in the lee of one of the mesas and picketed the horses there. Stark set them up with feed and water while Red Buffalo scavenged together some kindling from mesquite bushes and the dried ribs of downed cacti. He got a little fire going and proceeded to gut the hare. After a little while, he had some coffee brewing and had set the rabbit to cooking on a spit. Stark helped himself to a cup of black gold and took a seat beside Red Buffalo, staring out at the horizon.

"Hope the general gets here soon," he said.

"Why?" asked Red Buffalo. "Isn't my

company good enough?"

"Not really," Stark joked. "But for now, I guess it will have to do."

They were just finishing their meal when the wind kicked up. A strong gust blew across their fire, scattering ash and sparks. Stark thought it just a minor annoyance until the gust turned into a continuous wind. It persisted, growing stronger over the course of a half hour. When its howling force cast a clutch of pebbles into Stark's face, he knew they were dealing with something more than a mild annoyance.

"Sandstorm," Red Buffalo said. He began kicking sand over the fire.

"We better get the horses somewhere safe." Stark stood, brushing sand from his jeans and looking around. The foot of the nearest mesa was intercut by ripples and crannies, some quite deep. They would do. He and Red Buffalo guided Buck and the Crow's horse into a recess in the rocks. The wind was blowing something fierce now, the sand having filled the air to mute the sun. It was now just a pale disk against the blowing storm. Buck shied away, suddenly skittish.

"We'd better bag them," said Red Buffalo, and Stark knew exactly what the man meant. Concealed in their saddlebags were canvas bags they could use to cowl the horses in the event of this kind of fierce weather, or if they needed to be led across terrain that might otherwise spook them. They drew these hoods over the animals' heads and then hunkered down to weather the storm.

"Look there." Red Buffalo pointed. "A little cave."

"Good idea," said Stark. The sand was starting to sting his eyes.

Hunched over in the howling storm, they made their way by feel to the break in the rocks Red Buffalo had noticed. It was a short distance but a lengthy trip, with the wind whipsawing back and forth and turning their steps to a disordered stumble. Stark reached it first and placed a hand on one side of the triangular break.

Looks wide enough to enter, he thought. Peering in, he could see nothing. But visibility wasn't important. What mattered was getting out of this damnable wind! Hunching his shoulders, he lowered his head and shouldered his way inside.

Red Buffalo was right behind him. They paused inside the cave entrance, coughing up sand and taking full breaths for the first time since the storm started.

"Bigger than I expected," Stark said. He squinted into the shadows.

Red Buffalo took a few experimental steps forward into the darkness. He was able to spread his hands wide.

"Too bad that entrance is so narrow," he said. "It would be good to bring the horses in here."

"I was thinking the same thing." Stark reached into his pocket for matches. "But they should be fine out there."

He drew out his matches and began fishing one out of the pack.

"Those storms don't usually last —"

A sound rose somewhere in the darkness — a feral, low growl from the depths of the cave that rolled like thunder.

A light sweat broke out on Stark's body. Chills snarled his spine. Red Buffalo had heard it, too. The Crow was backing away now, his hands up. Stark struck a match and held it aloft.

The mother bobcat, curled protectively around her litter of cubs, was tensed, aroused, and completely focused on their every move. Stark knew from experience that threatening any mother with young in the wild was a dangerous proposition. Even deer could become suddenly and effectively violent. But a bobcat was another thing altogether.

"Let's go," he whispered to Red Buffalo.

Rather than make a sound, the Crow scout nodded, the eagle feather on his hat bobbing in the match light.

Perhaps it was the feather moving that did it. Either that or the shadows shifting on the little cave's walls. But whatever it was, it was enough to cause the momma bobcat to shriek, roll to her feet, and lunge forward.

She landed on the pads of her front paws with a soft *plop* scant feet from them. Stark's hand reached for his Colt. And that was when Red Buffalo began to sing.

It was a low, quiet song. Very soothing. Stark knew that some tribesmen had a personal "death song," a melody to be sung in their final moments. Perhaps that was what Red Buffalo was singing. Stark drew his Colt and cocked it, but the Crow reached out and laid a hand on his arm.

The bobcat remained, tensed, and still in the spot where she had halted.

Slowly, Red Buffalo began backing out of the cave, continuing his song. Stark followed him, keeping his eyes on the bobcat and the Colt aimed squarely at its head. Then he was turning sideways to fit through the narrow triangular opening. He never felt so relieved to return to the middle of a sandstorm.

"That was pretty impressive," Stark cried

above the wind, holstering his pistol.

"It's an old song," Red Buffalo said, leaning in close to be heard above the din. "A song from the days when men and animals held counsel together as equals. The mother cat recognized the song and so did not attack us."

"Whatever the cause, it seemed to work!" He cast a nervous eye back at the cave entrance as they retreated to the horses.

The storm persisted for another hour. And then, just as abruptly as it began, it died down. Within minutes, the sand in the air had settled back to the ground, and the temperature abruptly climbed as the sun reappeared and began to beam down on the desert.

"It's been an eventful day," muttered Red Buffalo, standing and knocking sand from the crown of his hat.

"That's an understatement," Stark agreed. He stepped over and untied the canvas bag Buck was wearing. The horse whinnied and stamped softly, pleased to see Stark again. "It was a close-run thing in there."

"It was. And speaking of close . . ."

The Crow tilted his head out beyond the twin mesas. A train was approaching.

Chapter 15

Stark remembered seeing private trains during the war. He had once been within a half mile of some tracks when President Lincoln's sailed past. It was on Lincoln's watch that Congress passed the act allowing the government to seize control of all captured Confederate rail assets. Soon afterwards, the United States Military Railroad was established to coordinate and operate all the rail assets necessary for the war effort. Military transport trains came into use, with some cars earmarked for use by high-ranking officers.

General Crook's train was a standard 4-4-0 locomotive, a great beast of black iron that belched smoke and emitted screeches from its whistle as it slowed toward Diablo Gap. Hooked immediately behind the tubular locomotive was a shallow coal car piled with fuel. The passenger carriage immediately behind brought up the rear of the train. It was an elegant railcar, reminiscent of the late president's. But knowing General Crook's reputation for hard work and efficiency, Stark reckoned any excess space inside would be filled with hardworking aides busily overseeing the war effort against Geronimo. The man had a Territory to run.

The 4-4-0 pulsed and rumbled and chuffed across the wastes, slowing, with an intermittent screech of steel on steel, as the brakeman applied his lever. The vast triangular cowcatcher at the engine's nose slowed, and the locomotive came to a halting rest with a massive sigh of hissing steam. The last of the haze dissipated above the smokestack, and a clanking of machinery locking into rest mode arose from the black iron beast. Men moved in the front cabin of the locomotive, the engineer and the brakeman. The former stepped forward and grasped the lanyard of a handbell, banging it twice. Shortly afterward, the front door of the carriage car opened and an officer stepped onto the carriage deck.

He was youngish, Stark noted, but with the straight back and confident bearing of the seasoned staff officer. He wore the fringe and fronds shoulder boards of an infantry major and exuded the gravitas and presence of a man who had seen military service in the field before attaching to a flag officer's staff. He strode out to where Stark and Red Buffalo waited by their horses, reins in hand.

"Major Anderson," he said by way of introduction. "I'm General Crook's aide-de-camp. You've come a long way. Those horses look like they could use some water and feed. If you'll allow me, I'll have them seen to while you visit with the general."

"Much obliged," said Stark. "We've come out from Fort Apache. And up from Tubac before that. There's Apache activity all across that area. We saw multiple farms and homesteads ablaze."

"It's raiding season," Major Anderson observed. "Geronimo is politically savvy. But his actions reflect the traditional calendar of the Apache year. That's part of his success. Men like him and the Prophet capitalize on Indian culture and tradition."

"Excuse me," said Red Buffalo. "What news of the Prophet? Have you heard anything?"

Anderson turned to Red Buffalo and gave him a long, measuring glare. Some men were uncomfortable around Indians, and others actively disliked them. Still others took active measures against them whenever possible, as Stark did in the course of his professional life. But then there were men who burned with a seething hatred of the natives beyond even that which Stark felt. Stark had been like that, too. But he was changing as a result of knowing Red Buffalo.

Stark reckoned Anderson had not.

"The Prophet is a dangerous man," Anderson replied angrily, glaring at the Crow as if he himself were responsible for the Prophet's existence. "He and his movement represent a clear and present threat to the sovereignty of the United States government."

"How?"

Red Buffalo's simple question caused the Major's face to darken. He was unaccustomed to being challenged by a red man. Stark suspected that had they been alone, Anderson might have made the mistake of becoming physically aggressive with Red Buffalo. As it stood, the presence of another white man forced a veneer of civilization onto the situation. On the pretense of observing this, Anderson tipped his gaze to Stark as if to say, *Can you believe this uppity Injun?*

Stark's response was a stone-faced "How?"

For some reason, Anderson was more amenable to answering the question when

Stark posed it.

"The dancing? The peyote ceremonies? They're the foundation of a religious cult. You know these people believe they possess the power to resurrect the dead?" Anderson pulled off his hat and smoothed down his brown hair. "It's a revolutionary movement. Like the one that gave birth to Mexico. There was a religious leader at the center of that one, as well."

"So Uncle Sam is afraid the dead will rise and go to war with the U.S. Cavalry?" Red Buffalo's eye twinkled with derision as he spoke.

Anderson ignored the remark. "The danger the Prophet's teaching poses lies in rallying the Indians to political resistance," he said. "Religions and fables have the power to unite and motivate groups of people. History has shown this conclusively."

Stark and Red Buffalo exchanged a glance. That the army's resistance to the Prophet was so carefully reasoned surprised them both. So far as Stark was concerned, the Prophet as Red Buffalo described him was simply a medicine man bringing a message of hope. It was obvious Washington thought him something much more sinister.

As Anderson finished, a young private climbed down from the carriage deck and hurried over, coming to attention and saluting Major Anderson.

"Private Coop, take charge of these men's horses. Feed and water and rest them a spell."

"Sir." The private saluted, then stepped forward and took the reins of the two horses. He guided Buck and the Crow's horse to the rear deck of the rail carriage, where he tied them to the railing and proceeded to remove their saddles and blankets.

"Come on aboard. The General is eager to meet you." Anderson said to Stark, then shot a glance at Red Buffalo. "You, too, I guess."

They took the steps to the front deck of the passenger car. Major Anderson knocked sharply twice, and the door was pulled open by a tall, slender corporal armed with a revolver. Immediately inside was a watchman's post with a desk, lamp, and padded bench. Stark noted the iron ring set in the wall and wagered to himself that the trunk beneath the bench contained irons in which any unruly intruders could be fixed and secured to the wall.

Another private holding a Henry rifle occupied the bench for now. He came to attention when Anderson entered. Behind him, a narrow doorway in the back wall led to an inner compartment.

Beyond the security post was a combined office and waiting area. Two privates labored over papers at two narrow workbenches. A third, Stark could see, was attended by another private and equipped with its own telegraphy setup. They would have wires on the roof allowing them to stop and connect to poles as necessary.

Stark guessed at least one of the men on board had the requisite professional training to engineer such an arrangement. He didn't envy that man his position. If he was caught at the top of a pole during an Apache attack, he would be a sitting duck.

"Wait here." Major Anderson left the two standing by a workbench and strode to a third door. He knocked twice, then opened and entered, shutting it behind him.

"I'm guessing that's where General Crook has his office." Red Buffalo raised his arms up high and gave himself a good stretch. "Do you think that nice white major is going to let me in? Or send me to be watered with the horses?"

"He doesn't like you one bit, that's certain sure," muttered Stark. "I wonder what put the bee in his bonnet."

"The same thing that put the bee in Geronimo's is my guess. Family killed by Indians. There's been enough killing to go around for all sides of that ugly war."

"I agree about that." Stark thought back to reports he had heard of the great slaughter of buffalo on the American plains, the effort being made by the U.S. government to weaken and wipe out the more hostile tribes by depriving them of their food source. As much as he generally disliked the red man, Stark would never countenance that kind of action.

Indians have a right to live, he thought. *Just over in their own area. Not with us.*

It seemed to him the height of common sense.

"You're coming in with me," Stark said firmly. "We've both been ordered to come here, and we've worked together before. We go in as partners."

"So long as that nice white major is agreeable." Red Buffalo smirked.

"It don't matter a damn what the nice white major agrees to or not."

"We'll see, I guess."

And they did. A few seconds later, Anderson reappeared. He held the door wide and stood back. He did not say a word when Red Buffalo passed.

■ ■ ■ ■

General Crook's office was sparse but well appointed. A number of seating options were available, which made Stark think that perhaps journeys were started with staff meetings in these quarters. A coal stove stood against one wall, available to provide heat in the colder months. The General's desk, actually a large, filigreed antique table, sat across from it. The desk was imposing, which was very much in keeping with its occupant.

Stark studied the general as he arose. Crook was a legend in the armed service, having been an active-duty soldier since 1852. His blue uniform with its twin rows of gold buttons was clean but obviously worn. The boards of epaulettes were firm and neatly squared away. His hair was short and slicked back. But the outstanding feature was the overgrown mutton chop sideburns. Stark had seen his share of muttonchop aficionados in his day, but nothing on a par with Crook. The man's whiskers grew out from his cheeks in great hairy layers, hovering there like a pair of overgrown kittens. They shook when he spoke, as he did now in a low, gravelly voice.

"You would be Stark and Red Buffalo. Thank you for reporting as ordered. I trust your journey here was not unduly dangerous. Please stand easy."

"Thank you, sir," said Stark, because it seemed dangerous not to say so. Crook was a man with an eagle's gaze, who tracked every event and registered every point and counterpoint in an exchange. Such men demanded acknowledgment and attention. Crook's was a commanding presence.

He turned and stepped back to the desk, pausing to lift up a sheaf of papers held together by a large clip. He shuffled through the papers, paging one to another until finding what he sought. He stood reading in silence for a time, holding the sheaf in one hand, the other balanced on his hip. Stark noted the ease and confidence with which he dismissed his visitors' existence.

It's all his world, here, thought Stark. *He's got everything under control.*

Crook coughed into a fist and closed the sheaf of papers.

Everything but Geronimo.

"Gentlemen, there is a time for diplomatic talk and a time for frank talk. To me, the time for diplomacy is over. Too much of it, as well as fear of telling the simple truth, has led us to this current pass. The situation out here is desperate and likely only to worsen. Some of what I am going to tell you about the front is classified secret. You will repeat what you hear to no one. Is that understood?"

"Yes, sir," said Stark.

"Yes, general," said Red Buffalo.

"All right." Crook crossed his arms. "We're losing the war. That's right. We're losing in Arizona Territory and losing badly. Geronimo runs the table out here. And he is well on his way to ridding the area of Americans and Mexicans entirely. He is a force of nature who kills everything in his path. And he is coming in to administer the knockout blow in the final battle. In short, gentlemen, Geronimo is coming. And he's bringing hell with him."

Chapter 16

It had all started, the general explained, with the Spanish.

The Arizona Territory was a reverse Eden. Where a garden should have been was a desert. Where fruit might have been were thorns. And serpents abounded.

In any paradise there were bound to be primitives, and so it was in the Territory. Nobody really had a clue about their earliest ancestors, those shadow tribes that had inhabited the caves in cliffs of distant canyons, whose trade and roads had run across the entirety of the area, whose legacy had been to disappear without a trace. But somehow their descendants, or descendants of those who displaced them, lived on.

It was the Spanish who landed on the beaches, took to the sands, dragging their cannons across the desert, sweltering in their brass armor and iron helmets. The conquistadors further south had fought the

Aztecs, but the ones who came to this region faced more scattered and primitive foes: arrow and arquebus matched up against obsidian blades and battle hatchets. The fighting had been brutal and its aftermath covered over by the desert sands with a weird thoroughness, as if the land itself were eager to forget all the blood that had been spilled here.

It was God, not guns that survived this erasure. A string of stone missions was established across this Territory in the early days, one of which was named for St. Jerome. A village developed around it, a mixture of native and Spanish and, later, American inhabitants. *San Jerónimo* was a stone fortress, a cathedral, and a home to those rising out of the sands of this anti-Eden.

And it was at St. Jerome that Geronimo first struck. In those days, he was called *Goyath'la,* the clever one, a war chief and widower. But his name was forever changed by the prayers that rose that day from the blazing wreckage of his wrath:

"San Jerónimo . . . Mio San Jerónimo, Santa Mio Jerónimo, Jerónimo, Jerome mio, Jerónimo . . ."

American contact with the region first came

twenty years before the War Between the States. The Jicarilla War had been an outgrowth of American expansion. Washington desired the lands of northern Mexico and was prepared to fight for them. Local chiefs had guaranteed the American military safe passage through their tribal lands if it meant bedeviling Mexico. However, the Apache were loosely organized and disjointed in their policies toward newcomers. Some welcomed and supported the wagon trains while others made war on them. The first American military presence in the region was established.

"The problem with the Territory is its vastness and inhospitable character," General Crook said to Stark and Red Buffalo. "We are forever struggling to establish a foothold — cities, towns, centers of trade and travel. But before we can do that, we must have safe lines of communication. And the enemy keeps cutting ours."

Maintaining contact with armies in the field proved a challenge during the Mexican War. The Butterfield Overland Stagecoach route was established but came under near constant assault by Cochise and his warriors. When the Apache chief took hostages at the stagecoach offices, the army had spearheaded negotiations under Lieutenant

George N. Bascom. Bad faith had hampered clarity on both sides, and after an ill-fated attempt to arrest Cochise and his party, hostages were killed. In reprisal, Bascom hung his Apache prisoners. When the Civil War intruded, it became a welcome excuse for the army to retreat back east and leave Eden to rot.

"We lost our strategic foothold in the area," Crook admitted. "It was a loss from which we were never able to recover."

Then came an exodus from the Territory. Farms and ranches, even entire hamlets, were abandoned and left for the desert to reclaim. Cochise and his ilk saw themselves as having won a remarkable victory. Their scouts fanned out across the sands, raiding abandoned farmhouses for equipment and supplies, tearing down the wooden shacks of ghost towns for firewood. A few stalwart settlements — Tucson, Bisbee, and the like — endured through these years. There was enough lifeblood left among the local government types to form an assembly, hold a vote, and opt to join the growing Confederacy as a slave-holding state. Challenging this became a priority for Washington. The army enjoyed a brief encore in the region.

"As rebs, they weren't much," admitted

Crook. "Some rabble in arms and a bunch of gentlemen ranchers playing cavalry. Our forces met them at Picacho Peak and it was a rout. After less than a day, Arizona was once again part of the Union."

But the cavalry would not stay. With the Confederates put in their place, a unit was left behind to watch things, but the main body returned east in preparation for the decisive engagements of the war. Although there was no parity in numbers between the federal forces and those of the local Apache, differences in tactics placed them at an uneasy stalemate until matters were decided between Washington and Richmond.

Return units were already en route when the late president had his fateful rendezvous with an assassin's bullet at Ford's Theatre. The cavalry would come and establish a robust series of forts across the territory, isolate and destroy the pockets of Apache resistance, and bring Arizona into full statehood. That was the plan.

But things didn't work out that way.

"Which brings us up to today." Crook stared out the window at the barren desert landscape. He cracked the window slightly, drawing it open an inch or two before lighting a cigar. "We have our string of forts.

And good intelligence on Apache positions in the hills. All this, plus fresh supplies and horses, and troops seasoned in battle. You would imagine this places us in an unassailable position. But it doesn't because of that damn Geronimo."

The stories about him seemed true. Geronimo's coming home to discover his village razed and his family murdered by horsemen with shod mounts meant his war against whites incorporated both Mexican and American nationals. In short, communications traffic heading either way was doomed under Geronimo's guns.

"The desert itself poses a tactical problem, too," Crook continued. "Sure, we have maps. But they're strangely incomplete — ineffective, almost — due to conditions out here."

The weather was changeable. A migration of coyotes, a sudden dearth of game animals, the odd fire in forested areas . . . any and all of these were apt to befall a rider or an armed column seeking to dominate the Territory. The Apache were like the weather: unpredictable and deadly. And everpresent.

"We learned we couldn't conquer the territory. There was no subduing it. We just had to adapt." The general shook his head. "Did you know that before the war, we tried camels? We did. We really did. Obtained a few from some Arab, off somewhere in the desert, and brought them over here. Nasty critters. Disagreeable as hell. We disbanded the unit when our business back east started up. Released the dromedaries into the desert, never to be heard from again."

But where camels didn't work, men did.

"Our first contact with the Navajo was a hopeful one. They were nothing like the Apache who were, in fact, their sworn enemy. The Navajo wanted to ranch and trade. The Navajo wanted good relations." Crook flicked ash from his cigar into a spittoon. "So did we. And once we began using them as scouts, we began to understand this territory and how to control it militarily."

Navajo scouts began cooperating with the federal cavalry, and the results were almost immediate. Apache ambush sites were located and destroyed. Columns of Geronimo's raiders were intercepted and routed. Areas previously inaccessible became open to settlers and cavalry alike. The tide was turning.

"And it continued to turn," Crook said, "until it didn't anymore."

Operations were left in the hands of regional commanders. But then their reports started to contain startling developments.

Patrols were again coming under fire. Ambushes were succeeding against transport columns. Ranches were burning again.

"Seems we had a problem. And it lay with our new allies, the Navajo." Crook's gaze met theirs. "This is where you two come in. Because this is a scout's problem. We can't see any other way to figure it."

Crook explained that he had dispatched one of his junior officers to the nearest Navajo settlement to gather intelligence. His report, when he returned, was troubling in the extreme.

"The long and the short of it," said Crook, "was that the Navajo guides had all gone on strike."

"On *strike*?" Stark sat forward. "A coordinated action?"

"The same." Crook frowned. "Seems those people had a grievance. Felt we owed them. And sure enough, their chief came to us with his demands a few days later."

The chief was a man of sixty summers, old enough to remember a time before Geronimo and the cavalry. He had been strong among his people, a leader for many seasons. And he had had children in middle age.

"The old chief had not expected to become embroiled in a war against the

Apache. But when the opportunity presented itself, he did not hesitate. He closed with the enemy. Contracted an alliance with the United States government. Made sure that his people would be front and center in any action against the Apache. Because he had a personal stake."

Many years before, when his son and daughter were yet young, Apaches descended in a raid upon the Navajo chief's village.

"They fought, but the Apaches were numerous and well organized. When the smoke cleared, the chief's wife was dead and his children were gone. He grew mad with rage. He vowed vengeance. And so, he told his scouts to be ruthless."

They had been. Prisoners were rare, the Navajo's preference being to merely execute any Apache taken in raids. But one was taken alive. And during his interrogation, he revealed stunning news.

"The chief's son and daughter were still alive. Being held by an Apache band near Purgatory Crossing. It's rough country, and the Apache who live out that way are exceptionally brutal."

The chief had appealed to Crook for help against the Purgatory Crossing Apache, but the manpower could not be spared. So the

Navajo chief had told his scouts to stand down.

"That was the genesis of the strike. The old man wants his children back and expects me to go get them. Well" — Crook spat a wedge of tobacco off his tongue into the spittoon — "that's neither here nor there. And certainly no obligation of mine. But the good Lord knows my life would be a great deal simpler if I had those scouts working for me again.

"I want you to go to Purgatory Crossing. I want you to find the Navajo boy and girl, who would be about sixteen or seventeen by now. I want you to free them and return them to General Miles at Fort Lowell. He'll see they get back to their Navajo family. But this needs to happen with some dispatch. For the raiding season is upon us, and Geronimo is on the move. Without those Navajo scouts, the carnage he inflicts upon us will be apocalyptic.

"Those are your orders, gentlemen. General Miles is expecting you. Godspeed."

They returned outside to find that Private Coop had done a fine job of caring for their mounts. Both horses had been brushed down, fed, watered, and re-saddled with professional care.

"Fort Lowell is a piece from here," said Stark, grasping Buck's reins and gazing south. "How far from here you figure, private?"

"Two, three days' ride, sir," said Private Coop, handing Red Buffalo the reins to his horse. "Through enemy country. I'd be careful."

"I would, too." Stark touched the brim of his hat. "We'll see you around."

Chapter 17

They rode in silence for more than two hours before Stark spoke.

"Army's bit off more than it can chew out here," he remarked. When his words were greeted by silence, he glanced over at Red Buffalo. The Crow scout had his head down, his attention turned inward. Stark bided his time. In the end, that proved a worthwhile decision.

"It's a family fight," Red Buffalo said finally. "All of this. From the War Between the States to Geronimo's war with the Navajo, to this. It's members of the same family refusing to listen to each other, refusing to get along. And when that happens, you get the worst fights."

Stark considered this carefully. There was a grain of truth to Red Buffalo's words. The War Between the States *had* been a family feud. The Confederacy had even adopted a great many of the same core principles as the Union from which it seceded. Because, ultimately, they *were* American whether they accepted it or not. They simply had a different version of America in mind, one that could not coexist with the original version.

And so, a desperate family quarrel, he thought. He could see Red Buffalo's point.

"I think it's the same with the Apache and the Navajo." The Crow fixed his gaze on the horizon. "This land is different from my home. It's brutal. Unforgiving. The Hopi Indians believe this was where the world began. That the Creator made this desert first and released from its womb the five races of men. Many tribes out here believe this or something similar. So you can imagine them all sharing certain beliefs in common and probably working together to survive a harsh environment."

"But fighting, too," Stark offered. "A land like this lends itself to —"

He paused. There was something scattered in the trail ahead. Red Buffalo noticed it at the same time Stark did.

"What's that?" asked the Crow, in mild surprise.

Stark squinted. Little white squares and rectangles dotted the pathway. It was only after a few seconds that he recognized them for what they were. Curious to test his idea, he reined Buck to a stop, dismounted, and bent to examine the nearest white shape.

"Paper," he said. Lifting one from the ground, he read the writing on it aloud: "*Miss Jocelyn Sayward, Special Delivery, San Francisco.* This is mail."

"Special delivery," Red Buffalo repeated. "Not so special, after all, I suppose."

"It leads in this direction," Stark said.

They mounted up and pressed on, following the trail of discarded letters and packages. It continued for quite some distance. Some new editions of local newspapers were mixed among the trail trash. Stark paused and hopped off long enough to collect a few from Arizona Territory.

"Want to catch up on the news?" Red Buffalo joked.

"You never can have too much information," Stark replied, remounting and stuffing two newspapers into a saddlebag.

"I don't trust newspapers," admitted the Crow. "They print them with something called 'movable type.' Those are words that can be moved from one place to another."

"What's the matter with that?"

"Well, if you can switch the position of words, you can just as easily switch what they mean."

"No! No, that's ridiculous. That could never happen."

"I think we Indians have signed enough treaties with you whites to know better."

Stark had to admit the man had a point.

The trail of paper extended for another quarter mile before cresting a rise that overlooked a shallow valley. They rode to the top and stared down.

The stagecoach had been intercepted somewhere back along the trail and pursued with feverish alarm. Stark could see arrows poking out from the vehicle, which had been knocked over onto its side. The horses — only two instead of the more common four- or six-horse hitch — had broken free of the traces but were lingering around, rueful and curious. Efforts to set the stagecoach ablaze had been unsuccessful. Smoke curled skyward from the crisp and blackened back end, but the progress of the flames had been stopped, whether by wind, moisture, or luck, Stark could not be sure. If luck it had been, it did not extend to the coach's driver.

The man lay spread-eagle where he had been fastened, wrists and ankles, to one of the stagecoach's large wheels. A short distance off lay the body of another man, facedown, two arrows protruding from his back.

"Somebody's not getting their mail," noted Stark, casting around at the postal items scattered across the surrounding half acre.

"A violent, terrible waste," agreed Red Buffalo.

A sound intruded, a high-pitched, thin wail that rose into the air. It was the man on the wheel, struggling to speak. Stark spurred Buck down the valley's edge and reined to a stop nearby.

"Please," whispered the man. "Water!"

Stark dismounted, grabbed a canteen and unscrewed it, hurrying to the man who smiled wanly and gobbled at the mouth of the tin canteen greedily. After a time, he gagged before lying back.

"Thank you, thank you," he whispered. "I've been out here for hours."

"Hold still." Stark drew his knife. "We're going to cut you loose."

Red Buffalo dismounted to assist. It took them longer to cut the man's bonds than Stark expected it would. When they were finally done, the man could barely move. His muscles had cramped from dehydration and lengthy extension in the awkward position. It took some more water and stretching before he could finally shamble to a boulder and take a seat.

"Thank God you two fellas came along," he sighed. "I figured I was done for. Either the Apaches would circle back to finish me or some wild critter would eat me for dinner." He gazed up at Stark and Red Buffalo. "Name's Bishop. Brad Bishop, Overland Stagecoach, at your service." He looked over at the dead man lying nearby. "Poor Billy."

"Apaches got you?" Red Buffalo knelt beside Bishop and looked him over.

"Sure did." Bishop reached for Stark's canteen again and took a good solid gulp before continuing. "We've been through this way before. Had a few close calls. But they were always too far off to get us. I figured this morning would be no different. But suddenly there were more of them. And more spread out,"

"Geronimo's on the warpath," explained Stark. "Looks like he and his people are making a major push against settlers and cavalry."

"That's just like Apache," Bishop said bitterly. With a glance at Red Buffalo, he added, "No offense. Present company excepted. But I'll tell you what!" He puffed out a massive sigh. "It's hairy out here for an honest man just trying to make a living. Figured the cavalry would sort everything out. Boy, was I wrong."

"How damaged is your coach?" asked Red Buffalo, rising and pacing around the overturned vehicle.

"Good as new. Leastways, so far as the driving goes," replied Bishop. "After they failed to burn it, they tried breaking the wheels. But you can see, the rims are reinforced with steel." He cackled. "Made 'em mad as hell! So they killed Billy, turned the coach on its side, hoisted me up there, and lashed me to that wheel."

"If we can get this upright, you can continue your journey," Stark said. "We're headed in more or less the same direction. We'll ride with you."

"I'd be much obliged," said Bishop. His gaze crept back to his dead colleague. "It's getting late. By the time I gather up the mail and bury Billy, it will be sundown. Why not camp here, and we'll leave in the morning?"

Stark and Red Buffalo agreed.

It took some doing, but they managed to bury the stagecoach guard and gather up a good amount of the scattered mail before night fell. Bishop shared the considerable supply of food he had packed for the journey and topped off the meal by producing a bottle of whiskey and offering to share it around.

In the end, he was the only one who sipped . . . and sparingly, at that. He put the bottle away and they bedded down, keeping near to the stage which now sat upright on its wheels.

They woke and broke camp early. Bishop begged for an extra hour to hike around and gather what mail he could, so Stark and Red Buffalo relaxed with a second cup of coffee while he conducted his search.

Bishop returned with a stuffed mailbag and two piles of letters cradled in his arms. Stark had to admit he admired the dedication with which the coach driver approached his duties. They doused the last of the fire as Bishop stowed the mail and clambered up onto the driver's box. The dawn's heat was already crawling in over the mountain peaks when they set off, sending up a plume of dust in their wake.

They rode for a solid hour, making good time. Stark took point, leading the stagecoach with Red Buffalo bringing up the rear. Bishop was a focused, talented driver, gamely guiding the conveyance around ruts and road scars that would entrap or hobble the big wooden wheels.

During the second hour, the road was rougher and it slowed them some. At one point, both riders dismounted to help

Bishop lever a rear wheel from a stubborn hole. Once it popped free, with some elbow grease from Stark and Bishop and a judicious filling of sand from Red Buffalo, they resumed course.

The morning grew hot as the sun reached its zenith. Bishop drew up in the shade of a cliff and they paused to rest and eat. The coach driver was again generous with his supplies. Stark brewed up a pot of strong black coffee, and they sat in the shade, sipping the stuff, as the heat of the day came on in earnest.

"So you're going to Fort Lowell?" Bishop asked. "You two assigned there?"

"We're going to help out," Stark said vaguely, and left it at that. Bishop didn't pry further but mentioned that things had been hazardous around Tucson of late. "And Geronimo's not the only problem."

"You're talking about the marauders?" Stark poured himself a second cup of coffee and extended the pot to Bishop, who nodded. When Stark was done pouring, the coachman seasoned his cup with a toot from his whiskey flask.

"Marauders have been a big prob— Say, what is that?"

Stark and Red Buffalo looked up simultaneously. Out of the haze over the desert, a haze so dry and hot it shimmered, forms emerged, traveling on horseback. Although not obviously bound for the coach, they seemed to be heading in its general direction. Bishop put down his coffee and climbed up onto the coach to take a look.

"Ha! Looks like Halloran and his bunch." He climbed down. "They're out this way pretty regular."

"Who's Halloran?" asked Stark.

"They're deserters." Bishop said this flatly, no judgment in his tone, but his eyes suggesting caution. "Halloran used to be their squad commander. They were transferred out here but didn't much care for it. So they left to try their fortunes at civilian life. You might not want to mention that you're involved with the cavalry. Or headed to Fort Lowell."

"All right." Stark shot Red Buffalo a look. "I'm thinking maybe we should light out."

Red Buffalo pondered this for a moment. "Let's stay long enough to be neighborly and say hello," he suggested. "Leaving too fast might arouse suspicion."

"Fair enough." Stark sat back and watched the riders approach.

It was a small group of eight men, and a more motley collection you weren't likely to see. The men wore handmade and mismatched clothes, hats of all make and manner, and their saddlery would fill a museum exhibit. But there was no mistaking the seriousness of their leader's gray-eyed gaze and the guns by their sides.

Stark braced himself for trouble.

Chapter 18

"Bishop! You old fraud! What's the matter? Don't you have a kind word for your old friend, Halloran?"

Stark studied Halloran as he reined to a stop and spoke these words. He knew a hard man when he saw one, and Halloran was just such a man. He wore a flat black Levine hat after the Mexican style, the wide strap dangling below his clean-shaven chin. Thick red mutton-chop sideburns framed his pale, sharp-jawed face, and the stare from his flinty gray eyes was penetrating and without the slightest flicker of compassion.

Stark noticed that the man's smile never rose above his mouth to include the rest of his face. Halloran was clad all in black except for the pants, which were navy blue and sported the distinctive cavalryman's yellow stripe. Any man wearing such pants, whether fraudulently or because he was a deserter, was begging for time in a jail cell.

But Halloran didn't seem to care.

"Well, hello, Jake." Bishop struggled nervously to his feet. "So nice to see you again. How have you been?"

Halloran ignored the question and directed his stare from Bishop to Stark and Red Buffalo. "Aren't you going to introduce me to your friends? Seems a mite rude of you not to, Bishop."

"Uh, sure, Jake. This is Mr. Stark. And his companion, Red Buffalo."

Stark noted how Red Buffalo's name prompted muttering and shared glances among Halloran's men. At close range, he saw them for the scruffy desperadoes they were. Unshaven, wearing rumpled clothes, they were a mismatched band of filthy ruffians, unredeemed by any show of strength or confidence. They were strong men, but cowed under the will of their leader, Halloran. Examining them was like staring at a pack of rats, cowering in the shadows just outside the light, preparing to pounce.

"Well!" Halloran flashed one of his cold, beaming smiles. "Mr. Stark, pleasure to meet you." He glanced at Red Buffalo but did not acknowledge him. "What brings you out here to this neck of the woods? To, ah, *our* little neck of the woods?"

Halloran punctuated this pointed question by producing a slim cheroot from his inside pocket and sticking it between his lips.

"On our way to Tucson," Stark said. "We have a line on some work."

"Well! Isn't that nice?" Halloran struck a wooden match on his saddle and held it to the point of the cheroot fixed between his lips, stabbing Stark with his eyes as he spoke. "And, ah, what *line* of work are you in, Mr. Stark?"

"We do custom woodwork. Furniture restoration. Paneling. That kind of thing." Stark smiled in what he hoped was a non-threatening manner. He sensed that Halloran held tight control over his little group, control that relied on consistent demonstrations of dominance. Such men, Stark knew, could be dangerous when challenged. Or when they *believed* they were being challenged.

"Well, maybe you could help Bishop here with his stagecoach!" Halloran uttered a loud, mirthless laugh. "Looks like it could use a bit of restoring. What happened to you, Bishop? Did you fall afoul of the savages again?" Another glance at Red Buffalo. "And where are your manners? Here me and my men pull up after a hard trail and you're not even offering us refreshment? What's come over you?"

"Sorry, Jake," muttered Bishop, springing to his feet. "Let me see what I can do for you."

And that was exactly what Bishop did. As Halloran and his men dismounted, the stagecoach driver dug into his storage compartment and brought out supplies, including a side of bacon wrapped in wax paper and burlap that Stark had not seen before. It seemed Bishop knew who to butter up and when.

Seems like Bishop knows how to survive, he thought.

Red Buffalo was sitting very still, his gaze off somewhere in the middle distance, present but not inhabiting his body. It was a look Stark recognized. He had seen it before in towns and around campfires where Indians were not welcome. The Crow scout knew how to be present without being present. It was a form of invisibility, of camouflage. And sometimes it worked.

"So, ah, Mr. Stark." Halloran stepped up close and placed his hands on his hips. "What's the story with your, ah, *companion*? Is he like a slave or something?"

"No," Stark said neutrally. "We're friends."

"Well!" Halloran uttered a short, sharp laugh. "Being *friends* with an Injun. Now how about that? Mister, I think you need to cultivate a better taste in friends! Try hanging out with your own kind for a bit."

Red Buffalo sighed quietly to himself and started to rise.

"You stay put, redskin!" snapped Halloran, gaze flashing to Red Buffalo as his hand dropped to the butt of his pistol. "To be truthful, I don't much care for the fact that you're armed. Danny? Relieve Mr. Red Buffalo of his weapons, would you please?"

One of Halloran's posse, a tall man with curly black hair, moved toward Red Buffalo. As he reached out to grasp the lapels of his jacket, the Crow rose and, in one smooth movement, thrust Danny's hands aside, causing him to stumble in the loose scree and fall to his knees.

"Well, ain't you uncooperative?" Halloran's thin lips spread in a wolfish grin. "I guess some extra persuading is in order." He uttered a short, sharp whistle.

Halloran's men descended on Red Buffalo, an uneven match of six to one. Stark stepped forward to help but felt Halloran's hand on his elbow.

"I'd stay put if I was you, Mr. Stark." Halloran's words, whispered behind him, were underscored by the distinctive *click* of a pistol hammer being cocked.

Red Buffalo shoved away the first man to lay hands on him but was kicked from behind by a second. Then a third. As Stark watched, his friend hit the ground and covered up as Halloran's gang delivered a wicked thrashing to the man. Red Buffalo turtled up on all fours, covering his head and neck, enduring it. After a minute or two, the group became weary of battering back and bone and turned away, leaving the injured scout to crawl a short distance off and curl up into a ball.

Stark turned to Halloran. "Very impressive, Mr. Halloran," he said quietly. "You're man enough to lead a pack of cowards and bullies who gang up on an innocent man who's done nothing to them. Congratulations."

Stark fully expected Halloran to strike out at him for this. But he was surprised when the gang leader laughed and dropped a hand to his shoulder.

"Ah, Mr. Stark. How little you understand about strength. Allow me to, ah, *enlighten* you."

Abruptly, his grip on Stark's shoulder tightened and he led him to a log by the cooking fire where Bishop labored busily. Stark could see that his own coffeepot and store of coffee had been retrieved from where he had set it aside and reopened for use by Halloran and his crew. Bishop was laying slices of bacon into the skillet as the men gathered around.

"Strength, Mr. Stark, is cumulative." Halloran helped himself to some of Stark's coffee, then gestured with the full cup. "It does not emerge from a man fully formed but is gained through conquest. One little conquest at a time. First, you put a worm under your boot. Then a dog. Then an Indian. Then a man. You see how it works?"

Stark said nothing.

"No doubt," Halloran continued, "you harbor romantic notions about challenging and facing down your enemies mano-a-mano. But why go to the trouble when you can get your employees to do it for you? Or, better yet, when you can kill them in the cradle and thus spare yourself the trouble of getting your hands dirty?"

Stark sensed this was a prepared speech, the sort of thing Halloran could rattle off from memory. It had a performative quality. He was speaking as much to his own men as to Stark — perhaps more. Coming off like the wise professor who knows everything about strength.

He's got them spellbound, Stark realized. Halloran was charismatic. Every bit as charismatic as he was evil.

"Now take your friend over there." Halloran drew his knife, reached into the sizzling pan, and speared himself a slice of half-cooked bacon. "What good does he serve, really? Just another filthy Indian. The country is rotten with them. They'll never be full citizens, any more than the freed slaves ever will be. No. They are our footstool, Mr. Stark. They are there to be ruled over, and stepped on, to reach even greater heights. That is the law of nature. That is the law of the strong."

Halloran punctuated this pronouncement by taking a good long sip of coffee.

"I disagree."

Those two words, spoken softly, caused an unsettling stillness to befall the group. Every pair of eyes except Halloran's turned to Stark.

Stark didn't care.

"No, Mr. Halloran. I disagree. To my way of thinking, a man is a man. His skin color or his religion ain't got nothing to do with it. A man becomes a man by mastering himself, then mastering a trade, then being of use to his fellow man. I've known white men who were as useless as molasses in a bucket. Lazy. Dishonest. Drunken. And I've known red and black men who are handy with a shovel or a gun, who raise good families and work hard for their communities. It's what you do, not where you're born that makes a man."

Halloran finished his coffee. All eyes were on him now. Stark knew that he had challenged Halloran's authority by daring to disagree with him, something obviously not done among his gang. So there was a balance of power that could tip either way. A vast silence had settled over the men as they waited for the matter to be settled. The only sound was that of bacon sizzling in the pan.

"Well, Mr. Stark," Halloran said finally. "I must say, you do talk awful pretty for a man who refinishes furniture. And mayhap those newfangled ideas of yours might become useful someday."

He stood and tipped the lees of his coffee into the sand, then sauntered over to his horse.

"But I daresay, Mr. Stark, that day is not today."

Halloran's hand flashed to his saddle and returned a second later grasping the haft of a bullwhip. His arm snapped and the thin end of the whip lashed Stark's arm as he moved to stand. Then the whip flashed again.

But Stark wasn't there when it landed. He

had thrown himself into a rolling dive. Halloran was drawing back the whip for another strike when Stark came to his feet and launched himself at the man.

He never got there.

A half dozen men collided with him, throwing fists and elbows and, when he fell, boots. It was Stark's turn to endure the beating Red Buffalo had suffered, and suffer it he did. For a full minute, the fury of Halloran's gang rained down on him. By the time they were done, he had a split lip and a mouse around one eye. His right hand still shrieked where the whip had struck, leaving a long red weal.

He knew better than to get up. He lay there, listening as Halloran held court, thanking Bishop for the excellent cooking, explaining to his men that the likes of Stark and Red Buffalo were nothing more than cowards masquerading as hard men. He, Halloran, was the towering pillar of strength in this region of the desert. It was Halloran who kept them together and kept them alive. It was he who would lead them to success.

The clatter of dishes and mugs signaled the end of the meal. Stark lay still, wondering what would come next.

Chapter 19

"Well, now! That was a fine meal, Bishop. Very fine!" Halloran wiped his lips on his handkerchief, stood, and stretched. Then he produced a pocket watch from his vest and frowned down at it where it lay open in his palm. "And shoot, look at that. Where *has* the time gone? Bishop?"

"Yes, Jake — Mr. Halloran?"

"I think it's time you packed up and went on your way. No doubt there are people anxiously waiting for their mail. So go ahead and pack that kitchen of yours into your stagecoach." He paused. "And while you're at it, pack Mr. Stark, too. You'll be taking him along."

"The hell he will." Stark struggled to all fours. "I —"

That was as far as he got. Halloran's leg shot out, and the tip of his boot connected with Stark's ribs. Stark's right hand came out from under him and he dropped to one elbow on that side. And then Halloran was all over him, kicking and stomping. Weakened by the beating he'd received from the other men, Stark was unable to muster the moxie to even fight back. So, like Red Buffalo, he turtled up and waited until Halloran exhausted himself.

"There! See?" Halloran turned to his men. "*That* is how strength is revealed! Not through character! Not through accomplishment! Not through faith or devotion or belief! But by one man forcing another to *bend to his will* and *beg for mercy*! Are you going to beg, Stark? Are you going to beg me for mercy?"

Stark said nothing.

Halloran wound up and kicked him in the face, sending Stark backward to land with a bone-shivering *crunch* beside Red Buffalo. The Crow squinted at him through blackened eyes.

"Go, Nathan," he whispered. "Save yourself."

"I'll go," he whispered back, then paused to spit out a tooth. "But I'll be back for you. That's a solid promise."

Bishop did pack up his field kitchen and supplies. Then he watered and fed his horses and did a walk-around of the coach before approaching Stark and kneeling beside him.

"How are you?" he asked, touching Stark's shoulder. "Can you stand?"

"Yeah, I can stand." Stark wobbled to his feet. He felt the unfamiliar absence of weight on his right side. He stared down at the empty holster. He seemed to remember having been disarmed at some point.

Bishop guided him over to the stagecoach. As the driver was opening the door and unfolding the stairs for him, Stark turned back. Two of Halloran's men had pulled Red Buffalo to his feet and were steadying him as a third fastened his wrists together with a length of rope.

"You'd best forget about your friend," Bishop whispered. "They're fixing to kill him."

Red Buffalo was released to stand upright on his own, which he managed. Stark watched in disbelief as the Crow's bound hands were fastened to a long length of rope that ended around the pommel of Halloran's saddle. The gang leader mounted and turned his horse around to study Red Buffalo from the saddle.

"You and me are going to be traveling companions, yes siree. Now, I generally go at a fairly sedate pace. But sometimes I like to gallop a little! So I hope your legs are limber and your lungs are strong, Injun, 'cuz you'll be doing some running."

Stark collapsed into a window seat as Bishop closed the door and Halloran's men mounted up.

"We'll make it to Table Pass by nightfall and camp!" he cried to his men. "Then we'll have us some fun with Mr. Red Buffalo, here!"

Laughter and cheers broke out as Bishop climbed into the driver's box and cracked the whip to set his team running.

Stark bided his time, gathering his strength. He didn't want to wait too long and let the gang of deserters make it too far along the trail. But having Red Buffalo afoot would slow them some. Halloran didn't seem inclined to kill the Crow before nightfall, so there was that. A plan was coming together in his mind.

After an hour, with his aches subsiding and his strength somewhat returned, he bashed on the wall of the coach right behind the driver's box. He had to keep it up for a few minutes before Bishop heard him over the clatter of hooves and slowed. But eventually, he did. Once the coach had come to a stop, he called out:

"What is it?"

"Help me!" cried Stark, and did his best to make it sound convincing.

He heard Bishop sigh. Then a squeak of springs as he rose from the driver's box and clambered down. Stark threw open the door and grabbed Bishop as he approached.

"Hey!" The driver's eyes widened. "Let go of me!"

"What do you have for weapons, Bishop?" Stark growled. He shook the man. "Come on! I know there isn't a stagecoach driver west of the Mississippi who drives without some kind of weapon at hand!"

"I — There's a shotgun!" Bishop looked frightened. "It's up in the driver's box! On the floor, under the seat!"

Stark shoved him away, climbed up and found a double-barreled shotgun and a box of shells where Bishop said it would be. He cracked open and examined the weapon. It was old and disused. A clutch of cobwebs shrouded the trigger guard. Stark brushed that away, blew dust from both barrels, and inserted a shell in each.

"I'm going after Halloran," he said flatly. "You can come with me or sit tight right here. I'll bring your stagecoach back when I'm done. But one way or another, I'm going."

"You think that's a good idea?" Bishop

sounded disgusted. "You saw what they did to you and your friend. What makes you think Halloran and his men won't do that to you all over again?"

"Because I aim to kill every single one of them. Now make a choice. We're burning daylight."

With a curse, Bishop clambered into the cabin and slammed the door shut behind him.

The stagecoach, despite the damage done to it by the Apaches, was a fine conveyance. The suspension was responsive, the springs well oiled, and the wheels rolled smoothly over the sand and scree. Stark guided the team around one hundred and eighty degrees, then lashed them into motion. They jolted into action, bolting from their stillness like licks of flame and hurtling after the deserters.

It took them an hour to return to their point of departure. Stark pulled the reins, brought the coach to a stop, and jumped down to study trail sign. There was a jumble of disturbed sand, the aimless half circles of hooves where riders had sat waiting, then twisted around in a circle to keep their mounts quiet while waiting for others to saddle up. The jumble resolved into a line of tracks: eight sets of hoofprints going in parallel lines of four. Behind were two lighter sets of tracks — Buck and Red Buffalo's horse. And wavering outside the main tracks, the hurried, blurred boot prints left by Red Buffalo as he staggered along behind.

A short distance further on, the boot prints became a wide smear where the Crow had fallen and been dragged for a time before regaining his feet.

Teeth gritted with rage, Stark resumed his seat on the driver's box and urged the team onward.

He knew they were raising a cloud of dust, but he kept his eyes firmly on the horizon, searching for a similar cloud marking the group's passage. It didn't take him long to find it.

By late afternoon, he had a pretty good idea where they were. He reined the team to a stop, dismounted, and thumped on the door to the coach. Bishop shoved it open and glared out at him.

"You done hijacking my stagecoach, mister?" he sputtered.

"Almost." Stark pointed at the team, paused in their traces. "I'm going to take one of your horses and scout ahead.

Shouldn't be long. But don't be getting any dumb ideas about taking off on me."

"I won't! Dadgummit!" Bishop snatched off his hat and threw it to the ground. "How in tarnation am I supposed to get a stagecoach running with one horse?"

"I'm glad to hear you're not that resourceful," Stark sighed. He marched up to the team at the front of the coach and looked them over. Both were basically draft animals, large horses more suited to pulling a load than bearing a rider.

But they were broken the same as any other horses. Deciding the smaller one would do, he set about unhooking her from the traces and guiding her free. By doubling up and tying the reins, he was able to fashion a shorter set to use as a rider. After a few experimental gestures with the reins and bit, he drew the horse close to the coach and mounted bareback with the help of the steps.

He smiled at Bishop. "You stay put, now."

"Can't see myself going anywhere!"

With a grim smile, Stark set out after Halloran and his group.

He followed their dust plume for an hour. When it stopped, he knew they were camping for the night. Keeping a careful eye on the spot, he slowed to a trot, approaching with care. So far as he could determine, they had decided to make camp just on the other side of a rock outcropping a quarter mile distant.

He dismounted, hobbled the horse with his empty gun belt, and crept toward the rocks cautiously. About five hundred yards out, he could hear their voices. Someone was speaking — Halloran, of course. His words were indistinct, but once he finished, the group exploded in laughter. Stark made it to the edge of the rock outcropping and peered over.

Red Buffalo had been stripped of his shirt and forced to stand with his hands tied, facing the group. They were clustered in a semicircle, watching with some amusement as Halloran, knife in hand, approached the Crow.

Stark tensed, ready to make a move if it looked like a killing was imminent. At that point, being outnumbered wouldn't matter. The chances of success in such a case were slim, but he refused to let the Indian die alone.

Halloran paused before Red Buffalo and spoke to him quietly. Stark couldn't make out his words, but it didn't matter. Because the point of the knife flashed, tearing a wedge of flesh from the Crow's chest.

Despite this, Red Buffalo made no sound.

Stark fought the impulse to stand up and start blasting. Halloran was laughing and wiping his knife blade clean on his jeans, gesturing at Red Buffalo. He spoke again and the men laughed. When this died down and he spoke again, Stark caught part of it:

". . . wait till dark and feed him to the coyotes!"

More laughter. Stark stared hard at Red Buffalo, willing him to look his way. He needed to let the Crow know that he was not alone, that his partner had not left him to the tender mercies of these desperadoes. No matter how hard he tried, he could not will Red Buffalo to look at him.

But he did have a plan.

God have mercy on them all, Stark thought. *Because I sure as hell won't.*

As quietly as he could, he made his way back to the horse and spurred it back to the stagecoach.

"What?" Bishop was furious and trembling. "Mr. Stark, there are limits as to what you can impose on a man!"

Stark just stood there, arms crossed, waiting.

Eventually, Bishop broke down and complied. Whispering curses, he stomped back to the storage bay of the coach, flung it open, and moved some items around until he found a large earthenware jar.

"There it is," he said angrily. "My stash of hooch. A full gallon of homemade moonshine."

"You also mentioned kerosene."

"Yep." He thumped a tin can. "Right here."

Stark nodded. "And you said you had some glass bottles?"

"There's a shipment of them in this box. But they're promised to a perfume store in —"

"They're being requisitioned for use by the U.S. Army," Stark said. Then he told Bishop what he wanted done.

Chapter 20

They left at dusk, following the tracks from Stark's journey earlier that day. When it became too dim to see, Stark made Bishop light a lantern and walk ahead of the coach, acting as a guide. The rock outcropping behind which Halloran and his gang had taken refuge appeared on the horizon just before full dark. By the time night descended fully, the glow from their campfire was blazing like a dim beacon before them. Bishop had blown out the lantern so that its light wouldn't give them away.

Stark climbed down from the driver's box, easing the shotgun down with him. He distributed the shells into several pockets and slipped a knife into his boot. He was almost ready to become reacquainted with Halloran.

"You get that bag I asked for?" he said.

"Y-yes." Bishop swallowed and lifted the burlap sack from its place beside the front left wheel. It clinked slightly as it moved. "They're all in here. A dozen, like you asked for."

"Thanks." Stark accepted the bag and shouldered it. "I owe you, Bishop. And I aim to repay the debt. Two gallons of premium hooch next town we come to. Now I need you to turn this stagecoach around and start heading back. If all goes according to plan, you'll soon see Red Buffalo and me on horseback, moving fast."

"All right." Bishop made ready to go then hesitated. "You sure you want to do this? That Halloran is a beast. Mean as a rattler. After what he did to you? Are you sure you want to go back for more?"

Stark said nothing.

"He's just an Indian, after all . . ."

"He's my friend." Stark felt strange saying that. He had spent a career hunting Indians, only to partner up with one he couldn't leave twisting in the wind. "As for Halloran, well . . . Every dog has his day. And his is coming to an end."

With that, he turned and marched forward into the darkness.

He heard the rattle and clatter of the stage as it turned and lumbered off through the dark, leaving Stark alone in a wilderness of black with only the dim orange glow of the campfire to steer by. He pressed forward, stepping carefully by feel, taking long, slow breaths in that left his body in equally long, careful exhalations, the bag of full bottles clinking softly against his back. When the glow from the fire filled most of the horizon, he paused and placed the bag by his feet.

Halloran had been canny enough to post a sentry. One of his men sat on the rocks on the slight rise above the campsite, peering down on the goings-on below. Stark could make out the ordinary sounds of a meal in progress, the clank of a coffeepot, the scrape of a ladle against a cauldron, the low buzz of voices. From the sound of things, they hadn't yet started in on their plan to kill Red Buffalo. For that Stark was grateful.

He bided his time, waiting for the right moment to act.

Eventually, it came.

The sentry on the rocks rose and stretched. He set the tin coffee mug that he held on the rock and turned and made his way into the shadows. There, visible to Stark as a dim silhouette framed against the orange glow, he turned his back, unbuttoned his trousers, and began relieving himself.

Stark drew the knife from his boot,

crouched, and moved up on the man from behind, praying that the sound of his boots would be muffled by the passing water. But the man didn't hear, didn't turn, and was fully immersed in the sensation of relief when Stark struck.

Two quick steps and he was behind the man, one hand over the mouth to muffle him while he drove the knife hilt-deep into his back. The man stiffened, spittle spraying Stark's fingers with a muffled scream before the man keeled over. Stark caught the falling body and lowered it to the ground soundlessly, relieving the man of his revolver. Then he crept to the rocks.

Red Buffalo remained standing where Stark had last seen him. Trussed up and shirtless, he stared into the distance, oblivious to the thick red smear of blood crawling down his stomach from the chest wound Halloran had inflicted earlier that day. His expression was blank, his gaze turned inward, as Halloran addressed the seated men finishing their dinner. This time, his words were audible.

". . . time to have a little fun with our pal here." He sniggered. "I promised you gents some entertainment, and that's exactly what we're gonna have! Now —"

He suddenly broke off, raised his head,

and listened as the distant yipping of coyotes rose over the desert.

"There they are — my *boys*! Yes siree, raising their voices in song! You hear that, Red Buffalo?" Halloran wheeled on the Crow. "Don't you redskins *worship* coyotes? I heard that somewhere. That you believe they're some kind of god. Well, you're going to get to unite with your god tonight. How does that sound?"

The assembled men exploded in laughter.

It seemed the show was about to start.

Stark crept back to collect the burlap sack.

Red Buffalo was preparing to meet his ancestors.

He knew Halloran was about to kill him. He felt certain the death would be grueling and painful. He was determined to endure the pain stoically, not give the deserter and his gang the satisfaction of seeing him in agony. So he had turned his gaze inward and prayed, thinking back on the line of his people and whispering the thoughts of his heart to the Creator.

Grant me a good death, he thought. *Do not let me disappoint my ancestors.*

Now Halloran was speaking again.

"We want to make sure everybody gets in on this. Jack?" He raised his voice and peered up at the rock outcropping. "Jack! C'mon back here! We're about to get started."

Silence greeted these words. Halloran frowned, accustomed to immediate obedience. When none was forthcoming, he shifted his stance, squared his shoulders, and tried again, this time in a soft, coaxing tone.

"Ja-a-ck . . . Whoo-hoo! You out there boy? You'd best get your butt back here, sonny Jack! Because it's *me* calling!"

Silence.

"Well!" Halloran shook his head. "How do you like —"

That was as far as he got before the explosion hit.

Stark lit the rags protruding from the remaining two bottles in front of him, hauled back his arm and threw first one, then the second. The perfume bottles containing a deadly mixture of kerosene and high-octane moonshine hissed through the night to drop, one to the left of the camp and one just inside, about where the cook fire was. The first startled the group and made them duck for cover. The second landed in the midst of them and exploded, killing two.

Stark dropped the burlap sack containing his homemade grenades. Grasping the dead sentry's pistol in one hand and Bishop's shotgun in the other, he stepped atop the rocks and stared down.

Two men lay dead by the remains of the cook fire. One screamed as he staggered across the campsite, flailing his burning arm. Another was twisting around and around, rotating on his bootheel, gun in hand as he searched for the source of the attack. The other two were rushing up to the rocks to Stark's right. And Halloran . . .

Halloran, hands raised, was backing away from the licking Red Buffalo was laying on him. Hands bound, the Crow nevertheless was managing to land blows on the bandit leader with his bootheels.

Stark shot the burning man. It seemed the merciful thing to do. Then he dropped the one twisting around and around in a circle. Return fire exploded from the two on the slope, forcing him back behind cover.

Halloran grabbed for his gun but Red Buffalo was too fast, launching himself feet first at the man and hitting him in the solar plexus just as the pistol was clearing leather. Halloran crumpled, dropping the gun into the dust. Red Buffalo fell to earth, landing on his left side and wincing at the sudden jolt of pain in his shoulder.

Halloran rolled onto all fours, shaking his head.

Stark, meanwhile, was biding his time. The two deserters returning fire were wasting ammo, blasting away in a panic. He calmed his breathing, counting shots. Waiting. Eventually, he heard an angry *"dammit!"* as a hammer clicked on a spent chamber.

Stark rose, waiting. As one man reloaded, the other surfaced from behind his cover, aiming his weapon.

Stark put a bullet right between his eyes.

Halloran was up now, limping toward Red Buffalo as he struggled to crawl away. He reached for his belt, drawing a knife . . .

Stark brought his pistol to bear, aimed at Halloran, and fired. A miss, but it was sufficient to drive the man back from Red Buffalo. Stark was readying a second shot when the man who'd been reloading finally finished and opened up again. Stark dove back behind the rocks.

Red Buffalo was rising to his knees. He got one foot under him and was just managing to plant the other when Halloran dove forward, blade first, slashing. He managed to nick the Crow's arm. Red Buffalo dove for the ground, rolling and twisting to get away.

More gunfire from the man behind the rocks. Stark shifted position, moving to flank him. Soon he was out of the line of fire.

Halloran was upright, chasing after the Crow who rolled again and again, seeking to get out of range.

The man behind the rocks rose. Stark ended him with a volley of pistol shots. His body collapsed in a heap, and Stark's hammer clicked on spent brass.

He threw the pistol down, brought the shotgun to bear, and screamed.

"HALLORAN!"

The man halted his pursuit of Red Buffalo and turned slowly. There was a weird expression on his face — a smile and gleam in the eye that suggested delight. Stark guessed Halloran saw this as a chance to demonstrate his strength, his *power*! He had faith in his ability to grasp hold of this situation. He would show these attackers who's boss! Stark smiled as Halloran's eyes widened and he started in sudden recognition.

"Mr. Stark! Well, *well*! Look at you! Back from the dead. I must say . . . I'm impressed."

Stark halted ten feet away and cocked both hammers of the shotgun.

"Nice gun you got there! It's a shame our

final confrontation is so unfairly matched. As you can see, I have only this knife. Now, if you were a *man,* you would put down that gun and face me one-on-one!"

Stark smiled coldly. Shrugged. And pulled the trigger.

The twin barrels of the shotgun roared across the clearing, taking Halloran in the chest and blasting him in half. The man's body twisted and fell, a shredded mess of blood, torn skin, and black clothing. His corpse smoked where it lay.

"Who's the strong one now, Halloran?" Stark asked. He turned his head and spat.

Red Buffalo struggled to a sitting position. "I would say that is the end that man deserves."

"Worm food." Stark sighed and bent. "Here. Let me help you up . . ."

Chapter 21

They recovered their horses, then unsaddled and released the rest before going through the saddlebags and pockets of Halloran and his men, replenishing their store of ammunition and supplies.

"Well, they have plenty of bullets," noted Red Buffalo, pawing through Halloran's saddlebags. "No surprise there."

"Coffee, too." Stark held up a burlap bag of beans. He straightened and gazed around the wreckage of the deserters' camp. "Aside from that and some dried food, I'd say we've cleaned them out. At least, of anything useful."

Red Buffalo scanned the camp, too. The bodies of Halloran and his men lay scattered about, twisted and tangled where they had fallen. Stark sensed a hesitancy in the Crow, as if Red Buffalo were about to suggest they take time to bury the men. He lingered like that for a long moment before turning to Stark.

"We should go," he said quietly. "We don't want to pitch camp here."

"Moon's high and bright enough." Stark studied the sky. "We should be able to catch up to Bishop right quick."

"Let's go then," said Red Buffalo, mounting. Stark stowed the supplies they had recovered in his saddlebags and climbed into Buck's saddle. Then he paused to glance back over his shoulder.

The wind hissed past, a high, keen whine that swept over the camp, fanning the flames of the dying campfire and ruffling the clothes of the dead men.

It was time to go.

They found Bishop's camp after an hour's ride. The coachman had parked his conveyance at the base of a low hillock and released both mounts from their traces. The horses ate feed and watered themselves at a small trough Bishop had set out while bacon sizzled in the pan on the fire.

Bishop stood when he heard them coming. Stark had turned the marauders' horses loose and the animals had followed Buck and Red Buffalo's mount, so it must have sounded to Bishop as if a large group was approaching. He held a skillet raised defensively in one hand until he recognized Stark and Red Buffalo and relaxed.

"I wasn't sure I'd see you two again," he admitted, lowering the skillet. "Figured you for dead, to be honest."

"We're hard to kill," said Red Buffalo. "And the good Lord knows they tried."

They shared Bishop's supper, then sat back with cups of coffee to settle themselves a bit before bedding down for the night.

"I saw more fires," the coachman offered, nodding to his left. "Off to the west there. Geronimo and his men have been busy."

"Forces in this area are at a disadvantage," Stark said. "We aim to do something about that."

"Well, God love you and best of luck," Bishop said, toasting them with his mug. "Because at the rate things are going now, there won't be anyone left out here to receive any mail. And I'll have to move back east."

After a few hours on the trail the following morning, Stark could tell they were nearing civilization. The path grew into a road — a wider, graded, well-defined road suitable for coach traffic. He saw wheel ruts and, along the shoulder, the sort of garbage that stagecoach passengers toss from windows:

bottles, apple cores, food wrappers.

But by midafternoon, they were passing folks departing from Tucson in coaches and on horseback. They paused to speak with some, learned the road ahead was clear and that the Apache were not acting up hereabouts. Stark thanked each one, his concerns allayed with each passing fragment of news.

"I don't mind telling you," Bishop said at one point during a rest stop. "I'm darned glad to have you two along with me. This road is just rotten with bandits. Stagecoaches get held up here all the time."

"I'm not surprised." Stark narrowed his eyes to the sun's glare. "Probably not much out this way in terms of law enforcement. And what there is must stay focused in town."

"They do." Bishop nodded. "Tucson is a wild place."

"So I've heard." Stark put a foot in Buck's stirrups and grabbed the pommel of his saddle. "How close is the fort to town?"

"About an hour's ride south." Bishop climbed back up onto the driver's box. "You plan to go straight there? Or maybe you want to wet your whistle at one of the saloons on Stone Avenue."

Stark and Red Buffalo exchanged a glance.

Saloons in a large town like Tucson meant professional gamblers, criminal gangs, and plenty of opportunities for men with guns to get up to no good. As appealing as it sounded, the well-appointed lounges and saloons of Tucson were best left alone.

"No thanks, Bishop," Stark said finally. "I think we're just going to head straight on to the fort."

"Suit yourself!" Bishop picked up his drover's whip. "I've got a stop to make at the Western Union office, then I'm going down to the hotel to get drunk. Nice ridin' with you boys. Take good care now."

He cracked the whip, steered with the reins, and plunged ahead down the road to the beginning of Stone Avenue.

Between the town and the fort, they encountered a different sort of traffic, mostly Indian, mostly on foot.

"Those are Tohono O'odham," said Red Buffalo, nodding to a passing group. "They are the People of the Basket. Also sometimes called the People of the Maize."

"They violent?" Stark studied the ragged group of barefoot Indians as they slogged past.

"No." Red Buffalo seemed quite sure of this. "They are very peaceful people. Maybe too peaceful. They often get raided and taken as slaves by other tribes."

"You figure that's why they hang around the fort?" he asked. "Protection?"

"And to trade." Red Buffalo shrugged. "They bring baskets. Blankets. Snakeskins."

"People like snakeskins out here?"

"I've seen a few hatbands made from them."

Stark suppressed a shiver at the thought. He preferred his dealings with rattlesnakes and the like to be kept at arm's distance. Better yet, bullet distance. The thought of wearing a dead one wrapped around his hat struck him as gruesome.

The fort appeared in the distance, an unwalled compound of scattered buildings surrounding a parade ground. Stark noted that the buildings were a combination of brick and adobe, and it occurred to him that both were materials immune to damage by fire. Using them in Apache territory was a smart move.

Of course, their approach was observed. A rider streaked out to meet them from the doorway of the adobe stables, galloping full bore. He slowed as he approached. Stark recognized the distinctive uniform and horse tackle of the United States Cavalry. The man wore a single chevron on his sleeve. A private.

"I'm thinking you must be our scouts," the private said, trotting over with a grin. "Boy, are we glad to see you."

"We are." Stark reined Buck to a halt. "We spoke with General Crook at Diablo Gap. He's ordered us to report here to General Miles."

"The general is ready to receive you. He's just finishing up a meeting now. Come on and follow me to the stable, and we'll see to your horses." The private frowned at the half dozen extra horses and added, "Do you always travel with so many extra saddle mounts?"

"They're not actually ours," Stark said. "We kind of . . . picked 'em up along the way."

"We came across them on our journey, and they followed us," Red Buffalo said. "I suspect that something unfortunate befell their owners."

That explanation satisfied the private. "Geronimo, more'n likely."

"Could be," Stark said. "Anyway, I reckon we can add them to our string, if that's all right with the army."

"I reckon that'll be fine, but you'll have to talk to the general to be sure," the private said. "I ain't exactly high enough in rank to make any decisions." He winked. "I bet you could probably do with a cup of coffee and a plate of food, though. We'll see to that, next."

The man was as good as his word. He conducted them to the vast adobe building that served as the stables and livery quarters for the horses, calling out as they arrived. A small Mexican man appeared at the doorway.

"This is Hector. He's a real old-time vaquero." The private dismounted and handed over his reins. "Your horses will be safe with him."

"Muchas gracias, señor," said Hector as Stark handed over his reins. "Beautiful horse, señor. Does he have a name?"

"Name's Buck," said Stark.

"Beautiful animal." Stark watched Hector's practiced eye wander over the animal's lines. He turned to Red Buffalo and accepted his reins. "And yours? What is his name?"

"Horse," said Red Buffalo.

Hector smiled. "That too is a good name, señor," he said, and led both mounts into the barn.

The fort was large enough to have a guest house for civilian visitors. The private pointed it out as he led them to the mess hall. The guest house was a pleasant two-story structure with a wide covered veranda that circled three sides. The mess hall, to which the private led them, was two buildings down from it.

The place was empty, save for a clutch of four cavalrymen who had obviously just come off the trail. They sat grouped together in a far corner of the room, guzzling coffee and eating eggs from their mess plates. They raised their eyes and studied Stark and Red Buffalo as they entered. Stark heard a suspicious buzzing arise as he and the Crow grabbed plates and held them out for the cook to fill.

"Coffee's fresh," the man said, ladling scrambled eggs onto Red Buffalo's plate. "Can't say the same for the eggs. Lunch'll be better."

"We're grateful for this. Thanks." Stark took a steaming mug of coffee and led Red Buffalo to a table. They sat and leaned in, going at the mountains of eggs on their tin plates, washing bites down with slurps of strong black coffee. They were so immersed in this that they didn't notice the cavalrymen until they were surrounded.

"No Indians in here," said one with corporal's stripes. His three pals, all privates, nodded in agreement. "This is a U.S. Army mess hall."

"I see." Stark put down his fork. "Well, what about employees of the army?"

"Civilian employees and the like can eat here," said the corporal.

"Well, then he can eat here. We're scouts."

At this, the corporal raised his eyebrows and laughed. His friends joined in. Feeling his oats, the corporal, who was a large beefy man, leaned over the table toward Stark.

"He's a scout? For the army? Out *here*?" The corporal laughed again. "Mister, you're out of touch. You don't know how things are, out here in the Territory, between Indians and white men. We each keep to ourselves and our own kind, and don't cotton much to mixing."

"Is that right?" Stark narrowed his eyes at the man, starting to not like him.

"That *is* right." The corporal narrowed his eyes, too. And his men crowded around closer. "See, that's the way it is out here in the Territory. None of this being friends with the redskins nonsense like they do back east. No, sir. Out here we don't like Indians."

"I see."

"And you know what we like even *less*?"

"What's that?"

"Indian lovers." The corporal stood up to

his full height, raised his eyebrows, and folded his arms as if daring Stark to take issue with his words. "That's white people who mix with Indians. We can't stand them. And you look like the sort that does." He glared meaningfully at Red Buffalo.

"You know what I don't like?" Red Buffalo asked.

The corporal's shock at the Indian's interruption was visible. He stood speechless as Red Buffalo continued.

"I don't like bullies." The Crow put down his fork and turned. "Men who need to get their little gang of friends together before they go talk tough. Like you're doing now."

The corporal flashed a smile at his friends, leaned in, and poked a finger at Red Buffalo. "*You* work for the army? You trying to tell me you're a guest here?"

"Yep."

"*Whose* guest?"

"They're my guests."

The group turned.

General Nelson Miles lounged in the doorway of the mess hall. A tall, rangy man with slicked-back hair, a mustache, and a Vandyke beard, his uniform, while neat, was a tad rumpled and dust-stained. He looked like any other cavalry officer at the fort yet exuded an unmistakable aura of command.

Standing there peeling slices from an apple with a penknife and popping them into his mouth, he had the easy confidence of a man accustomed to obedience. And that's exactly what he got when the corporal and his men snapped to attention.

"Don't mind Corporal Harrison, gentlemen." Miles ate the last slice of apple and dropped the core into a refuse bucket. "He's just flexing his authority. Aren't you, Harrison?" He flicked an annoyed glance at the man. Turning back to Stark and Red Buffalo, he finished: "You two eat up, now. Then come see me in my office."

Chapter 22

They finished their meal in peace. Corporal Harrison and his boys didn't so much as glance in their direction after the general's departure. They left their plates in the tub by the doorway before stepping out into the blazing Arizona sunshine.

It was a short walk across the parade ground to the cottage where Miles had his office and residence. A corporal standing guard outside greeted the two men by coming to attention and holding the door for them. Another man inside invited them to be seated while waiting for the general to see them. But they had no sooner done so than a voice rose from a back room.

"Corporal? Is that them? Send 'em through."

Stark suppressed a smile as he followed Miles's aide to the general's office. Miles seemed inclined to forgo formality in favor of immediate action. Stark figured he would enjoy working for the man.

The general was pacing back and forth in his office when they arrived. Something about Miles exuded the energy of a caged animal. He seemed to force himself to take a seat so that his visitors could do likewise. Stark suspected the general would prefer nothing better than to be on horseback, pursuing hostiles down some desert trail. Ironically, his demonstrated skill in doing just that had landed him here, commanding hundreds of others in a task he himself would prefer to be doing.

"You'd be Stark." Miles regarded the scout with a penetrating authority. "I've heard about your exploits. You've been of invaluable service to the army." He turned to Red Buffalo. "I know less about you. But if you're good enough to ride with Stark here, that's recommendation enough for me. What tribe are you?"

"Crow."

Miles nodded. "What do you think of the Apache?" he asked.

"Good horsemen," Red Buffalo replied crisply. "Good fighters. Very dangerous."

Miles smiled. "That's the understatement of the year." He swiveled his chair toward the window and stared out. "The effect this war is having on the people hereabouts is devastating. We've got plenty of friendly Indians around here. The Navajo, the Papago, the Yaqui — good people. Friends and neighbors to the whites. But because of Geronimo, I've got settlers now who refuse to leave their homes if they so much as see a friendly native walk past. Geronimo's war isn't just on us. It's on everybody. Including his own people."

"The White Mountain and Cibicue Apache are our allies, aren't they, sir?" Stark asked.

Miles was nodding. "They are. Those Navajo scouts really turned the tide for us." He paused, lips firming and shoulders hunching. "Then fate decided to intervene and have a little fun with us."

As he heaved a heavy sigh, Stark could see fatigue suddenly drape the man like a wet blanket. Circumstances had taken their toll, not just on the military situation here in the Territory, but on Miles himself. Stark found himself almost feeling sorry for the general.

"Atsa is the name of the chief we've been working with." The general produced his penknife, opened it and tested the sharpness with a thumb. "The name means 'eagle' in Navajo. The man's good. Navajos are generally a peaceful lot. Keep-to-themselves sort of folks. But Atsa?" Miles shook his head. "The man can ride. The man can fight. And what's more, he can *lead.* His scouts made the raid at Tanque Verde possible. With his help, we were able to rout a hundred of Geronimo's men at Santa Cruz. But then . . ."

"Atsa," said Stark. "Is he the man whose two children were taken by Apaches?"

"The very one." Miles flicked a glance Stark's way. "I see General Crook briefed you some. The two youngsters are named Mosi and Chayton. They were taken by the southern Apache during a raid almost fifteen years ago. They were just little kids at the time. Everyone thought they were dead. Until one of the Apache captured at Santa Cruz let drop that they were still alive. Next thing you knew, Atsa was here in my office, demanding that a cavalry detachment go and recover them."

Red Buffalo sighed and stared at the floor. The gesture did not go unnoticed by Stark. Or Miles.

"Of course, I understand," Miles continued. "If it were my children, I'd go get them come hell or high water. But the situation here makes that impossible. I can't just send a raiding party of cavalry off to Purgatory Crossing. That would leave Tucson and the surrounding homesteads unsecured. I tried explaining that to Atsa, but — Well, he's a parent. And one that is seeing red right now."

"General Crook said he's called a general strike of Navajo guides."

"That's right. Like I said, the man can lead." Miles shook his head. "Once he told his men to stand down, Navajo all over the territory joined in. We can't get any members of the tribe to work for us now. And that's a state of affairs that leaves us vulnerable to attack.

"The Purgatory Crossing Apache are Geronimo's. Their chiefs and war leaders follow his lead and are among his strongest supporters. They're right at the juncture where Arizona Territory meets Mexico, not far from the hamlet of Isaacson. It's hilly, rolling country out thataway. Plenty of places to hide. And those people are like ghosts. Just when you think you've got a fix on them, they vanish like a desert wind. We don't even know the name of their chief or how many are in their band. But one way or another, we've got to find them and get Atsa's children back."

Stark and Red Buffalo exchanged a glance. This assignment would prove no simple matter.

"General" — Stark sat forward — "is

there anybody we can talk to who knows the area? Having the chance to meet with someone familiar with Purgatory Crossing would make a big difference for us."

"Fortunately for you, there is." Miles spread his hands. "Unfortunately, he doesn't work for us. Or Geronimo. He's a rather unusual case. Johnny Two-Face. He's a half-breed — part Apache, part white. He's spent most of his life on the fringes of both cultures and is accepted by neither. But he knows the area. And while Atsa's scouts were working for us, he assisted and proved extremely helpful, particularly in the Santa Cruz action, which took place near Purgatory Crossing."

"He knows the Apaches there?"

"Well enough to know some on a first-name basis. I reckon he spent time there growing up, although the tribe itself wanted nothing to do with him long-term. If you're to find Atsa's son and daughter, he's the man to talk to."

"Where do we find him?" asked Red Buffalo.

At this General Miles's lips skinned back from his teeth and the officer let slip a slightly uneasy smile.

"That's where things get complicated," he said.

■ ■ ■ ■

Slavery. The Civil War. The Snake War. The Yavapai War. The Apache Wars. The Territory had been bathed in blood for decades. Eventually, a large enough group grew sick of it to break away and found a community of their own. And the Free State of Mescalero was born.

It was a tough bunch of men and women who had banded together in the badlands north of the border to create the Free State. They were a motley crew of whites, freed blacks, Navajos, and dissident Apaches. They had forwarded Miles a letter, a declaration of independence from the United States. Johnny Two-Face had delivered it personally.

Miles hadn't taken the declaration seriously. Ordinarily, such a thing would be tantamount to insurrection, but he had bigger fish to fry. Plus, it seemed unlikely that the Free State of Mescalero posed any great threat to Uncle Sam. To his mind, they were just a bunch of loony eccentrics holed up in a box canyon somewhere between Tucson and Isaacson. They engaged in no illegal activity — no cattle rustling, train robbery, or gunplay. They seemed content to just mind their houses and herds, stand guard over the boundaries of their "state," and be left alone.

Eventually, they would be brought to heel. Their little experiment in democracy would have to be drawn back into the Union's fold. Miles felt confident that would happen in due course and without resort to violence. Provided the Apache didn't wipe them out in the meantime.

"Geronimo and his men know to steer clear of the Free Staters. He tried a raid two years back. Cost him dearly." Miles shrugged. "If you can convince Johnny Two-Face and some of his men to help, they would prove powerful allies, indeed."

Red Buffalo was quiet for a long time after their meeting with General Miles. His gaze was turned inward as he and Stark walked back across the parade ground to their accommodations.

"You're awful quiet," Stark observed.

"I suppose so."

"Something on your mind?"

Red Buffalo stopped dead and studied the desert beyond the fort. "The Free State of Mescalero," he said quietly. "Whites, free blacks, and Indian people all living together. Helping one another." He turned to Stark.

"I like the sound of that, Nathan Stark."

Stark had to admit that it sounded attractive. Sort of a miniature version of America. Or what America was *supposed* to be.

"It takes a hearty breed to tear a living from the land out this way," he observed. "I bet their lives are full of backbreaking work."

"Maybe so. But they have each other to rely on."

Stark grinned. "You thinking of maybe throwing in with them?"

"Might do it."

Stark said nothing. But he was surprised by how Red Buffalo's admission made him feel.

Sad, he realized. *I'd be sad if I couldn't work with Red Buffalo anymore. He's . . .*

Stark caught himself.

He's just another damn Indian!

What had gotten into him? He had no idea.

They were halfway across the parade ground when a familiar figure approached. Short, portly, clad in an ill-fitting corporal's uniform and sporting a walrus mustache, his reappearance was a surprise to Stark.

"Corporal Buell?"

"The same!" The stubby little corporal ran over and pumped their hands. "We just got in here early this morning, sent by order of Colonel Livingston. Now I hear tell you're fixing to go to the Free State!"

"We are," affirmed Red Buffalo. "We just have to find our way there."

"Well, you're in luck!" Buell beamed. "I just finished speaking with one of General Miles's aides. He sought me out."

"Thought you were mostly retired, Buell," said Stark.

"I am. But like I said, I know this area well. Used to hunt up in the White Mountains. And down here. The area of Purgatory Crossing where the Free Staters have set down is generally avoided by the army. But I used to bag javelina out thataway. You guys like pork?"

Stark shrugged. "Don't have anything against it."

"I like a nice bacon sandwich," Red Buffalo admitted.

"Damn good hunting down there!" Buell chuckled and rubbed his hands together. "I'm to take you boys down. And I figure I can shoot me a peccary or two while I'm about it. We'll bring Lampkins along."

"You ever mix with the Free Staters?" Red Buffalo asked.

"No, but Lampkins has. He knows a few. Who are you looking for?"

"A man named Johnny Two-Face," said Stark.

"I've heard the name," admitted Buell. "I think he's in your line of work. Scouting, I mean. That kind of thing. If he's there, Lampkins will help you find him."

"He's agreed to come?"

"He has." Buell nodded. "And that's a good thing. Because if you two had just showed up unannounced, they'd more than likely shoot you."

Chapter 23

They set out early the following morning, a party of five: Stark and Red Buffalo, Buell and Lampkins, and another cavalryman named Bertram Johnson. At Buell's suggestion, they allowed Lampkins to take point, due to his familiarity with the area.

"The Apache follow certain well-established routes when they travel," he explained. "We aim to avoid those. It'll be rough going, in some places, but worth it, if we can avoid their raiding parties."

For two days they rode south, first passing through a level area of desert that was like a vast ocean of sand and saguaro. By night they camped. Despite the rigors of the journey, Lampkins was only too happy to dismount and set up his camp kitchen lickety-split. On the second afternoon, Buell shot a wild pig with his long gun. They enjoyed some fine dining, courtesy of their guide.

Near the end of the second day, the desert gave way to valleys and rolling hills. Mountains crowded in around them, the elevated areas well forested. It was into these thickets that they disappeared when dust plumes suggested other riders were approaching. Lampkin's knowledge of the area proved invaluable. At one point, they retreated into the trees and watched as a massive war party passed, heading north.

"Look," Buell said, offering Stark his telescope. "The head of that group there. See him?"

Stark centered the scope on the lead rider. He was a slight man of small stature but from the way he sat in the saddle, it was obvious he was in command. Stark studied the round, brown face, the keen black eyes, and the twin braids of black hair that floated out past his war bonnet. His expression was one of calm resolve.

"That's him," Buell whispered, almost reverently. "That's Geronimo."

"I hope that's the closest I ever get to the man," Stark said, handing back the glass.

"Me, too!"

They descended from the forest, once the Apache war party had disappeared to the north, continuing into the wilderness of rolling hills dotted with mesquite trees and bushes. The trail thinned and grew hard to distinguish out there. A sense of real menace hung in the air. Stark became convinced they were being watched.

"We're entering the area of Purgatory Crossing," Lampkins told them. "We're not far from the Free State now."

"They're watching us," Red Buffalo said.

"Oh, you bet they are," Lampkins affirmed.

They came upon the sentry soon afterward.

He made no effort to conceal his presence. Stark reckoned the man could just as easily have taken cover behind the rocks on the little hillock where he was posted, but for some reason he had chosen to show himself. At this distance, there was very little about him that was distinguishable, just the silhouette of a man with a rifle.

"Corporal, if you fellas will wait here, I'll go talk to him," Lampkins said.

"I'll cover you," said Johnson, the third cavalryman.

Lampkins shook his head.

"You'd best stay back, Bert," he said. "I'll go talk to him alone."

Johnson seemed on the point of objecting, when Buell made the decision. "He's right. Johnson, you stay here with us. Go ahead,

Lampkins."

They watched as the cook rode up ahead at a sedate pace, raising his hand and waving to the sentry. The man gave no reply, but the fact that he didn't shoot as Lampkins approached was acknowledgement enough. Soon they were talking.

"Do you think he'll check our travel documents?" joked Red Buffalo.

Buell laughed. "He'd probably like to. But I rather suspect their customs inspections are a bit less formal than all that."

A short time later, Lampkins came galloping back. He looked relieved as he reined up in front of them.

"We're on the right track," he said. "That man is a sentry for the Free State. He's prepared to offer us safe conduct to their settlement."

"You explained who we're here for?" Stark asked.

"I did," replied Lampkins. "Johnny Two-Face comes and goes between the Free State and us fairly frequently, so a visit is reasonable to their way of thinking. I don't think we'll have any trouble."

"All right," said Buell. "Let's go follow the man."

They put the spurs to their mounts. The form of the sentry grew more distinct as they approached. He was a black man, a freed slave who valued his present circumstances sufficiently to be scrupulously careful in his examination of each approaching rider. Stark noted the crisp, efficient way he evaluated them, appraising each man's clothing, weaponry, and degree of fitness before speaking.

"No guns allowed in camp," he said. "I'll lead you to the edge. But anyone who wishes to go further will have to lay down their firearms."

"Wait just a damn minute!" snapped Johnson. "We're U.S. Cavalry. We don't —"

"Relax, Johnson," Buell said easily. He turned to the sentry. "My name is Buell, and I'm in command here. We will observe whatever regulations you require of us in your territory. These two men here" — he gestured to Stark and Red Buffalo — "are scouts in our employ who are seeking your man Johnny Two-Face. I will accompany them into your camp to make an embassy to your leaders. These other two will remain back with our weapons if that's amenable to you."

"That'll do," the sentry replied. "Follow me."

He led the way around the base of the hillock and then upslope, into a forested area. The ground cover seemed wild, untrammeled by human passage. Stark could tell they were entering a remote sector.

"If the Free State has their main encampment nearby, you couldn't tell," Stark said to Red Buffalo.

"Only if you don't look up."

Stark did. And saw, high in the branches of a tallish tree, the camouflaged platform guarded by another armed sentry. The two sentries waved to each other and the column continued on.

They rode for an hour before the ground rose, then dipped into a forested valley. A third sentry waited there. Their guide halted.

"Our main camp is down there," he said, pointing into the valley. "This is where you leave your guns."

Buell, Stark, and Red Buffalo removed their gun belts and handed them across to Lampkins and Johnson.

"You boys wait here," Buell said. "I'll be back shortly."

"Godspeed, Corporal," said Lampkins.

The guide spurred his horse and they followed. The way into the valley was all soft grass and flowering plants. In the middle distance, the sound of a running stream could be heard. Birds twittered in the trees.

"This is good land," Red Buffalo observed. "Soft and generous."

"The soil is good here," offered their guide. "Much better than the cotton fields I worked in Georgia. We get a fine crop of vegetables every year."

The fields in which these vegetables grew soon appeared. A large level section of the ground had been cleared and tilled, and was now being worked by a team of farmers. Stark saw two black men, who waved to the guide, as well as a woman who appeared to be Native. A second woman, white, looked up and shielded her eyes. As they passed, she turned and spoke to the other woman in what sounded like Apache. Stark had no idea what was said but the two women doubled over in laughter.

Beyond the fields was a path. The guide followed it through the trees into the main encampment. The Free State was a motley collection of tents, lean-tos, and simple log cabins. Despite this, the structures were neatly organized along the trail. Stark saw an open circular area with benches that he reckoned was probably used for town meetings and church services. A cross stood on a simple wooden altar. Before the cross was a large ceremonial pipe.

"Do your people follow the Prophet?" Red

Buffalo asked the guide, gesturing toward the altar.

"Some do," came the reply. "We have two preachers, one white and one Indian, like yourself. They hold services both separately and together."

"Do they do the peyote ceremony?" Red Buffalo asked.

"Sometimes," admitted the guide. He left it at that.

At the far end of the row of dwellings was a larger cabin with a front porch. The door opened as they drew near, and a man emerged. He was a white man, tall and broad-shouldered, wearing a white dress shirt, buttoned to the neck, and black pants held up by suspenders. Like Buell, he wore a walrus mustache, and when he folded his arms, the shirt bulged out around his muscular physique. He looked like he could lift a horse.

"Well, well," he said in a low, deep voice. "What have we here?" Turning to their guide he said, "Joseph, who are these people?"

"They came from the road to Purgatory Crossing," replied Joseph. Then to Stark and company, he said, "This is Randall, leader of the Free State of Mescalero."

Buell rode forward.

"Mr. Randall, my name is Buell. I'm a corporal with the United States Cavalry. We are entering your territory on an official embassy from the United States government, on a matter of national importance. We have come unarmed and pledge to abide by the laws and customs of your land while we are on it."

Stark was impressed. He had figured a telegraph operator would be gifted with words, but Buell had the true silver tongue. Upon hearing them, the big man, Randall, relaxed slightly. His expression of suspicion was replaced by one of curiosity. Then he became conscious of the other citizens of the Free State, who came trickling out of their dwellings to have a look-see. Aware that he was being watched, Randall lifted his chin and went into leadership mode.

"Welcome, Corporal Buell. I'm Randall, President of the Free State of Mescalero. You have my guarantee of safe conduct. No harm will come to you or your friends while you are our guests here."

"Thank you, Mr. Randall." Buell turned his horse slightly toward Stark and Red Buffalo. "Allow me to introduce the gentlemen under my protection. This is Mr. Nathan Stark. His companion is Moses Red Buffalo of the Crow nation. Sir, they are assisting the army in a matter of national importance. And —"

"Geronimo." Randall smiled as he interrupted. He held up a hand. "What else could be considered of national importance here? Unless, of course, President Cleveland cares to offer us diplomatic recognition . . ."

Stark, Buell, and Red Buffalo were careful not to laugh at this, lest they bring offense. But everyone else did. The Free Staters were under no illusions about the precarious nature of their experiment.

At least they have a sense of humor about their situation, Stark thought grimly.

Buell smiled. "Well, I'm just a lowly corporal, sir. Not fit to speak on behalf of the president. But I *can* assure you that any assistance you can render us would be viewed most favorably by the U.S. Army *and* the U.S. government." He turned to Stark. "I'll let these gentlemen explain the nature of their mission."

Stark cleared his throat to speak but paused. Studying the motley assortment of those who had gathered to listen, he noted they were representatives of just about every race in the country: whites, blacks, Indians, Mexicans, and even a few Chinese. But what they all had in common was poverty. Their clothes were ragged, and a great many went barefoot.

But they radiated an unmistakable sense of pride — in themselves, their community, and their leader. They were outsiders, all. People who had suffered and been rejected by society. They would understand someone who could speak to them on their level.

He turned to Red Buffalo.

"You talk to them," he said quietly.

"Me?" The Crow scout seemed surprised.

"Yes, you. These people don't need a speech from a soldier. They need to know they're dealing with people who understand and respect them. An outsider."

"I understand," said Red Buffalo. He nudged his horse forward.

Chapter 24

The Crow reined to a halt before the porch. Randall's eyes fell on him with cautious interest.

"*Sho'daache Kahee* — hello. I am Red Buffalo, of the Crow Nation. I have come with my friend Nathan Stark to request your help. We come in aid of Atsa, the Navajo war chief." He paused, drew in a deep breath as if adjusting to the weight of this burden. "Atsa's two young children, Mosi and Chayton, were taken by the Apache many summers ago. For a long time, Atsa believed his son and daughter to be dead. Or worse. But now we learn that they are alive and well. They would be a young man and woman by now. Once the old chief heard this, he withdrew from the world of men. He dwells in grief now, unable to attend to his obligations or do his work. This has harmed many people, both Indian and white men. We hear that Mosi and Chayton are with the Purgatory Crossing Apache. We seek the help of Johnny Two-Face, a scout who lives among you. We would ask him to accompany us to their camp that we might rescue the chief's son and daughter and return them to their family. That is who I am. And that is why we came.

"These words are true. *Ahóoh* — thank you."

A murmuring rose as Red Buffalo finished his brief address. His request seemed to be generating some controversy. Johnny Two-Face, if he was among the group, did not step forward. Nobody did. All eyes went to Randall where he stood on the porch. Stark had noted how carefully the man listened. Randall was obviously accustomed to dealing with people of many different races and customs, and knew well to take a moment of silence to consider his reply.

"You've come. You've followed our laws by leaving your guns at the border. You've been plainspoken and respectful," Randall said. "You've shown honor and trust for the Free State, and that is recognized and appreciated. We have no official treaty with the United States." He directed this pointedly to Buell. "If we did, we would oblige in the name of our country. But we have no such treaty. And so the decision whether or not to help you is Johnny's alone. We are a *free* state, which means that men are allowed to exercise their *freedom* and to make their *own* decisions. So, here is what we are going to do . . ."

In the ensuing silence, one might have heard a pin drop — if such luxuries as pins could afford to be negligently dropped in the poverty-stricken Free State.

"We will counsel with Johnny Two-Face and present your request. In the meantime, we'd ask you to withdraw back to the border of our territory to await a reply. I guarantee your safe passage back. Somebody from the Free State will convey Johnny's decision to you as soon as he makes it. That is all."

"God, I need a drink!"

Buell dismounted with a heavy groan and rooted in his saddlebag as Stark and Red Buffalo rode up just behind him at the border of the Free State, where Lampkins and Johnson waited. Buell produced a flask from his saddlebag, tipped it to his lips, and then offered it to Stark.

"No thanks." Stark drew Buck out into some nearby brush and released him to graze. He turned to Red Buffalo. "That was quite a speech you made. I think you tipped the balance in our favor."

"Right you are!" affirmed Buell, toasting the Crow with his flask. "Well said, Red Buffalo. Now let's hope that our friend Johnny Two-Face heard you and decides to do the right thing."

"That's up to Johnny," Red Buffalo said, dismounting. "I get the feeling Randall will counsel with him and offer his opinion. He's a cautious man."

"It's actually quite remarkable what they've achieved down there," Buell mused. "It takes a lot to walk away from — well, everything."

"It does," Stark agreed. "It also gives them a good reason to say no to our request. What do they gain? Not much. They're well protected here. And like General Miles said, even Geronimo gives them a wide berth." He shrugged. "They might be just as inclined to let Uncle Sam and the Apache battle it out without them."

Lampkins had set up his field kitchen and was whipping up something that smelled really good. It turned out to be a stew: pig meat, carrots, and potatoes in a thick brown broth. They sat in a circle around the cook fire and ate, trail fatigue silencing any further conversation. Dusk fell as they finished up. Their after-dinner coffee was consumed in a similar silence. The men were just reaching for their bedrolls when a rider appeared.

It was Joseph, the black sentry they had first encountered. He stopped short a dozen yards from the border of the Free State.

"Johnny Two-Face has made his decision. He and Randall are asking to speak with you back at our camp."

"Of course," said Stark. He stood and went to Buck, grasping the reins. "Is he coming?"

"That ain't for me to say," replied Joseph. "He can tell you himself."

As they had earlier, Buell, Stark, and Red Buffalo left their weapons with Johnson and followed Joseph back to the porch of Randall's house, the lanterns on the porches of the smaller dwellings lighting their way. Joseph took the reins of their horses as they dismounted.

"You're to go in," he said, nodding to the front door.

They climbed the steps to the porch. Buell knocked, and the door was opened by a white woman, in a gingham dress, with her hair tied back. She went barefoot and stepped aside, holding the door for them. Stark and the others stepped into a good-size front room, which held a number of visitors.

Randall stood by the mantle of a primitive brick fireplace, arms crossed, his posture unchanged from their earlier conversation on the porch. The barefoot woman in the gingham dress took a seat in a nearby chair. Standing around the walls were several men, a mixture of white and Indian. Two women, one black and the other Chinese, sat on stools by the door.

"Gentlemen, welcome back," Randall began. "Your request has prompted a great deal of discussion among us here in the leadership council." He paused. "The courteous and diplomatic way you have approached us made a great difference, I can tell you. But we have some questions."

"Certainly," said Buell, taking the lead, as he had done before.

One of the men by the wall stepped forward, an older white gentleman with silver hair and a wrinkled face who stood leaning on a cane. "When you contact Johnny Two-Face, assuming you can find him, do you intend to return here to the Free State?"

Buell shook his head. "No, sir. Leastways, not unless you want us to. Our business lies south of here. We don't intend to bring any of that here."

The old man looked at Randall, nodded,

and limped back to his place by the wall. Next to speak was the black woman seated on a stool.

"Do you plan to return to the Free State at any time in the future?" she asked. "Do your plans include making visits like this again? Relying on our support in the future?"

"Not at this time," answered Buell. "Our embassy here is for a single cause, with a single purpose. Once our business with the Purgatory Crossing Apache is concluded, we have no intention to return." He turned to Randall. "It is my intention to brief my superior officer on our visit here. I intend to report that you were courteous, cooperative, and that you accorded us every diplomatic privilege. I will also report that you prefer we leave you alone. That is a sentiment I can understand and agree with. I will urge our officers to comply."

Randall nodded.

A long silence fell. Stark had the sense that everyone in the room was waiting for something. And when that something finally did happen, he understood.

One of the native men by the wall shuffled forward. He was a short, slender man with long black hair tied in braids that fell to either side of his head. Stark guessed his age at about twenty-five. His clothes were rumpled but clean, and his hands had the roughened look of a man accustomed to hard work. When he spoke, his voice was strong and confident.

"I'm Johnny Two-Face," he said. "I'm the man you're looking for. You want my help finding the Apache in this region? I can provide that help. But you must promise that you will do everything in your power to avoid harm coming to this place and these people. If you promise this, I will assist you."

Stark stepped forward. "My name is Nathan Stark, U.S. Army scout. You have my personal guarantee that we will conduct this mission in a way that will leave this place and these people completely out of it. We just need to go and get those kids. You guide us there, help us get oriented, and then you can leave. We'll take it from there."

Johnny Two-Face considered his words, then nodded once.

"Johnny," said Randall. "This is your personal choice, and we support you. If the Apache capture you, you can just say these two men must have followed you to their location. That way" — he turned pointedly to Stark — "we can avoid any mention of our meetings here." To the group, he said,

"This will be kept completely within council. Agreed?"

Every member of the Free State leadership council nodded. A few murmurs of agreement rose.

"Unless you have anything else for us, we'll be on our way back to camp," said Buell. "Johnny, you can meet us where your sentry Joseph was posted."

Johnny Two-Face and Joseph exchanged glances, then Johnny nodded again.

"All right." Randall smiled. "That concludes our business."

"I have a question," said Red Buffalo quietly.

Randall turned to him.

"It may be that once our business with the Apache is finished, I might want to return here," Red Buffalo said. "I see what you are doing here, and I approve of it. I would like to learn more about you. May I have your permission to return for a visit? To share in worship with those among you who follow the Prophet and eat the Flesh of the Gods in their company?"

Randall listened until Red Buffalo was finished, then turned to one of the native men standing by the wall who had not yet spoken. He was an elderly man with a deeply lined face and thick braids. Stark noted that he was dressed in a white man's suit jacket and trousers. The quality of his boots was excellent, suggesting a custom fit, and a strange fetish hung around his neck.

"Do you know the Prophet?" he asked Red Buffalo.

"I have worshipped with his followers," the Crow replied. "I took peyote with them and remained among them for a while. The Prophet's teaching speaks to my heart. I would like to learn more."

"I am Spotted Owl," the old man replied. "The Prophet is my brother. Red Buffalo, if you return, you may come and worship with us. We will eat the Flesh of the Gods together and I will teach you the Ghost Dance. You are a traveler. You must teach the Ghost Dance to other Indian people you encounter. And I will give you a quantity of peyote to take with you. Teach the others about the cross and the pipe. Teach the others about the ancestors' return. Keep the ancient ways and dwell in goodness, and you shall be my brother, too."

Red Buffalo nodded and they turned to the door. Stark was surprised to see tears in his friend's eyes as they left.

Chapter 25

"Well, Mr. Stark" — Buell climbed into the saddle of his horse and settled there with a smile — "looks like this is where we part ways!"

It was the next morning. A low mist shrouded the trees near their camp. Johnny Two-Face lounged in the saddle, his horse nearby, plumes of vapor streaming from its nostrils in the chill.

"Seems so." Stark squinted back in the direction from which they had come. "Maybe you'll bag another javelina on the way back."

"I aim to." Buell paused to consider Johnny Two-Face as he bent to adjust his saddle. "You take care, now. And" — he lowered his voice — "you keep an eye on that Apache half-breed. He seems like a decent enough lad, but . . . he *is* part Apache. And we know they're part animal. Or apt to behave like animals, leastways."

"We'll be careful," Stark replied.

"Good. See you down the trail. C'mon, men!" He touched the brim of his hat by way of salute, wheeled around, and began following the trail back toward Fort Lowell, Lampkins and Johnson trailing behind, skillet clanking against Lampkins's saddlebag as he galloped.

Stark mounted up and patted Buck's withers. Red Buffalo was already in the saddle. As he had so often been in the past days, the Crow had withdrawn into himself, plumbing his inner depths, ruminating about all the memories these travels had stirred up inside him. Stark paused Buck beside him and lowered his voice.

"Ready to go?" he asked.

Red Buffalo nodded.

"Buell says we should watch ourselves with Johnny, here. Seems to feel he might revert to savagery if we turn our backs."

At this, the Crow stirred. "We should watch ourselves," he said quietly. "The anger is very close to the surface with these people. And that's unusual for Indian people."

Stark chuckled. "Really? Most of the Indians I've dealt with seem plenty mad."

"That's in the heat of battle." Red Buffalo's eyes flicked to him. "In regular life, anger is discouraged among us. In many native languages, the word for crazy is the same as the word for angry."

"That right?" Stark's forehead creased in surprise. Then he laughed. "You know, that makes a lot of sense, really. Because when you're angry, you're *not* in your right mind, are you?"

"No." Red Buffalo's attention turned inward again. "It's just one of many things I have on my mind right now."

"I understand."

Johnny Two-Face finished adjusting his tack and turned to them.

"Purgatory Crossing Apache move their camp often," he said. "This is one of the worst places in the Territory to settle. You've got American cavalry going through here a lot. Mexican Army sometimes, too. But also other bands of Apache. They're the enemy. As well as the scalp-hunters. Makes better sense to move around out here so as not to become a target."

"It does make sense," Stark allowed. "You know where their traditional camping grounds are?"

"I know them. And I have an idea which one they might be at. But if they're not there, we'll check the others."

"Fine," said Stark. "You guide us to their

present camp and orient us. We'll take it from there."

They lit out, Johnny Two-Face in the lead. He guided them, past the rock outcropping that was the border of the Free State, into the chaos of hills and valleys that comprised the Purgatory Crossing territory. He seemed, so far as Stark could tell, to be following no discernible path or trail. But he appeared to know where he was going, so Stark decided just to follow along and familiarize himself with the territory as best he could.

After an hour, the level ground gave way to a shallow slope that led down into a dry wash. Johnny Two-Face began following the wash in a generally southern direction toward the border with Mexico.

"This is where the Mexican Army sometimes crosses," he said. "We'll hear them coming from a long way off, if they're around." He paused before adding, "When the Prophet and his people come through, they use the same path."

"I noticed the cross and the pipe on the altar at your encampment," Red Buffalo replied. "Has the Prophet ever conducted a ceremony there?"

"I don't know," Johnny replied breezily. "I don't attend those ceremonies."

"You don't?" Red Buffalo raised his eyebrows. "Why not?"

"Because I don't believe in all that stuff. Jesus and the sacred vision of the Ghost Dance. It's garbage. All religion is garbage."

The shock was plain on Red Buffalo's face at these words. "How can you say that?" he demanded, real anger in his voice. "As Indian people, we are tied to the spirits of this land. And as men, we are all tied to the spirit of Jesus! To deny this is foolish."

Johnny Two-Face brayed laughter at this. "No. What's foolish is to believe fables and fairy tales. Jesus dying on the cross and rising again? It's a story, nothing more. Same with that lie about the Ghost Dance. A dance to raise the dead? And the idea that the buffalo can return — nonsense!"

"That 'nonsense,' as you call it, *matters,*" Red Buffalo objected. "Religion ties us to the sacred. Reminds us that people and animals are sacred!"

"People are not sacred." Johnny Two-Face spat into the sand. "People are just animals that have learned to talk. They care about themselves. The Free State is the only place I have found that accepts me. I live for them — a real, live community of living people. Not the ghostly community of our ancestors. They died. They're dead. That's all there is to it."

"I feel sad for you," Red Buffalo said softly.

"Feel sad for Geronimo's victims," Johnny shot back. "For the women and children he has slaughtered. They died unjustly. And for similar stupid ideas! Those Indians?" He spat again. "They died because they were stupid. Couldn't adapt to the white man's ways. The iron road is coming. The Black Wires are coming. White men like your friend here are coming. Intelligent men reject religion and fables, and focus on the real world that's happening all around them. Doing anything else is foolish."

After this, they remained quiet for a long time.

"The camp is up this way." Johnny Two-Face had reined to a halt at the base of an incline. A narrow goat path twisted up into the mesquite forest. "They like to be here at this time of year. Good fishing in the nearby river. You two wait here, and I'll go and see if they're there."

"All right," said Stark.

Johnny started up the goat path at a sedate walk. Stark and Red Buffalo watched him go until he disappeared into the trees.

"He's a strange one," said Stark.

"He has no respect for the old ways." Red Buffalo sounded sad. "I think he has forgotten who he is."

"Well, he's a half-breed." Stark shrugged. "Perhaps he never knew who he was to begin with."

Red Buffalo shook his head. "No, Nathan Stark. When a person has Indian blood, they know. A part of them cries out to the Earth, the wind. Johnny Two-Face has cut off that part of himself, and he did so deliberately. He is like a man who cuts off his nose to spite his face."

Stark had to admit that it did sound sad.

Johnny returned a few minutes later at a light trot. "They are not there," he reported. "But there is something you should see. Come."

They followed him up the hill into the trees. The path meandered through the growth, widening, the deeper they moved into the forest. After a quarter hour, they emerged at a broad clearing. Grassy, sheltered from the elements, it was the perfect camping ground for a small tribe of maybe one or two hundred Apaches. Stark squinted at a smudge in the grass a dozen yards off.

"Somebody has been here," he said. "That's an Indian-style fire pit right there, dead certain."

Johnny Two-Face was nodding. "They were here, I agree. But come see."

He guided them away from the fire pit to the far edge of the meadow. The grass ended, leaving a stretch of dirt. As they arrived, Red Buffalo slid from the saddle to examine the ground.

"Horse prints," he said. "Fresh."

"Look closer," said Johnny Two-Face.

Red Buffalo continued staring at the ground for a time. Then he turned to Stark and said, "White men. These horses wore shoes."

"But who?" asked Stark.

"Not soldiers." Johnny sounded confident. "The bluecoats don't come up here. These tracks are from someone else. Could be Mexican soldiers."

"Could be marauders," Red Buffalo offered. "Or those scalp hunters."

"I'm thinking it's another group," replied Johnny. "There's a renegade bunch of cavalry deserters led by a man named Halloran. They're hell on horseback. They—"

"Wasn't them," said Stark.

"Why do you say that?"

"Because they're dead. Halloran, too."

Johnny cocked his head. "How do you know?"

"Because I blew him in half with a shotgun and left him for the buzzards."

Johnny Two-Face considered this. "I'm glad to hear it," he said finally.

Red Buffalo was the first to sense they were being followed.

About an hour out from the first camp and well on their way to the second, Johnny Two-Face mentioned there was another spot the tribe favored in the summertime, a canyon studded with old cliff dwellings.

"The Old Ones lived there," he explained. "The Purgatory Crossing Apache like to camp there sometimes. They live in the old ruins and hunt game in the area. It's a long journey to the nearest water. In fact, we just passed it."

"Why the cliff dwellings?" Stark asked.

"They're well hidden," replied Johnny. "And big enough to bring their horses inside. When they camp in the Old Ones' homes, nobody can tell they are there."

That was when Stark noticed Red Buffalo was lagging some distance behind them. He turned. The Crow scout had paused in the middle of the trail and was studying the rocks at the top of a nearby mesa. Stark wheeled Buck around and galloped back to him.

"What's going on?" he asked.

"I spotted someone," Red Buffalo replied. "Or thought I did. Up there." He pointed. "Just for a second. Looked like somebody's head peeking over."

They sat staring for a time, perhaps a couple of minutes. Just when Stark was ready to give up, he saw a suggestion of movement. Like a shadow shifting among the rocks. Distant. Indistinct. But definitely there.

"Okay." He sighed. "We've got company."

Johnny Two-Face rode up. "What's going on?" he asked.

"We have someone following us. At the top of the mesa. Don't look," said Red Buffalo.

Johnny looked.

"Hey." Stark bumped Johnny's horse with his own. "What are you doing? You want to let them know we're on to them?"

But Johnny ignored this, continuing to scan the mesa top for a long interval. When he was done, he turned to them.

"I wanted to make sure it wasn't them. The Apache." He resumed riding the trail, with Stark and Red Buffalo following. "I can tell when it's one of their sentries. But these people are not Apache."

"How can you tell?" Stark asked.

Johnny Two-Face ignored the question and kept riding. Stark heaved a sigh and dropped back to ride next to Red Buffalo.

"Strange kid," he muttered.

"Yes." Red Buffalo uttered a muted chuckle. "But knowing it's not the Purgatory Crossing tribe is good. That narrows it down."

"Scalp hunters. Or marauders. Possibly Mexican military."

"I'd scratch that last one off the list," the Crow said. "They travel in large groups on this side of the border, and you can hear them coming from miles away. Being unobtrusive is not their strong suit."

"So it's one of the other two groups." Stark narrowed his eyes. "Could just as likely be highwaymen. Thieves. You know the type. They'd lie in wait for a rider or small band of riders to pass before pouncing."

"One thing we do know."

"What's that?"

Red Buffalo smirked. "It's not Halloran."

Chapter 26

Thievery was a risk any traveler took when journeying across open country on horseback. The stagecoach lines had learned to mitigate that risk by posting guards alongside drivers. Such men scanned the countryside ahead, alert to signs of ambush. Coaches bearing cargo, such as gold or cash boxes, were escorted by additional armed riders to make them a less attractive target. It was in this way that companies like the Overland Stagecoach line managed the risk of operating in Indian country or the ruined, lawless remains of the Confederacy.

But such resources were scarce here in the Territory. Stagecoach lines fortunate enough to be in the employ of the government received cavalry escorts. But independent coach lines, or travelers journeying in columns, on horseback, had to make do with whoever made themselves available for that service. Given the risks associated with conflict or capture, volunteers were hard to come by. The prizes to be had were more plentiful out this way, and the motivations of the robbers, different.

Ten dollars per scalp, Stark thought.

It was a princely sum.

"I wonder," Stark muttered to Red Buffalo as Johnny rode ahead. "You think the army is paying for white scalps, too?"

"How can they tell the difference?" the Crow asked. "One scalp looks pretty much like another. And I'm sure the Mexican Army doesn't care. Probably pay extra for cavalry scalps."

The claim didn't strike Stark as outlandish. He knew that variations of scalps commanded different prices. A man able to take a scalp with the victim's ears still attached, for instance, could earn twenty-five dollars. A grisly commodity made for a grisly market.

Their shadow continued to follow them. Both could feel it. Once a man senses that heat on the back of his neck telling him he's being watched, he can't ignore it. When they paused on the trail to rest or eat, Stark would keep a surreptitious watch on their flank. Twice now he had seen distant movement. Whoever was on their tail was cautious enough to keep well back. Those forms he could see were so indistinct as to render horses indistinguishable from men.

Johnny Two-Face, meanwhile, kept leading them toward the valley with the cliff dwellings that the Apache sometimes used as a camp. The country was drier out this way for lack of water. When they came to a stream, it was a slack current that was drying up. From the look of it, Stark figured it would slow to a trickle within weeks in this damned heat.

"This is the last chance we'll have to water the horses and fill our canteens," Johnny Two-Face said, dismounting. "The valley is another hour or two ahead. We should take advantage of this now."

Stark and Red Buffalo didn't have to be told twice. They dismounted and let the horses drink their fill while they bent to lower their canteens into the water.

"I can see them," Red Buffalo said quietly, kneeling beside Stark. "They're coming closer. Probably making plans to come at us around nightfall."

"We'll take turns keeping watch," Stark muttered back. "And I think we should keep this between ourselves."

"I agree."

Something wasn't right about this situation. Stark was beginning to consider the possibility that Johnny Two-Face might be leading them into a trap. He had given his word at the Free State, to be sure. But given how strapped that little enclave of nonconformists was for cash, it stood to reason that a betrayal might prove more profitable than a straight-up scouting arrangement.

So they would be careful, too.

Very careful.

The valley appeared as a sudden drop-off in the trail ahead. It turned out they would have to circle around a good piece of it before finding a place to descend. A wide clearing surrounded the lip of the valley, keeping the tree line at bay. Their shadows were confined to the tree line, prevented from moving out into the open for a stretch. Stark figured this was good.

They followed a treacherous, broken trail of loose rock. Johnny Two-Face dismounted partway down and led his horse. Stark and Red Buffalo followed suit. It took them another half hour to reach the valley floor. Stark could tell at once why the Old Ones had chosen to settle here.

The remains of a riverbed cut through the middle of the valley. This place had once been well watered. Likely, it had been a cool and lush oasis in the midst of the desert.

They had made their fire circles and stone quarries, and scaled the cliffs to cut their homes into the rock. These became visible now as they crossed the riverbed's remains and the nearest cliffs came into sharp view.

"Here," said Johnny Two-Face. "This is where they had their city."

It was an impressive sight. Beginning at a point ten feet off the ground, a series of square doorways had been chiseled into the cliff face. These rose in tiers from the valley floor for two hundred feet or more. Against a few of the tiers, the remains of the tall wooden ladders the Old Ones had used to access their homes rested.

But these were barely ladders anymore: mostly splintered structures, falling apart, their sinew lashings having dried out and crumbled years before, leaving only skeletal remains. A ghostly wind swept over the cliff face in the approaching dusk. Here was a ghost town.

"There's a large home here." Johnny Two-Face started up an incline of rock and soil someone had piled there recently. The Old Ones would not have compromised their safety so. But this man-made dirt hill allowed folks access to the mouth of the nearest dwelling.

As he guided Buck beneath the lintel and

into the stone chamber, Stark found himself marveling at the ingenuity and industry of these ancient tribes. The interior was more than just comfortable; it was beautiful in a functional way.

This was once someone's home, he thought.

There was ample room for them as well as the horses. Red Buffalo took charge of feeding and watering all three mounts. Stark stepped back outside with Johnny Two-Face and helped him gather firewood for the evening, then took advantage of the last half hour of twilight to examine the approaches to the dwellings.

The way they had come was the only way, a relatively narrow section of the valley. It was fed by the same path down which they had descended. Stark chose a location halfway between the cave entrance and that point as a forward position, one he could get to even in the dark.

We'll hear them coming, he thought. *Or should, at least.*

Johnny built a fire on the valley floor, right by the foot of the earthen ramp leading to the cliff dwelling's entrance. Each contributed something from their supplies, and so each got to eat roasted potato, a few slices of bacon, and some dried apples. They were enjoying an after-dinner mug of coffee, when Johnny started talking about the cliff dwellers.

"They were here long before any of us." He directed these words pointedly at Red Buffalo, emphasizing the last. "The Old Ones controlled all of Arizona Territory and all of old Mexico. Some of the paths we followed to get here have existed since their times."

"That's a big territory," Stark observed. "You're telling me there are paths that connect the whole thing?"

Johnny was nodding. "They had a trading empire. All of the tribes and peoples hereabouts — the people of the flatlands, the people of the mesa, the people of the basket, and the people of the war ponies — all paid tribute to the Old Ones. Their powers stretched to the horizon."

"What happened to them?" asked Red Buffalo.

Johnny shrugged. "Nobody knows. There was no great war or famine. No plague. But for a time, they were here, and then . . . they just weren't, anymore. It's like they vanished. Perhaps it all just became too complicated for them, so they walked away from it. Abandoned their own civilization. Left us this." He gestured toward the dwelling's entrance.

Stark definitely felt a presence here, and not from whoever was following them. Something ancient echoed in the air, in the way the cook fire threw flickering shadows against the rocks, causing the entrances of the dwellings to appear and disappear in the shimmering light. Stark felt a sense of something gathering around him in the dark. Not the presence of living enemies, but the memories of ancient tenants, who may well have gathered around fires, just like this, in the distant past.

"The Hopi say man was created out this-away," observed Red Buffalo. "They say in the Fourth World, the gods created the different races who climbed out of the underground kivas and went out in separate directions to populate the world."

"Sounds like a lot of hogwash to me," snapped Johnny Two-Face. "I believe in what that white man from England, that Charles Darwin fella, says. We evolved from lower creatures. He figures apes, but I say different men evolved from different creatures. The red men evolved from buffalo, to roam the plains and live free. I think the Mexicans evolved from coyotes, clever and patient, to survive in the desert."

"And white men?" Red Buffalo asked.

"White men evolved from snakes." Johnny Two-Face spat into the fire. "To deceive and poison us all."

Stark shrugged. "The Hopi say one thing. Bible says something else. Neither one matters, because we're here. We're stuck with it. And we just have to figure out what to do about it."

Neither Johnny nor Red Buffalo had a reply for this.

They finished up their coffee, gathered up their plates and cookware, and kicked sand over the fire. The valley dropped into a moon-shrouded darkness as they made their way back up the earthen ramp to the dwelling entrance.

Stark and Red Buffalo waited until Johnny bedded down before setting up their bedrolls by the door. Stark volunteered to stand first watch, and so Red Buffalo settled into his blankets, while Stark took up a post just outside the door. He found a spot among shadows and sat, his Henry rifle across his knee, his eyes fixed on the narrow section of valley through which an attacker must pass to be a threat to them. He settled down to wait.

He didn't have to wait long.

He hadn't reckoned on the stillness, on the way it caused small sounds to be amplified and echo around the valley. When he heard stones shift, he thought at first it was close by. But when he cocked his head and listened again, he knew: it was rocks shifting on the path down to the floor from the valley's edge.

He rose and moved silently, across the valley floor, to the sheltered forward post he had scouted at dusk. From there, he had a direct line of sight to the path down from the top. And he could discern, just faintly in the gloom, the suggestion of lanterns moving slowly, slowly . . .

They're coming in the dark, he thought, marveling at their persistence.

He hurried back to the dwelling entrance, ducked inside, and shook Red Buffalo awake.

"We've got company," he said. "They're coming down from the top now. Wake Johnny, get your guns, and meet me by the fire we had earlier."

Red Buffalo rolled to his feet and grabbed for his rifle. Stark made his way back out to the forward post in the riverbed.

The distant lights had reached the valley floor and were making their way over. He figured maybe half an hour before they were on top of them.

He hurried back to where Red Buffalo and

Johnny Two-Face were waiting. The last of the smoke from the evening's cook fire was wafting away in the moonlight now peeking over the valley's edge.

They began planning their ambush.

Chapter 27

Stark crouched behind the rocks at his forward position, scanning for signs of those approaching. The moon had risen sufficiently to flood the valley floor with light. The faint sounds of slow and careful hoofbeats, half-whispered voices, and the creak of saddle leather came clearly to him now.

So it was no surprise when shadows shifted into silhouette and silhouettes brightened into shapes emerging from the darkness to assume the forms of men. A threesome.

What Stark saw chilled him.

The man in the lead was an Indian. Rail thin, with long gray hair, he rode a bony palomino that moved with its head down, plainly trail-worn and exhausted. Tied to the pommel of the saddle and draping down either side of his horse were huge bundles of dried scalps. They shifted as the horse moved, their dried skin rustling like leaves.

Moonlight twinkled off the pistol holstered at the man's hip.

Behind this first man came a second, a wide, fat man astride a donkey. He wore the wide black sombrero and classic mustache of the vaquero. Across his ponderous belly he clutched a sawed-off shotgun. Like the man in front, he had a bouquet of scalps suspended from his saddle.

The last man was the strangest. He was a tall, thin black man astride a milk-white horse. Although barefoot, he wore a fine suit of clothes and a top hat. His lips were spread in a permanent grin, showing off a ferocious set of white teeth. He had a long rifle strapped to his back but kept a hatchet at the ready in his right hand, even while riding. It took Stark a second to recognize what he wore around his neck. At first, he thought it might be some sort of elaborate collar. But then he rode into a patch of moonlight and Stark saw it for what it was: a wreath of scalps.

Slowly, this trio plodded through the narrow gap from that portion of the valley floor linked by a trail to the ground above. Now they were closing in on the cliff dwellings. They paused, clustering together and conferring briefly before they split apart. The tall black man with the top hat went off to the left, to encircle the cliffs from that side, while the Mexican with the sawed-off did the same to the right. The Indian with the bundle of scalps continued straight on.

Stark returned inside the doorway to their dwelling, where Red Buffalo and Johnny Two-Face crouched next to him. He signed what he had seen by gesture. His companions watched, nodded their understanding, and then conferred with each other before splitting up and going their separate ways.

Stark settled down and waited for the Indian headed his way.

Red Buffalo crept down the earth ramp to the valley floor, his eyes on the fat man astride the donkey. He recognized the man as dangerous, even from behind. He had the look of a brawler, an eye-gouging, testicle-kicking biter of a fellow. The sort of man who would break a bottle over someone's head or go after them with a sharp stick or shard of glass. Red Buffalo would have to be careful of that shotgun.

The man abruptly halted his donkey and half turned in the saddle. Red Buffalo got down as quickly and quietly as he could, lowering his face into the shadows until he was just a shape, and waited.

When he heard the donkey jostle back into motion, he crawled after it.

Johnny Two-Face was also moving on hands and knees. He was at the high end of the earthen ramp, and anxious not to be spotted by the tall man in the top hat. He knew that he was at an advantage, that the tall man would be vulnerable to an attack from above. So long as he was careful not to reveal his position.

He dropped down to his belly, wiggling through the dirt to the ramp's far edge. He could hear the clopping of hooves. The man was close. Johnny moved as close as he could to the edge, paused for three breaths, and then peeked over.

No sign of the man.

Johnny frowned, scanning the valley floor from side to side. He couldn't find the man. It was only when he turned his gaze downward that he saw the bright grin and gleaming whites of the eyes glaring back up at him.

Stark watched the Indian approach. He was tensed, prepared to spring into action as always. But there was an added tension in his frame, a strange coldness in his heart. There was something about this man that was unusually troubling. As he reached to caress the butt of his Colt, Stark was surprised to feel his hands trembling.

Something about the man scared him. He was still trying to figure out what, studying the long gray hair that covered the face now visible. Something about the skeletal horse, the silence, and the ghostly movements of the man suggested an otherworldly spirit. Stark wondered if he might not be some sort of shaman — a spirit healer or suchlike. He had that feel about him, the feel of a man accustomed to haunting ritual lodges and graveyards, who moved with the rhythms of life and death, giving and taking away . . .

Stark got hold of himself, reached and quietly drew his Colt from its holster, bringing the gun around in front of him, very deliberately *not* cocking the hammer, although nothing would have pleased him more. He was playing it cool, being cautious with this man. Reckoning surprises were likely.

He got his first one when the man looked up. His face was a smear of black and white war paint fashioned to create the horrid impression of a skull.

The second surprise came when Johnny screamed.

■ ■ ■ ■

Then he screamed again. The man in the top hat holding the hatchet was staring right back up at him. Had been sitting there waiting for him to peek over the edge. *How had he . . . ?*

Johnny didn't even let the question finish forming in his mind. He was too busy scrabbling backward through the dirt, reversing awkwardly on all fours, hands and knees working furiously as the black man's laughter rose to crash down over him like a tidal wave. Deep rich, rolling laughter that got louder, because, well, obviously the man was coming, and coming fast.

Up the bank he scrambled, launched from the saddle of his horse, scrabbling his way up the dirt wall with hatchet and clawed fingers. Then the black man in the fancy suit and bare feet was at the top and flashing his toothy white sinister grin. He said something Johnny Two-Face didn't understand, something that sounded like it might be French, but it didn't matter because now the man was hurling himself forward, hatchet raised to bring it down into Johnny's forehead.

Johnny rolled. A rush of wind passed close

by and then a body hit the ground where he had been a moment before. Johnny was up on his feet now and then — *whoosh!* — narrowly able to duck the hatchet that immediately whipped at him out of nowhere. He overbalanced and fell backward.

The black man with the top hat lunged a second before Johnny drew and fired.

Johnny's scream caused the fat man on the donkey to turn and see Red Buffalo.

The Crow scout figured a blast of that shotgun would come the moment it centered on him. So he dove away, rolling into the sand in a tight somersault. But then the unexpected occurred.

The man on the donkey was turning in his saddle, bringing the barrels of the shotgun up when his weight got the better of him and he overbalanced. He pitched forward out of the saddle, one of the shotgun barrels going off as he fell. This spooked the donkey, which bolted, dragging the fat man a short distance before his foot came loose from the stirrup and he collapsed, face first, into the sand.

The donkey took off, braying, to disappear up the canyon.

Red Buffalo was on the move now, drawing his knife as he sprinted toward the fat man, who was thrashing and cursing in the dust, struggling to rise, the sawed-off flailing in all directions while he thrashed. Then suddenly, he was on all fours and facing Red Buffalo.

Red Buffalo noted the man's attention fix on him. Saw the man raise the gun . . .

Then he collapsed, face first, back in the sand, unable to support his own weight on one arm. Red Buffalo almost felt sorry for the hombre. But he launched himself forward, landed on the man's back, and let his knife do the talking.

The gunshot spooked the skeleton-faced man's horse. His scalps rustled dryly, bouncing as the horse jounced. Then Stark was steadying his rifle atop the boulder and preparing to shoot.

Yet somehow, suddenly and all at once, the man looked up from the ground before his horse's hooves, saw Stark, and got the horse to veer right a split second before Stark fired. The bullet grazed one of the man's saddlebags but left horse and rider untouched.

Cursing under his breath, Stark struggled to bring the rifle around for a second shot.

Then the skeleton rider was shrieking, wheeling his mount and bearing down on

Stark with savage intensity. In his fist had appeared a thin wicked lance. He charged at full gallop, the point of the lance aimed at Stark as he shrieked at the top of his lungs.

Stark dropped and rolled an instant before it connected. The skeleton rider sailed past but stopped short, wheeling in a cloud of dust and moonglow to raise the lance skyward, letting out a horrific shriek, more like something a bobcat or wolf would vocalize than a human. Stark brought the rifle around.

The skeleton rider slammed his mount's front hooves down to the ground, reset his balance on the mount, and spurred its flanks.

The tip of the lance rushed forward, mere yards away.

Stark's rifle roared and the skeleton rider was blown backward out of the saddle, with a final shriek, to land in a heap on the moon-washed floor of the valley.

A short time later, Red Buffalo limped over. He was covered in blood and leading a donkey.

"That Mexican varmint sure was big," he said, pausing beside Stark and the dead Indian. "What about him?"

"He tried to skewer me on that stick of his." Stark spat. "Damn near did it, too. But I managed to put a bullet in him first."

Johnny Two-Face appeared and wandered over. He was wearing a top hat.

"So you got the one in the suit," Stark said.

"He was tricky," said Johnny Two-Face. "Had a sort of hoodoo about him. Tricked me into revealing my position and then jumped up. He tried to chop me into little pieces, but I shot him and took his hat. It's a nice one, eh?"

"It's a good hat," agreed Red Buffalo.

"They're scalp hunters, all right." Stark kicked a bundle that had fallen loose from the rider's saddle as he fell. "Must have a thousand dollars worth or more here."

"You figure they were the ones tracking the Apaches?" Red Buffalo asked.

"Makes sense to me," said Stark. "A small tribe, off by itself. They'd probably hang around and look for strays. Lone hunters. People who wandered off by themselves. Kill them and take their scalps."

"Scavengers," spat Johnny Two-Face.

"That's about the size of it," agreed Stark. "Come on, let's see what we can recover from the gear that makes this mess we made here worthwhile."

Chapter 28

Once the scalp hunters were dead, their bodies and saddlebags ransacked for supplies, and their horses unsaddled and released, it occurred to Stark what the attack on them confirmed: their attackers had not yet found the Purgatory Crossing Apache.

"All these scalps?" He kicked at the bundle dropped by the skeleton rider. "They're old. Dry. Nothing fresh here."

"The Apaches are too clever for them," replied Johnny Two-Face with a touch of pride. "They are well hidden. And their camp is guarded."

"Will you be able to find them?" Red Buffalo's question was intended honestly, not as a jibe. But Johnny didn't take it that way.

"Of course, I can find them," he snorted. He began to head south.

Stark and Red Buffalo exchanged a shrug, mounted up, and followed.

The desert rolled away beneath their hooves as they traveled forward into the dry and stone-strewn land. Stark found himself boggling at the weird, unending sameness of the Territory. A man could go mad in a place like this. Some had.

He recalled stories of some of the earliest settlers drawn to Arizona Territory. The Mormons were driven out this way by violence and prejudice. Some miners and prospectors had come willingly. Others were just down-on-their-luck homesteaders, hopeful that a fresh start in a new place might bring a change in their luck.

Many of those tales ended with ruin. Whether by attack, drought, or death by madness, the Territory had taken its pound of flesh from settler and frontiersman alike.

Two hours after lighting out, they were passing through a wide valley, when a rider appeared in the narrows ahead. Stark's hand went immediately to his gun but fell away as the rider approached. He was a young white man astride a fine bay. He galloped up to within a hundred yards of them and stopped.

"Heya, fellas!" He yanked off his hat and

waved it. "Got a big drove of cattle coming through this way! You might want to get to higher ground!"

"Which ranch?" asked Stark, checking the boy for hesitation as he answered. But there was none.

"Bar J Ranch, sir! Belong to Mr. Horace McKellan!"

"Sounds right," he said, turning to Red Buffalo. "I think he's telling the truth."

"He is," replied Johnny Two-Face, pointing to the boiling gray-black cloud of dust approaching the mouth of the pass. "Because that's either a thousand Apache or about two hundred head of cattle."

They withdrew to a flat space above the valley floor. The young man thanked them with a wave of his hat, then spurred his horse toward the oncoming herd. An outrider met him at the valley mouth, an older man who sat tall in the saddle and had the bearing of an excavalryman. He conferred briefly with the young man before turning to squint at the ledge where Stark, Johnny, and Red Buffalo waited. Then he spurred his mount up the incline to meet them.

"Howdy, gents!" The man's mouth was curled in a smile, and he touched the brim of his hat by way of greeting. "Sorry for the inconvenience. We should be through here in a minute or two."

"Where you bringing them?" Stark asked.

"This lot? They're heading for the train station in Tucson," the cattle boss said. He drew a packet of chewing tobacco from his vest pocket, fished out a chunk, and stuck it in his cheek. "They'll be on the hoof until Chicago, where they're due for the slaughterhouse."

"How has your drive been to this point?" Stark asked. "Any sign of Apache?"

"As a matter of fact, yes." The cattle boss swiveled in his seat and pointed. "Back about eight miles or so, we had a run-in with a small raiding party. No more than five braves, all young. Weren't even armed with guns. They came at us like greased lightning and tried to pick off a few stragglers by bow and arrow. We drove them off, but it took some doing."

"Did you see which way they went?" Johnny asked.

"They retreated into the hills," the man said. "Disappeared into the trees just behind the old mission."

Johnny Two-Face smiled. "That tells me a lot, sir," he said. "Thank you."

The cattle boss listened to this, nodded once, and then chuckled. "If you boys are looking for Apache," he said, "don't worry.

Out here? *They* find *you*."

With that, he spurred his horse and returned to the valley floor, where the outer wave of the herd was coming on. A vast wavering storm front of cattle entered the valley, jostling and mooing, and kicking up clots of dirt. Soon the air was filled with clouds of dust and their cries. The men on the ledge fixed bandanas over their noses, hunkered down, and waited for the wave to pass.

The vast herd of livestock cleared the valley, attended by their half dozen drovers, in just under a quarter hour. The sand and dust settled and the three riders were able to continue on their journey.

"You said the news about the mission was helpful," Stark said to Johnny. "Any particular reason?"

"They're in the spring campground," he replied confidently. "It would be the last place I would look. But that may be why they chose it. They're trying to go unnoticed."

A low brown structure appeared in the distance ahead, tucked in at the foot of the wooden slope.

"That's the mission there," he said, pointing. "San Marco. The Spanish built it way back in the old days. Back when they were trying to bring Jesus to us savage Indians." He chuckled, ignoring Red Buffalo's look of annoyance. "It didn't work out very well. Cochise and his warriors laid waste to the place a long time ago. Nobody has been there since. It's believed to be cursed. Haunted by the ghosts of the dead missionaries. Nobody goes there anymore. Not even the Apache."

The mission grew in size as they approached. But even before the high adobe walls, with their tall wooden gate, sharpened into visibility, Stark could feel a chill. It wasn't a drop in temperature, but a quality of the air, of the light around them that suddenly seemed colder. Clouds passing over the sun, rendering the area in gray light. Something about the forlorn wind, the bent posture of the trees, gave the area a sense of foreboding. The aura of the wasteland prevailed in this area of the desert, a wilderness, deeper than the wilderness itself, that spoke of dashed hopes and wrecked lives.

The mission bore signs of decay. Portions of its great adobe wall had been fractured, the missing sections allowing a view into the courtyard. The gates themselves appeared fire damaged. The one on the left side was open, skewed from its mountings and hanging by just the bottom hinge. It creaked in the wind as they rode past it.

Inside, the sense of ruin only deepened. The outer portion of the courtyard was dirt, but the section closest to the mission's entrance was paved with brick. A fountain stood at the center of the brick section, dry as bone, its bowl shattered in places. The doors to the mission itself stood wide, and sections of the dirt beneath the horses' hooves were blackened a darker color than the sand.

That was where people fell and bled out, Stark realized, reining to a stop and dismounting. But where were the bodies?

"I want to take a look around here," Johnny said, as he also swung down from the saddle. "Our little group of cattle rustlers might have come through."

As a group, they left their horses tied to a hitching post and made for the open doors to the main chapel. A bird twittered in the roof beams as they crossed the threshold into the derelict sanctuary.

The place had once been a wide, high-roofed chapel. Its purpose was clear in the span and design of the room, with its perspective tapering toward the altar in front. Stark could imagine the place holding hundreds gathered for worship.

Now it was a forlorn wreckage of its former self. The rows of benches had been scattered, and those not charred or burned to ash were thrown in haphazard piles against the walls. He saw more dark spots on the ground here, and shapes on the walls that Stark recognized as dried blood spatter. A few old arrows still stuck in the benches where they had stopped midflight. The place had been attacked and raided, leaving virtually nothing standing.

"It's been like this for years," Johnny said, reaching the front. The altar cloth had been torn, and the chalice and candlesticks lay in disorder across its surface. As Stark watched, Red Buffalo stepped forward, grasped the large brass cross that had been knocked over, and reset it on its stand. Then he stepped back, placed his hands on his hips, and looked around.

"Terrible shame," he said quietly.

Stark examined the interior of the large chapel. A room like this would have been home to a dedicated congregation. He knew that the old Spanish missions had functioned as centers of community, with tenant farmers and ranchers working the land around the walls. The missions themselves served as both centers of worship and protection, providing a place to retreat in case of attack. Stark recalled Lampkins's story about taking refuge in an old mission building during his childhood. This place had once served the very same purpose.

Until the Apaches broke through, he thought.

They made their way into the rear of the church via a hallway behind the main altar. Narrow doorways lined both walls. Stark peeked into rooms as they passed. He saw a sacristy, a small office, and what appeared to be a storage room. All the rooms had been stripped of furniture and other goods. The back wall of the storage room was scarred by a huge burn mark. Something had been set afire in here and blazed briefly before being extinguished.

The last room was a kitchen with a massive hearth. Stark was still studying the doorless cupboards and damaged counters when Red Buffalo walked past him, heading straight for the hearth. Upon reaching it, he knelt, reached out, and put his hands into the ashes.

"Still warm," he said.

Johnny Two-Face started and rushed over. Kneeling, he passed his hand over the ashes.

"They are!" he marveled. "This fireplace was used no more than a few hours ago!"

Stark smiled. "I bet I know who used it," he said.

He turned and marched to the side door, Red Buffalo and Johnny on his heels. Stepping outside, he scanned the dust. It didn't take long to find what he was looking for.

"See here?" He knelt. "These tracks here are old. Couple months. Probably some traveler passing through who stopped to take shelter from the day or night. Now long gone. But there . . ."

He scooted over to another set of tracks, hoofprints that were sharp and clear in the dust.

"The old ones were from a shoed horse." He stood, wiping his hands on his pants. "These aren't."

Johnny Two-Face knelt and examined the tracks for a long moment. "These would be our little raiding party of young Apache," he said. "The ones that tried to pick a few cattle out of that cattle drive."

"Got tired of playing raiders and decided to take shelter. Possibly for the night," said Red Buffalo. "They built a fire, cooked, then left. Not more than a few hours ahead of our arrival."

"Johnny?" Stark asked. "What do you think? Are these kids Purgatory Crossing Apache?"

"No doubt about it," replied Johnny Two-Face. "No other Indians around here. From the look of it, these kids woke up and decided to make a beeline for home." He pointed. "These tracks lead in the direction of the spring campground."

"So that's where we'll find our Apache," said Red Buffalo.

"Come on." Stark turned back toward the horses. "We're burning daylight."

Chapter 29

Stark had to hand it to the gang of Apache youths. They were cautious.

A dozen times while they were following their tracks, Stark, Johnny, and Red Buffalo found themselves flummoxed and forced to turn back, retrace their steps, reconsider the route. Had they gone left? Or right? It required the combined skills of two Indian trackers to keep up with the little gang. For once, Stark found himself truly appreciative of the company of Indians.

Part of the need for the constant doubling back was due to the fact that their quarry was young — essentially, a bunch of snot-nosed kids out for a lark. This land of mesas, canyons, and arroyos was more familiar to them, and no more intimidating, than the few city blocks in which their white urban counterparts ran wild.

In several places, the tracks of the group abruptly halted, then scattered in different directions, when their attention became captivated by some passing animal — likely a rabbit or coyote. At this point, the group would transform into something like a pack of wild dogs, with a predatory, "every-man-for-himself" mentality. It didn't take long for the two Indian scouts to figure this out, and rather than pursue wildly erratic sets of tracks through the scrub, they searched for the area where the group reformed and resumed the journey. This was often time consuming.

Two hours into the hunt, they found the spot where the group had stopped for a midday meal. Stark noted the remains of a campfire and the scattered bones of whatever small animal they had killed and cooked for lunch. A patch of nearby grasses had been grazed down to stubble by their ponies.

"They were here an hour or two ago," observed Johnny Two-Face. "Fresh tracks. Right over there."

Red Buffalo picked up some of the discarded bones and sniffed them. "They ate some sort of little critters for lunch. I'd guess rabbit."

Johnny Two-Face nodded. "There are plenty around here," he said.

Stark studied the line of tracks leading off

into the desert. Slowly but surely, they were catching up to the boys.

It was only a matter of time now.

"How much farther to the spring campground?" Red Buffalo asked.

"Not far," replied Johnny Two-Face. He had removed his new hat and was studying it as they clomped along a trail that girdled the side of a forested hill. "On the other side of this hill is a valley. Once we cut through that to the valley on the other side, we're there."

"Getting close, Nathan Stark," Red Buffalo said, slowing down until he rode beside his partner.

"That we are," Stark said. "We'll have to post up. Find an observation point from which to observe the Apache camp while Johnny makes contact. Get the lay of the land. Find Chief Atsa's children and spirit them away from the camp."

"It won't be easy," noted the Crow.

Stark sighed. No, it wouldn't be easy. But it had to be done.

They were on the downhill slope to the first valley, still among the trees, when they heard the commotion.

Stark brought Buck to a halt and closed

his eyes, cocking his head to listen. It was a small sound, distant and indistinct. The suggestion of movement. The odd click or *thunk*.

"I think I hear horses," he said finally.

Red Buffalo cocked his head. "I think you're right," he said.

Then the sound of a gunshot, thin and flat, split the air. Although more than a mile distant, it was without a doubt the report of a weapon.

"I wonder if our boys ran into a posse of scalp hunters," Johnny Two-Face mused aloud. He didn't seem in a terrible rush to learn the answer. Stark had to agree with the sentiment. Wading in now would reveal their presence and risk losing the trail to the camp.

"No matter," Stark said. "We should pursue, but cautiously. No way to know what we're walking into."

Two more shots, spaced fifteen seconds apart, sounded.

"Come on," said Johnny, spurring his horse. The other two men followed.

Within minutes they heard the sound of voices yelling. The rumble and crunch of hooves rose, and then Stark heard the distinctive *twang-smack!* of an arrow nocked and fired from a bow. He knew they had found their little party of raiders.

The trees tapered out toward the bottom of the hill. Johnny was the first to arrive at the tree line. Stark saw him rein to a halt, gape, and turn to them, gesturing wildly. Stark stopped beside him and looked.

In the clearing at the edge of the valley floor, a covered wagon was under attack from a group of young Apache. There were five of them astride their ponies, moving in a blur around the wagon. Stark saw lances, arrows, tomahawks.

On the driver's box of the wagon, a man stood, firing periodic shots from a repeating rifle. Crouched below the wagon, between the front two wheels, were two huddled figures. Stark recognized a woman and a young girl.

"Johnny! Get your rifle and snipe here from the trees!" Stark wheeled his horse around. To Red Buffalo he said, "Come on!"

They burst from the trees, galloping down on the raiding party. The kids were fierce and strong, but inexperienced enough to leave their flank uncovered out here in a territory they felt they owned. The startled look on the nearest kid's face was priceless as Stark drew his Colt and fired a round that barely missed the brave.

Then the kid was yelling to his friends. Red Buffalo opened up with his Henry rifle, firing from the saddle while gripping the horse with his knees. The bullet took one of the Apaches high and in the shoulder, spinning him off his mount to crash to the ground. Two others spun and made straight for Red Buffalo.

Stark fired at one of the others. No hit, but the kid was forced to break off his attack on the wagon. He scooted out of the way, whirled his horse around, and glared at Stark with palpable hatred. Slowly, he drew a tomahawk from his belt.

The man on the driver's box of the wagon, seeing that help had arrived, adjusted his angle of fire. Throwing the rifle to his shoulder, he fired and took down one of the two closing in on Red Buffalo.

Stark saw the kid with the tomahawk bearing down on him now, murder in his eyes. His face was painted in black and red war paint, and his bone breastplate clacked as he came on, screaming and waving the tomahawk. Stark leveled the Colt at him, held his breath, and pulled the trigger.

Click.

A misfire! He didn't have time to grab the rifle before the kid was on him.

Much to Stark's surprise, he didn't go for Stark immediately but went instead for Buck, swinging the wide stone head of the tomahawk toward the horse's head. Stark jerked the reins, forcing Buck's head to the left. The tomahawk came down hard, tearing a strip of flesh from Buck's shoulder. The kid's horse was jostling right up against Stark's now, so Stark was able to rear back in the saddle and kick the kid in the ribs, hard.

Crack! Another gunshot. This one from Red Buffalo. The remaining kid who had been closing in on him wheeled and fled, along with another.

Two on the ground. Two fleeing.

And the one with the tomahawk.

Stark hauled Buck around, the two horses crashing chest to chest. Then Stark was galloping clear, forcing the Apache kid to chase him. He made for the tree line, where Johnny Two-Face waited.

But it was a longer stretch than Stark had reckoned. He felt rather than heard the hoofbeats behind him, sensed the kid's menacing rage closing in on them, and made ready to do an abrupt turn when . . .

Crack!

A single shot from the trees ended it. Stark turned in time to see the kid stiffen and fall from his horse. He landed on his back, a puckered red hole in his chest where Johnny's bullet had struck. Beyond the bodies, and the wagon from which the driver was now climbing, he could make out the distant forms of the two surviving Apache kids hightailing it back to safe ground.

Stark waved Johnny out of the trees and turned to where Red Buffalo sat, stuffing his Henry rifle back into its saddle scabbard.

"You all right?" Stark asked.

"I'm okay. You?"

"I'm good. Buck will be a little scarred, but he'll live." Stark patted Buck and nodded to the driver, who was helping the woman and girl out from under the wagon. "Let's go say hello."

The man finished helping his wife clamber out and stand upright, then turned to Stark and Red Buffalo with a relieved expression.

"I can't tell you how happy I am to see you fellas!" he exclaimed. "You came along just in the nick of time!" He stuck out a hand. "Thank you! Thank you!"

"Eat up now, boys! There's plenty more where this came from!"

Robert Ebson, the father of the family

Stark and company had just rescued, ladled another heaping helping of stew onto Stark's tin plate. He had already eaten two servings, but the Ebsons were such enthusiastic hosts he was having a hard time saying no.

And Kitty Ebson, it turned out, was almost as talented a cook as Lampkins. No sooner had Robert introduced himself, her, and their daughter, Lisa, than Kitty had built a fire and commenced to fixing them something to eat. From her pans and cookpots had flowed a veritable cornucopia: stew, fresh biscuits, coffee. And it just kept coming.

"Where are you folks headed?" Stark asked.

"Well" — Robert lowered his eyes to the ground and laughed — "I hate to admit it, Nathan, but we're a mite lost. See, we came out this way as part of a wagon train from Illinois. Headed for Salt Lake City. And we got, uh, separated from them . . ."

"Robert insisted on pressing on rather than turning back," Kitty explained, leaning in to top up their coffee mugs. "He promised it would only take a few days to track down our friends."

"Well, I didn't exactly *promise,* Kitty!" Robert objected good humoredly. "I said I *figured.*"

"You were so sure of yourself, Robert..."

"I said I *reckoned*..."

Kitty just smirked, shook her head, and wandered back to the cook fire, to see to the stew.

"You're a good ways off from Salt Lake City, Robert," Stark said.

"We are?" Robert's voice contained a tone of sudden dejection. "How far is 'a good ways'? — if you don't mind my asking."

"Well, I don't know *exactly*..."

"A good guess'll do!"

Stark thought for a minute. "I'd say about eight or nine hundred miles."

Robert was silent for a long moment. Then:

"Oh, Lord."

"I'd make for Fort Lowell, if I was you," Stark advised. "It's a few days' ride north of here. You'll be going through Apache country. But if you're careful, you should be able to make it."

"You'll be safe at the fort," Red Buffalo said. "And they will be able to help you get back on your way."

Robert was shaking his head, tears standing in his eyes. "I'm such a fool," he whispered. "Darn near got my wife and beloved daughter killed by savages. All because of my damned pride."

"Now, Robert" — Kitty hurried over and put her arm around him — "everyone makes mistakes. Don't be so hard on yourself."

"Ah, Kitty." He looped an arm around her waist. "I don't deserve you."

"You don't," she teased. "But I'm not fixing to go anywhere." She turned to Stark. "Which way are you fellas headed?"

"That way." Stark pointed. "After those braves."

"Well, godspeed, Nathan," Robert said. "If you ever make it to Salt Lake, look us up. Same goes for all of you." He toasted them with his mug. "When things were at their worst, the Lord sent you as guardian angels. Praise be."

Chapter 30

The two boys they tracked were good horsemen. Studying their trail, Stark could see they handled their mounts well, compensated for changes in terrain, and made sound choices where cutting trail was concerned. They were fast, knew the country, and traveled with a definite destination in mind.

They were also scared.

"They're not making much effort to hide their trail," Johnny Two-Face noted. "Apache boys old enough to ride out from the tribe on their own should know better."

"They probably do," retorted Red Buffalo. "But they've forgotten."

"Why?" Johnny was puzzled.

"Because they're frightened," Red Buffalo said, gesturing down at the tracks. "They're running back home for safety."

Stark had to admit it made sense.

They were in deep desert now. The forested hills had slipped behind them, and the rolling hills softened to an undulating floor of cacti and dried-out mesquite bushes. They were off the wagon trails now. This was unexplored territory, an area unfamiliar to and avoided by white men. Only the Apache and rattlesnakes lived out this way.

"Good place for a hidden camp," Stark observed.

"It's got more moisture in the spring," Johnny told him. "Those creek beds usually have some flow. And there's plenty of small game out here. Rabbits. Birds. Snakes."

"What about these buzz worms?" Red Buffalo asked, nodding to the body of a dead rattler by the trail's edge. "Are they good eating?"

"Not my favorite, but yes." Johnny shrugged. "Tastes like chicken."

Stark rolled his eyes. Everything that wasn't ordinary fare was characterized as "tasting like chicken." He determined to give rattlesnake a wide berth if it was served up at a cook fire.

An hour after this exchange, Johnny slowed his horse. Stark looked around. Was this windswept, godforsaken plain the spring camp? He tended to doubt it.

"We're close now," Johnny said. "Come see."

Up ahead was a pile of boulders ten feet high that stretched a hundred feet in either direction. Johnny spurred his horse up to the edge, dismounted, and then began scrambling through a break in the rocks.

"Why don't you stay here and watch the horses?" Stark asked the Crow, dismounting. "We'll just be a moment."

Red Buffalo nodded and remained in the saddle as Stark followed Johnny.

Stark clambered through the rocks. It was tough going: uneven, treacherous surfaces alternated with low, sharp overhangs that forced him to duck and, occasionally, sidle through sideways. He caught up to Johnny standing on a flange of rock that jutted out into empty space.

"Here," he said, pointing.

Beyond the rocks, the ground dropped away sharply in a chasm that widened in a V shape, deepening as it progressed. Deep below was a thin wash with a trickle of water. The wash cut through a series of forested slopes that echoed the more fecund areas of the desert.

"Beautiful, hey?" Johnny Two-Face shook his head. "This was always my favorite of their campgrounds. It's like the cliff dwellings except forested and protected by depth instead of height."

"So they're down there somewhere?"

"Look."

Stark followed Johnny's finger. A tiny wisp of smoke climbed skyward from a point several miles into the valley.

"We'll descend there." Johnny pointed to a narrow trail that led from the desert floor into the chasm. "Once we reach the bottom, it's a bit of a journey. But we'll close in on their camp by late afternoon, most likely."

"No sentries," Stark noted. "Or are they just hidden?"

"They don't post them up at this end of the valley," he said. Stark followed him as he turned to go back. "They usually have someone guarding close by the edge of the camp. But I know the spot."

"Can we evade notice?"

"Oh, yes." Johnny grinned. "Easy to do. You'll see."

The trail down was rocky and narrow. Negotiating it safely required each rider's undivided attention. There were a few hairpin turns that Stark would have preferred to dismount for and guide Buck around, but there wasn't room for him to swing down from the saddle. So he gritted his teeth, clung on tight with his knees, and did his best not to look down.

After an hour or more, they reached the valley floor. Looking up, Stark could see the pile of huge boulders as a tangle of pebbles in the distance. At his feet lay the narrow wash. Coming to a halt, he dismounted, moved toward the trickle sluicing down its center, and bent for a drink.

"Not much here for a whole tribe," he noted, rising to his knees and wiping his mouth.

"Darn little," Johnny agreed. "But better than nothing."

They remounted and continued on, following the wash. The further they went, the more impressed Stark became with the Apache's choice of campground. This was a different world down here, one completely separate from the desert above. Many of the same creatures resided in the chasm, of course, but the abundance of trees and the freshness of the air was nothing like the desert above. The place was, truly, a little oasis.

"Okay, stop here," Johnny said after three-quarters of an hour. "The area where they post their sentries is up ahead. I'm going to go take a look-see. You two stay here."

As Stark watched Johnny vanish through the trees, he turned to Red Buffalo. "What do you think?" he asked.

"It's very nice down here," Red Buffalo said, looking around. "Also, not the sort of place the U.S. Cavalry is likely to risk sending troops into. Too easy for them to get cut off and surrounded."

"I was thinking the same." Stark studied the rock walls rising upward from the trail. "It's a perfect hideout. I bet the tribe has been coming here for generations."

It didn't take Johnny long to finish his scouting trip and return. Within a half hour, Stark spotted him winding his way back through the trees. He returned and mounted up, glancing back along the trail before speaking.

"The sentry is near," Johnny said, keeping his voice low. "We're going to cut around him, through the trees, to a point above the camp. Stay close. Stay quiet."

He set off, Stark and Red Buffalo following. In this portion of the valley, small trails had been cut through the woods. The ground was soft, and the going easy. At one point, Stark glanced back, grateful that the ground retained little trace of their passage.

Johnny stopped, turned, and gestured with his chin. Stark followed his line of sight and caught a glimpse of the Apache sentinel. He was an elderly man, likely a warrior whose days of riding to battle were over. He sat swaddled in a government-issue blanket, a rifle in hand, staring back up the valley toward the chasm with the path to the surface. At the distance of a quarter mile, he did not register their presence.

Johnny brought them safely past the sentry, and on for another half mile or so, before dismounting in a clearing at the edge of a cliff. Stark left his horse and crept to the precipice.

Below, the valley floor flattened into a wide, open area in the shape of an oval. There, the Purgatory Crossing Apache had made camp. Stark saw perhaps twenty tents, scattered in a circular pattern, around a central area with cook fires. He saw the forms of women moving to tend the fires, fetching water from the stream, keeping an eye on small children, who ran loose, getting up to mischief as little ones tend to do.

At the edge of the camp were the horses. Tied together after the Indian fashion, they loafed, foraging on what grasses were available to them. As he watched, a young girl came out from the camp with a basket of flora she had gathered. He turned away as she began to distribute it among the horses.

"So this is where we'll camp," Johnny said. "Actually, where you two will camp."

"And you?" Red Buffalo asked.

"I'm going to go back the way we came and then approach along the valley floor. Present myself to the sentry. He'll know me. Or at least the people in camp that I'll mention by name."

"What will you tell them?"

"That I'm returning from Mexico. Just resting on my way back to the Free State. They'll let me stay with them tonight. I'll find out what I can and return in the morning."

"All right." Stark extended a hand. "Be careful, Johnny."

"Sure." Johnny seemed amused as he shook Stark's hand. He waved to Red Buffalo, mounted up, and started back down the trail the way they had come.

"Well" — Red Buffalo dismounted and stretched — "looks like we're done traveling for the day."

"Now we wait." Stark sighed. Waiting was always the hardest part.

They didn't dare build a fire so close to the camp, so there was no coffee or hot food that night. Stark and Red Buffalo dined on jerky and hardtack washed down by water from their canteens. As was customary when out in hostile territory, they took turns keeping watch as the other slept.

During his watch, Stark saw the large cook fire and the small individual fires that the Apache families stoked for warmth. The camp was quiet, with very little activity during the night.

He slept, then was roused by Red Buffalo a few hours before dawn for the final watch. Stark perched on a rock overlooking the camp as the sky grew brighter in the east. Johnny Two-Face returned up the same path they had taken to get here, his horse plodding quietly through the trees. Stark went and shook Red Buffalo awake before going to meet Johnny.

"Any luck?" he asked.

Johnny nodded, and the three of them sat together and ate a breakfast that was identical to last night's dinner as they heard his report.

"Mosi and Chayton are there. I didn't see them myself, but I heard about them. Didn't even have to ask." Johnny washed down a piece of hardtack with some water. "The friends I was staying with talked about them. Mosi has apparently grown up to be quite the beauty. Desired by many young men in the tribe."

Great! Stark thought. *I'm going to have to dodge a bunch of suitors to get to her.*

"Chayton is a different story." Johnny paused, marshaling his words. "He's a man now. Or a young man, anyway. While his sister is celebrated, he's a bit of a joke. They say he rides and shoots like an Apache, but they never stop commenting on the fact that he's Navajo. It's driven him a bit crazy. He's always picking fights, eager to prove himself."

Another treasure, Stark thought, and did his best not to groan.

"They've been adopted by Taza, one of the war chiefs, and live with his family." Johnny pointed. "That big tent at the far end, the one with the red stripe, that's Taza's home."

"Anything else about them you were able to learn?"

"She wears an owl feather. And her brother is often with her, protecting her from the Apache boys."

"They should be easy to spot," Red Buffalo said.

"The trick will be getting them away from the camp. They —"

Just then, the air was split by a man's cry. Looking down, they saw a small group of young men galloping out of the camp, waving their bows and spears. Off for an early morning hunt, from the look of it. The group reminded Stark of the ones they had fought off while rescuing the Ebsons. Within moments, their dust had settled and quiet had returned.

"So we post a watch and wait," Stark said. "And see."

Red Buffalo took a drink and capped his canteen. "I'll take first watch," he said quietly, and perched on the rock lookout to observe the camp.

Chapter 31

They caught sight of Mosi within the hour.

With dawn came the first stirrings of morning. A young brave was the first to appear, emerging from a tent near the edge of camp where the horses were kept. He yawned, stretched, and then wandered over to check on them.

While he was walking around, muttering to each of the horses and occasionally touching their flanks and withers, another tent flap opened and a man emerged who Red Buffalo supposed was the tribal medicine man. He stepped into the morning wearing his ceremonial shirt and clutching a staff to which was affixed an eagle feather. He meandered across the campground to another tent. The flap parted as he approached and a woman beckoned him inside.

"Healer," said Johnny Two-Face.

Shortly afterward, women began emerging from the tents and wandering toward the central cook fire. One bent to stoke the smoldering ashes and feed fresh wood into the embers. Soon the flap of Taza's tent parted and two women emerged, one older, one younger. The younger woman sported an owl feather in her hair.

"That's got to be Mosi," said Stark. He pulled a telescope from his saddlebag and trained it on the girl.

She was indeed lovely. Her black hair radiated a silky delicacy, and her eyes were large and captivating. Chiseled cheekbones framed a slender, good-humored face, and her mouth was soft and expressive. The other women looked up and smiled as she approached. It was immediately obvious that she was liked and admired among the mothers and grandmothers of the tribe.

"Let me see?" Johnny Two-Face put out his hand for the telescope, and Stark handed it over. He watched the young half-breed put the glass to one eye and stare for the longest time.

"She is very lovely," Red Buffalo said in a hushed voice.

"Attractive girl," Stark agreed.

But Johnny Two-Face was riveted. Motionless, mouth slightly open, he continued studying the girl at the other end of the telescope. Stark and Red Buffalo met each other's eyes with a rueful smile.

"I think we're going to need a napkin," Stark joked.

"To wipe up all the drool, you mean?" Red Buffalo replied.

Johnny, if he heard them, said nothing. Just kept staring at Mosi.

Stark began to worry.

The camp came completely to life over the course of the next hour. Some families emerged from their tents to gather around the cook fire for breakfast, while others took theirs inside, with mothers gathering up helpings from the cook pot and walking it home to their tents.

Once breakfast was done, the daily life of the camp clicked into gear. Children tumbled out to begin the day's play. Men emerged, yawning and stretching before meeting up in groups of two and three to set about the day's work. One pair resumed raising a partially assembled tepee. Another trio went to a small pit at the camp's edge and set about knapping flint and assembling arrows. Others, mostly elders and war chiefs, assembled around the cooking fire for discussions.

The watchers kept their eyes on Taza's

tent. After a time, the man himself emerged and began circulating around the camp. He went first to the boy tending the horses and conferred with him before stopping at the tent into which the medicine man had vanished. He had a few words with the woman at the tent flap before checking on the flint knappers. That done, he joined the group around the cook fire.

"Doing the rounds," said Stark.

"Checking on everyone," said Red Buffalo. "He's a good leader."

Stark reckoned so. The tribal chief, an older man with gray hair and an eagle feather, welcomed Taza with a shoulder clap, inviting him to speak to the assembled leaders with a roll of the hand. Like many tribes, the Purgatory Crossing Apache had both civil and war chiefs. It seemed obvious that this elder intended to hand off the job of chief to Taza someday, and that the men assembled by the cook fire were inclined to view this as the natural order of things.

While the men talked, the flap of Taza's tent moved and Mosi emerged by herself, carrying a water pot. She took a few steps in the direction of the creek before the tent flap opened again and a man emerged, calling out to her.

That would be Chayton, Stark thought. The

young man's movements had a shambling, disjointed quality. He kept flexing and rolling his shoulders as if to demonstrate his forcefulness. He was slightly shorter than the average Indian and stocky in build. He crossed the distance between himself and Mosi, then began to remonstrate with his sister. It was obvious from his manner, even at a distance, that he was displeased with her about something.

"I wonder what that's about?" Stark wondered aloud.

"I imagine he's upset that his pretty sister is walking around in camp alone, without her chaperone," Red Buffalo chuckled. "He's protective."

"He's a bully," Johnny Two-Face said flatly. "Look at the way he gestures at her. Like he's about to hit her!"

It was true. Although he hadn't laid a hand on her, there was an explosive quality to Chayton's gestures. Stark could tell Chayton was an angry kid: angry at being isolated, angry about his lack of acceptance in the tribe, angry (for all Stark could tell) about being short. But what was clear was that he viewed his sister as belonging to *him*. His property, his commodity, to do with as he wished.

The discussion ended. Mosi hung her

head. Then she followed him sedately back to the tent and waited outside while he went in and retrieved his bow and quiver of arrows. Now they were moving away from the camp, into a patch of grassland that rolled and undulated across the valley floor.

"They're leaving the camp!" Johnny Two-Face was plainly excited. "They're going into that field over there!"

"This could be our chance," Red Buffalo said.

"All right." Stark nodded. "I think you two should make contact. I'll cover you from here."

Without another word, Johnny and Red Buffalo left the lookout, moving into the trees overlooking the field to intercept Mosi and Chayton. Stark hurriedly packed up camp, checked the horses, then settled back on the lookout with his telescope to watch the proceedings.

Mosi and Chayton were now out of sight of the tents and moving through the fields, gathering edible plants. The young man had his bow unslung and was casting around for game. He had his back to the trees when Johnny and Red Buffalo emerged.

The two men moved cautiously, approaching the pair as they might a group of sleeping deer, anxious not to spook them. As they came closer, they could hear snatches of conversation. Although Red Buffalo could not understand the words, the tones were plain enough. Chayton's was impatient and frustrated. Mosi's was patient and weary. It seemed this game of control was a tug-of-war that had been going on between the siblings for years.

It was Mosi who saw them first. She turned to bend toward a flowering plant when she caught sight of Johnny beaming at her from a few yards away. She was too surprised to speak, merely marveling at the attention he was lavishing upon her. When he spoke to her in Apache, she smiled. Chayton whirled.

"Who are you?" he demanded, lifting his bow and nocking an arrow into place.

"Relax." Johnny Two-Face held up a hand. He spoke in English, for Red Buffalo's benefit. "We are friends."

Chayton relaxed a bit when he realized Johnny had just addressed his sister in Apache. He flicked suspicious eyes to Red Buffalo.

"And him?" he demanded. "Who is he?"

"This is my friend, Red Buffalo. He is of the Crow tribe. He is a friend to the Apache. And to you."

Chayton seemed skeptical. Mosi, on the other hand, was friendly to the newcomers, much to her brother's annoyance.

"Welcome," she said in English. "I am Mosi. And this is my brother Chayton."

"We are very pleased to meet you," said Johnny. Something in the warmth of his tone was suspect to Red Buffalo — and to Chayton.

"What do you want with my sister and me?" he demanded. "Where did you come from?"

Red Buffalo stepped forward. "Chayton, we have traveled a long way. From the traditional land of the Navajo."

Upon hearing the word, both froze, their attention rapt.

"You both know that you were taken as children," Red Buffalo continued. "Do you remember the time before?"

"I remember my father," whispered Mosi. "So kind and strong. And my mother . . ."

"Mosi, your father's name is Atsa. He is a chief, and he is very worried about the both of you. He wants you to come home. And he has sent us to help you find your way back."

Red Buffalo paused and studied the effect these words were having on her. For all her time spent among the Apache, Mosi was still Navajo. Buried within her mind and heart were the memories of her people. She still felt a connection to them. Now here was an opportunity to return.

But Chayton was having none of it. He shook his head furiously. Both fists clenched, one down by his side, the other wrapped around the handle of his bow. An arrow lay discarded at his feet. With a curse, he lunged forward and stomped on it, splitting it in two.

"Lies!" he shouted.

He whirled on his sister. "Mosi, can't you see what is happening? These men are scalp hunters, trying to lure us away from camp. Now come on. We're going home."

He turned to go.

"No."

Mosi, for all her feminine softness, spoke the word with iron firmness. Red Buffalo saw flashing in her eyes the fires of determination. He doubted she typically defied her brother. But he supposed there was a first time for everything. And this seemed to be one.

"W-what?" Chayton, visibly irritated, seemed more surprised than angered.

"I'm sick of living in that village!" she said. "I am tired of being the Navajo girl, the one every warrior and his brother is panting over. It's not our home, Chayton, and you know it! We'll never truly fit in there!"

"Yes, we will! Once I become a warrior, we —"

"They'll never let you become a warrior, and you know it, Chayton! You're too small. And you're not as strong as the other boys."

"Stop!"

"When you're not around, they laugh at you. They think it's funny that you consider yourself a 'true Apache.' Chayton, they hold you in contempt."

A thousand expressions flickered across the boy's face in an instant. Red Buffalo saw shame. Then sadness. Then self-righteous anger. He punched the air and stood quivering as he replied.

"I'll show them. I'll show them all! You're wrong, sister — I *will* be accepted into the warrior society. And I will prove it by bringing home two captives — these two — *today*!" He raised his bow. "Right now."

"Don't," said Johnny, reaching for his gun.

Chayton drew a fresh arrow from his quiver and was about to nock it when Red Buffalo moved.

Like lightning, he sped across the space between them, tackling the boy and knocking the bow from his hands. Before he could recover, Red Buffalo seized the bow and threw it away in the tall grasses, as Johnny seized Mosi's hand and ran.

Stark watched all this happen from up on the lookout, saw Red Buffalo tackle the boy and dispose of his bow, saw Johnny and Mosi running for the trees and, a few moments later, Red Buffalo following.

Chayton stood, rigid with anger, before turning to run back toward the village.

Better get the horses ready, Stark thought.

Chapter 32

From his vantage, Stark could see Red Buffalo, Johnny, and Mosi sprinting through the trees toward his position and Chayton dashing into the village, yelling and waving his arms.

This is going to be close, he thought.

The camp was packed up, the gear returned to saddlebags and the horses ready. Stark climbed into Buck's saddle, the reins to Johnny's and Red Buffalo's horses in hand. The animals were skittish, feeling the frenzy in the air. It was all he could do to control them. But soon, the trio was rushing into camp.

Down below, Chayton had made it to the communal fire at the center of the village, still yelling and waving his arms.

To Stark's surprise, the reaction of the other Apache was one of brief annoyance, followed by indifference.

He's well-loved down there. You can tell,

Stark thought.

Red Buffalo accepted his mount's reins and climbed into the saddle. Johnny grasped his and turned to Mosi.

"Ride with me, Mosi," he told her. He climbed into the saddle and gave her a hand up. She settled in behind him, wrapping her arms around Johnny's waist, which Johnny didn't seem to mind at all.

Down in the village, Chayton's caterwauling was finally getting some attention. Some of the warriors were striding toward him now. Stark sensed more annoyance than alarm in their steps.

"We need to go!" Fear showed plain on Johnny's face.

He began leading them down the trail toward the mouth of the valley. Stark kept an eye on the village below, as Red Buffalo rode past. Two of the warriors were with Chayton now, listening. Their stances still betrayed an attitude of skepticism.

At least they had that on their side, he thought. Then he urged Buck on and followed Red Buffalo down the trail.

"What is it, Chayton?" Taza stood before his adopted son, hands on his hips, a look of barely restrained anger on his face. "I hope this isn't more false panic! Last spring, you put the village into turmoil with your report of cavalry that turned out to be nothing more than a stagecoach!"

Calla, Taza's lieutenant, looked down at the ground. The stagecoach incident had been particularly upsetting for his family. But he did not wish to show anger at Chayton who was, after all, a member of the war chief's household.

"They took her!" Chayton's voice cracked with emotion. "Two Indians came out of the forest — *there*!" He pointed. "They claimed our father, a chief, wanted us to come back home!"

Taza's nostrils flared and his head tilted back. Such words were dangerous. Chayton and Mosi had been taken in a raid and so were technically his property. But like most slaves or prisoners captured by Indians, the children had been absorbed into the tribe.

"What Indians?" he demanded. "Navajo?"

"Not Navajo." Chayton shook his head firmly. "One looked like maybe part Apache. The other, I don't know. But they beat me up and threw away my bow and they *took* her! They took my *sister*! *We have to go after them!*"

Taza and Calla shared a look. Doubt flickered in both their expressions. But Taza's died on a shrug.

"It can't hurt to check, I guess," he allowed quietly. "Calla, gather two men and our horses. We will go see."

"I'll come too!" Chayton objected.

"No," — Taza started to refuse, but then remembered: Mosi was the boy's sister. He had a right to come along.

"Very well," he said at last. "Go get a pony, boy. But hurry."

Chayton grinned and dashed off toward the horses.

Stark's party made their way down through the trees to the floor of the canyon. Johnny moved slowly once they reached the rocks, not wanted to create a dust cloud or too much noise. Red Buffalo rode between him and Stark, who brought up the rear. He glanced back over his shoulder several times but saw no trace of pursuit.

Now the trail up to the surface appeared. Once they were on it, they would be vulnerable to arrows from below. But if they could make sufficient headway and put some distance between themselves and the bottom, they would be safe even from that. Anticipation tingled in Stark's gut. Once they were out of the canyon, they could lay on the speed and get well clear.

"Johnny's taken quite a fancy to Mosi,"

Red Buffalo observed quietly as Stark rode up beside him.

"Seems like many do," he replied.

"That could be a problem down the road," the Crow said.

"We'll burn that bridge when we come to it," Stark said. The path was directly ahead of them now. As he watched, Johnny urged his horse up the narrow stony trail. They followed.

Taza's annoyance was growing. Chayton had led them out of camp at a gallop toward the trees. But now he had stopped in the grassy fields and was riding back and forth around a section of it, peering down into the grass.

"I thought his sister had been taken!" Calla said impatiently. "What is he doing riding around in circles like that?"

Taza didn't know and didn't care. Chayton had wasted their time once before. He would not be allowed to do so again. He was just on the point of ordering the riders back to camp when suddenly Chayton stopped, slipped from the back of his pony, and dug in the grass. A moment later, he stood, clutching his bow.

"See?" he cried. "This is proof ! This is where that Indian threw my bow."

"Proof he threw it? Or proof Chayton dropped it?" Calla whispered.

Taza flicked an irritated glance at Calla. He was annoyed at his adopted son, annoyed at his lieutenant, annoyed at the situation. But he was a chief, and the tribe's safety was his responsibility. He would follow through on this search.

Strung out in a line, with Johnny and Mosi in the lead, Stark and the Crow behind, they made their way up the narrow treacherous path from the valley floor to the surface. Stark kept an ear cocked for the sound of hoofbeats. So far, there was no indication that the tribe had sent out a search party, but one would be coming sooner or later, of that he felt sure.

Despite the unstable stone underfoot, he felt safer now that they were on the trail. Soon they would be out of range of arrows and spears, and even aiming a rifle at them for an accurate shot would prove difficult. He would feel a lot better once they were out of the valley and on the straightaway.

That's when we light a shuck and get as far from this place as we can, he thought. Mentally, he began working out routes back to Fort Lowell.

"You all right there, Nathan Stark?" Red

Buffalo's voice drifted up from his place on the trail behind him.

"So far," said Stark.

Taza could feel Chayton's nervous energy quivering behind him as he rode. They had reached the trees and there *were* fresh tracks here — two sets of boots and a third in soft moccasins. Taza was following them, but not fast enough for Chayton's taste. The boy could stand to learn a little patience.

The tracks wound up the flank of the hill to a rock overlooking the camp. Taza's practiced eye could tell at a glance that people had camped here. They had been careful to leave nothing behind. But the patterns in the grass where bodies had stretched out in sleep and the horse droppings all pointed to the inevitable truth.

Someone had overnighted here recently, unobserved by the tribe. The tracks that had led them here attested to the likelihood that there was some truth to Chayton's story. He turned to Calla.

"Ride back to camp. Gather a dozen men and supplies. Have them ride fast to the trail that leads down here from above. We'll meet them there."

Calla nodded once, wheeled his horse

around, and galloped hard back toward the camp.

"You see?" Chayton cried. "You *see*? I wasn't lying!"

Taza ignored him. There were fresh tracks leading down the other side of the hill. He was fairly sure he knew where they went. But he would follow them carefully, regardless of Chayton and his nonsense.

It took some doing, but Stark and his party eventually made it out of the valley. He breathed a sigh of relief when Buck's hooves took their last steps on the shifting rock and they emerged onto stable, safe sand.

"Everybody all right?" he asked, looking from rider to rider. He saw nods all the way around.

"They'll be coming," Johnny Two-Face said.

"They will," agreed Red Buffalo.

"Then we better get a move on," Stark said. "From here on, we go flat out until the horses need resting. Try to put as much space between us and them as possible."

Johnny nodded once, looked over his shoulder to smile tenderly at Mosi, and then spurred his mount to a gallop. Stark and Red Buffalo followed.

■ ■ ■ ■

It didn't take the warriors long to assemble and meet Taza and his party at the path. Sure enough, the tracks from the camp overlooking the tribe led here. Which meant Chayton had been right — he *had* seen his sister taken. And those responsible had made their escape this way.

Once the group had assembled, Taza signaled for silence and rode to a place where all could see and hear him.

"Our Mosi has been taken!" he cried. "Indian men who are allies with the Navajo came at the chief's request to return her to him. It's true, she and Chayton were taken in a raid. But many years have passed, and they have become part of our tribe. This is an offense against our tribe. This is an offense against the Great Spirit. We will not tolerate this. We will find Mosi and reclaim her. And we will kill the men who did this."

He turned to Chayton.

"Chayton, you have done well. But now you should return home. Go."

"Father, let me come! It's time for me to prove myself and become a warrior!"

"It's not time," Taza said woodenly. "You heard me. Go."

Chayton's anger was visible on his face. But as he sat there trembling, one of Taza's warriors rode up to the chief and spoke softly.

"Taza. It's his sister. He has a right to come with us."

Taza considered this. He was accustomed to being obeyed, but he was not a man to refuse to hear out those with whom he disagreed. Nor was he a man to consider changing his mind a disgrace. Perhaps the warrior had a point.

"Very well," he said quietly. "Chayton, you may come with us. But mind your place, and follow the orders of the senior warriors. This will be a test for you, as this dangerous trail will be a test for all of us. We go."

With that, he urged his mount toward the rocky trail to the top.

Stark was galloping hard. They all were. Leaving the valley with the Apache camp as far behind them, as fast as they could, came with a certain exhilaration. For a moment, Stark was young again, riding hard with his Confederate comrades against Billy Yank. But the feeling didn't last. The gravity of their circumstances banished it.

Johnny Two-Face abruptly slowed. Stark was about to shout a query as to why, when he saw the young Apache half-breed wheel his horse around to stare back at the valley's edge, now just a thin black line in the distance. Stark did likewise.

It was impossible to see men at this distance. But the thin telltale plumes of dust beaten skyward by hooves was visible.

"They're coming!" Johnny cried.

Chapter 33

They ran north at full gallop, crossing the dusty, rolling plain, back to the forested hillocks. The Apaches were behind them and coming fast, but Stark took charge and led them in a hard gallop into the guts of the Territory — moving fast, switching direction frequently, his goal to find an optimal place to take refuge when night fell.

For he felt certain the Apaches would continue for as long after sunset as they possibly could. Once full dark fell, they would have no choice but to stop for the night, as all men must who journey on the frontier, where life is not carved up into chunks of time by clocks or schedules but by light and dark. And men knew just how vulnerable they were when the sun went down.

Stark led them into the hills, taking a circuitous path until he found the last arroyo they had traversed. It was oriented in a more or less east–west direction, which was perfect for his purposes. Leading them down into the dry wash, Stark proceeded to gallop west, scanning the terrain as he went.

He found what he was looking for at a portion of the wash that branched off from the main section, a narrower arroyo, just wide enough if they went single file. It led to the foot of some cliffs a quarter-mile distant.

He reined in, whistled sharply to get everyone's attention, and waited until they gathered around.

"Here's the plan," he said. "We're going to ride hard back to where we left the trail. The Apaches will be within sight before sunset. So we'll ride on past this wash, then double back and get here ten minutes before sunset. We'll head up this narrow wash to the base of this cliff and spend the night here. The night patrol won't be able to follow our tracks very well, so they'll be going by feel. This maneuver should fool them enough that we can catch a few hours sleep. We'll be gone by morning."

He looked around. Johnny and Red Buffalo both nodded, approving the plan. He turned to Mosi.

"How are you holding up?"

She smiled and nodded, and that was answer enough for him.

"Okay, then." He tilted his gaze up to check the angle of the sun. "It's getting close. Let's ride."

It was close.

Stark returned them to the trail the Apaches were still following, the northern route back to Fort Lowell. He rode them hard, as if their lives depended upon it. And in the half hour of precious dusk, he was glad he did.

The Apaches had already sent out advance riders. He could see the dust clouds of their horses widening on the horizon, fresher and closer than those kicked up by the main force. They would reach the point where Stark had resumed their journey northward just around nightfall. It was time to turn back to the arroyo.

He wheeled Buck around, waved to the others behind him and took off toward the dry riverbed.

He reckoned the scouts continuing to search after dark was a dead certainty. The job now was to make sure the cost of investing the time and energy outweighed the benefit. It was a modified version of the rabbit trick: doubling back to take refuge in a strong position, backs to a cliff so that they could not be surprised.

Stark could see the dust plumes of the outriders rising just off to the left, behind some hills, as he guided the other two riders down the narrow wash. Dusk was deepening. Full night was falling. The plumes continued north as the outriders attempted to make use of daylight until the last possible moment.

By the time Stark and the others arrayed themselves at the bottom of the cliffs, the last light was gone and the stars were just beginning to peek from behind the veil of night. Even in full daylight, it would take three hours of hard tracking for the Apache to catch up to them. At night, it would be impossible.

Stark reined in at the bottom of the cliff, slid from the saddle, and stretched. He watched as Red Buffalo's horse meandered over. And noted how Johnny Two-Face and Mosi were hanging back. Quite a distance back. Not so far as to be in danger from their pursuers, but far enough to ensure their privacy. Which got him to thinking.

"Johnny's got a little crush for that Navajo girl," Red Buffalo observed.

"I noticed." Stark kept his voice low. "I'm hoping it's not going to cost us at some point down the trail."

"They've paused outside of camp."

"Noticed that, too."

"They're probably out there somewhere in the shadows, hugging and kissing."

"I'd bet a hat that you're probably right."

Red Buffalo saw to their horses while Stark set out the basics of a camp. As had been the case so many times before, they could not risk an ordinary cook fire, so he dug a pit for a stealth fire. The small blaze was burning, muted but hot, and supper was almost ready by the time Johnny and Mosi came into camp. Both had weary, satisfied expressions on their faces.

Stark sighed. It was going to be a long ride home.

"Hey."

Stark snorted, moaned, and tried to settle back to sleep.

"Hey." He felt movement. Then he realized it was Red Buffalo shaking his shoulder.

Stark rolled upright, opened his eyes, and blinked last night's dreams from under his lids. "W-what . . . ?" he whispered. He could see it was not yet dawn.

"They're gone." Red Buffalo pointed to the smear in the sand where the other two had slept. "Several hours ago, from what I can tell. That damn fool boy has decided to kidnap himself a Navajo bride."

"All right." Stark grimaced, stood, and stretched. "Mount up, I guess. We're —" He paused, weighing his options. "Actually, it just occurs to me. We may be missing a real opportunity here."

"Opportunity?" Red Buffalo frowned. "I don't understand."

"If we split up, we can kill two birds with one stone. We can get the girl back, and we can lead our Apache friends on a wild-goose chase."

Red Buffalo raised his eyebrows. "Go on," he said.

"Johnny made tracks. Say, I follow them, and you ride out to where we cut off to switch back in this direction and make more tracks toward the horizon. Lead them on a good long merry chase headed due south. Go as long and far as you can before starting a wide circle back. We'll each head back to Fort Lowell. Likely meet up on the trail."

"If I leave early enough," Red Buffalo said, "I can get a good head start before they're on the trail."

"Yeah, you'd better get going." Stark said this and then, for some strange reason, looked down at the ground.

He couldn't think of what else to say.

Neither could Red Buffalo.

The Crow scout mounted his horse, nodded once to Stark, and took off in the wee hours.

Stark had Buck saddled and was mounted and on Johnny's trail within a few minutes. It was still mostly dark, but light enough to see the outlines of their tracks. Besides, it didn't seem Johnny had made much effort to conceal himself.

That stupid kid. Stark was annoyed at Johnny's selfish actions but, at the same time, grudgingly understanding. He had once been young and done stupid things because of women. It wasn't the women's fault — he had just been young and dumb. Johnny was no different.

Red Buffalo made it back to the point at which they had branched off from the main trail and began the trek south, drawing the Apaches off their intended trail by a full one hundred eighty degrees. He made a mess at the point of intersection and then took off, careful to leave a set of deep, clear prints in his wake.

The Apaches would notice, of course, that he was alone. But they would follow that trail as it was the only fresh one in sight. Others might pick up the set they had made last night when they turned back to the narrow wash that led to the cliffs. But all they would find there was a deserted campsite. Stark would be long gone.

The sky brightened to the east. The sun was getting ready to poke its flaming head above the horizon. Red Buffalo turned back and saw two bright columns of dust coming fast in his direction. He gave a smile of satisfaction, spurred his horse, and rode as hard and as fast as he could due south.

By the time the pursuers arrived at his starting point, he would be miles away.

Taza, with the main body of warriors, was awake and mounted by dawn. Most of his men were ready, as well. He sat watching as a messenger rode back fast from his scouts' forward position. There was news.

The messenger galloped into camp, reining to a canter and approaching the chief respectfully. He was one of the young warriors who was known to be careful and steady and so was entrusted with carrying important news.

"The scouts found the trail and followed it as far as they could until nightfall," he said. "They have picked it up again this morning. But it seems some of the party vanished in the night. There is now only a single rider."

Taza weighed this news carefully. The messenger, meanwhile, finished up.

"They are searching for a second trail."

"We won't split up the war party," Taza said firmly. "That is what they would want us to do. To cut our numbers and make ourselves more vulnerable. No, we'll trust the scouts to choose the route they judge best, then go all together. We'll trust that they know their business." He nodded to the messenger, who assumed his place in the ranks.

Chayton bustled up on his pony. Taza gave the youth a hard stare. The boy had shown strength, keeping up with the war party, not complaining about last night's rough food or rough sleeping conditions. He was showing more character than Taza would have expected.

"Father. May I ride up front with you today?"

On the verge of saying a solid no, Taza opted instead to give the boy a chance, recalling again that it was his sister who was missing, after all.

"Very well," Taza said. "But make sure to keep up."

Stark cantered along at an easy pace, reading from the scuffle and smear of Johnny's tracks the pace of their speeding up and slowing down. He reacted accordingly. The notion of moving on them too fast and spooking them was far worse than losing them altogether.

Because Johnny was out of his mind.

There was no doubt about it. The longer Stark reflected on what was at stake — the success of the Apache Wars, the safety of Fort Lowell and the Navajo, the welfare of the Free State of Mescalero itself — the more disgusted he grew at Johnny's antics. The young man's actions went beyond mere selfishness. They were destructive and apt to end as many lives as he and Red Buffalo hoped to save by delivering Mosi to General Miles and getting the Navajo guides back to work for the cavalry.

He stumbled upon the second set of tracks near the edge of a wash and did a double take.

No doubt about it. Someone — or, more correctly, some group of people — had begun shadowing Johnny and Mosi. He could tell by the way the fresh hoofprints overlaid Johnny's own, breaking up their pattern and shape, signaling that a force was on his trail, determined to catch up with him.

These hoofprints have shoes, Stark

thought. *These are white men.*

That meant scalp hunters, Mexican Army, or marauders.

Stark spurred Buck hard and went after them.

Chapter 34

The daylight brightened and spread as Stark rode. Uneasiness settled over him. The trackers had been following Johnny and Mosi at some distance for quite a while. He couldn't say how far behind he was, but he could tell that the trackers knew what they were doing.

Which got him thinking again about scalp hunters.

There was something ghoulish about the profession. It had a bleak, demonic quality to it — a weird calling along the lines of being a witch or hoodoo medicine man. It reminded him of Otoway.

The Apache Wars weren't the only Indian problem that seemed to vanish during the War Between the States. The matter of the great Cherokee Nation was forgotten during the national convulsion. The Five Tribes of the Nation allied with Richmond early in the war. If the promise of land titles and money weren't enough, a guarantee of the right to property, including human property, was sufficient to sweeten the deal. Some tribes kept human chattel. Otoway had been such a slave.

Taken during a raid on a Lakota camp, Otoway had been traded through the Cherokee and eventually into the hands of a white landowner named McLellan. Otoway's training as a medicine man served to make him a valuable asset to any homestead, and his talents were particularly useful to McLellan. He had donated great sums to the Confederacy, and so when he asked the army's assistance in tracking down his renegade Sioux, Stark had been dispatched to see to it personally.

Otoway had escaped in the early autumn, having cleverly chosen a morning when the frost hit and the ground was frozen. He had left few tracks and had been clever enough to forage for food over the next few days. Stark had had a difficult time keeping up with the man, even on horseback. And Otoway's ability to trick Stark, to redirect and distract his attention, to get inside his mind and turn it inside out, had been absolutely frightening.

Fortunately, the man was unarmed, because on at least a half dozen occasions, Stark walked right into some ideal ambush site. Had Otoway been equipped with a gun or spear, Stark would have been dead. But instead, it had served only to prolong the chase. Early autumn became mid-autumn. The leaves colored and fell, the temperature dropped, and still he was no closer to apprehending the man.

But that he was on the move was evident. By Stark's reckoning, he was making for his ancestral homelands in the Midwest. Knowing this eventually allowed Stark to capture the man, although he nearly lost his life doing it. For on the final day, Otoway had indeed laid a trap for him.

It was of such traps that he was wary now. He already knew the trackers were professionals. He couldn't discount the possibility that there were Indians among them.

Otoway had lured him into an orchard, dropping from the branches of an apple tree onto Stark's back and shoulders. The resulting struggle had become a mad and desperate scramble that Stark had only barely won. He had put a bullet through the medicine man's heart just before Otoway could use the knife he had plucked from a sheath at Stark's waist. He had been a split second away from burying that cold steel in Stark's body.

Instead, it was Otoway who wound up lying on the ground, nothing more than a sack of meat.

Now the scalp hunters were close. Stark could tell by the tracks, by the lack of any sounds from small animals, by the sense of *presence* his finely honed tracker's intuition picked up on. *Somebody* was in the area. Or had been, recently.

He stopped dead. Cocked his head. And listened.

He heard not voices, but the ghosts of voices. Someone was speaking perhaps a quarter mile from his present position.

It was time to go on foot.

He tied Buck to a tree and began following the tracks. Instead of staying right on top of the trail, he positioned himself off to one side, taking cover whenever possible in the trees. He followed the tracks as if a man were making them just a few feet ahead — more cautiously than he would a group on horseback a quarter of a mile distant.

He found them sooner than expected.

The group of trackers had fetched up against the base of a hill, having dismounted to stretch their legs and swill water from canteens. Stark got as close as he could and settled behind some scrubby vegetation and rocks. When he was satisfied that he hadn't roused their attention, he lifted his head from behind a parapet of stone to see who he was dealing with.

Three men. One, the obvious leader, was a white man with sharp features. Shaggy white hair and a white beard and mustache framed his face, and his eyes were alert and searching. Beside him sat a youngish man, not much older than a teenager, in a brown coat and brown hat. The third member of the group was —

A woman, Stark realized in amazement.

You didn't see many women who came out to ride the trails, and this one seemed the unlikeliest of all to do such a thing. She was enormously fat — what Stark would kindly call "a big gal" — with fiery red hair barely concealed beneath a conical peaked sombrero. The bandoliers of ammo strapped across her chest and the long black shotgun she clasped across her knees showed her to be a shooter well accustomed to having iron close to hand.

So it was the Graybeard, the Kid, and Shotgun Momma. That's who he was dealing with.

Stark slipped noiselessly back down to his horse and waited.

That they were scalp hunters was obvious. They were too motley and disorganized a crew to be anything else. But they still managed to surprise him.

He was resting with Buck, just out of sight, on the other side of a row of bushes. If he was very still, he could hear the occasional buzz of a voice. By shifting slightly, he could spy them through a gap in the brush. After a few minutes without noise, he looked and saw they were gone.

No matter, he thought. That they were so quiet was a prerequisite in their line of work. Stark mounted up and resumed his pursuit of them, even as they pursued Johnny and Mosi.

Stark went cautiously, pausing, more often than he had to, to check for sound. It wasn't long before he heard their voices echoing just up ahead. He was close on their trail. It would not do to make a mistake just now.

It continued that way, with the trio alternately traveling and resting, and Stark keeping pace with them, until midafternoon. The group had paused, as in the past, and Stark waited. But this time they managed to evade him. Stark cursed himself for falling for it.

He doubted they were aware of his presence, but they were canny enough to build little tricks like this into their routine just in case. He sighed and resumed the search for their trail.

He didn't catch up to them until near sundown. As dusk approached, he found a scuffed patch of sand and a bent mesquite twig that told him they had recently passed this way. He was maybe a half hour behind them now. He would close to within a few minutes' distance, then reconnoiter on foot before settling down for the evening.

That was the plan. Unfortunately, things worked out differently.

He pushed himself, traveling hard until he'd closed to within a quarter mile or so. Leaving Buck by a stand of cottonwood, he crept toward the small clearing beyond the hill. He was reasonably sure they had decided to stop there for the night.

And indeed, they had. But he wasn't prepared for the presence of Johnny and Mosi.

Yet there they were. Stark got to within one hundred yards of the clearing when he spotted them. He dropped down. Just in time, too, as the Kid was just turning to scan the landscape behind them. Johnny and Mosi had been taken unawares and were now trussed up like a pair of Thanksgiving turkeys, while Graybeard and Shotgun Momma gloated over their misfortune.

"She's real pretty," Shotgun Momma was saying, studying Mosi.

"Sure is," agreed Graybeard in a baritone voice. You could tell he was one of those honey-tongued devils who could talk the birds down from the trees.

As for the Kid, he merely looked at Mosi and grunted.

He's a man of few words. Looking over at Shotgun Momma, Stark thought, *She's about the ugliest damned woman I've ever clapped eyes on.* And of Greybeard: *The mastermind of this cabal.*

Stark was savvy enough to be aware of the recent rise of dime novels as a form of cheap entertainment. His own exposure to them had been limited, but he knew enough to sense that his current situation made for the kind of fanciful setting such adventures recounted. No doubt the conventions of gallantry and daring would have insisted he storm the camp immediately and bravely free his friends with a few well-placed shots.

But of course, things don't work that way — in dime novels, maybe, but never in real life. Reality required patience and planning, a willingness to adapt, and a certain talent for stomaching risk. He would rescue Johnny and Mosi. But he would wait until conditions were right. This meant waiting at least until nightfall. Which meant remaining here motionless for several hours. It would be difficult but, he hoped, worth it.

None of them seem terribly inclined to wander far from camp. Graybeard was a lazybones, lolling on his side on a blanket. Shotgun Momma was plopped down on her prodigious backside. And the Kid, while mobile, was a pacer, moving back and forth, covering the same stretch of ground over and over again.

Perfect glamorous heroes for a dime novel, Stark thought wryly. Then he arranged himself carefully, so as to maximize his own comfort over the next few hours, and settled down to wait.

The light slipped from dark toward deep nightfall. Enough light shone from the scalpers' fire for Stark to make out what was going on.

The scalpers moved as silhouettes against the glow. The Kid was herding Johnny and Mosi together for the night.

What worried Stark most was what they were going to do with Mosi.

She was by far the more important of the

two prisoners. Perhaps they even sensed it, having made a special effort to keep her tightly secured. Stark continued his watch and began figuring.

Chapter 35

There were times when, returning to the Christian mission where he grew up, Red Buffalo would sometimes get roped into looking after a group of kids for a while. His preferred method of babysitting was to run around the mission schoolyard and have the kids chase him. But if they were particularly small, he would have to pause every now and then to allow them time to catch up.

This chase with the Apaches was no different.

The group of riders on his trail was large enough to slow them down. Also, he had to make allowances for the fact that they were tracking as they rode, which meant frequent pauses and backtracking to ensure they were headed in the right direction. So, like an indulgent minder pausing in play to ensure the kids caught up, Red Buffalo would pause now and then on the trail, allowing the pursuers time to close the gap some.

Compared to me, he thought, *they probably are kids.*

He was growing old.

Not so old that he couldn't scout, ride, and shoot. Not so old that he couldn't make a living and support himself. Not so old that he was unable to hunt or keep house or live well. But old enough that long trips in the saddle were starting to get to him. Old enough that the absence of a home at the end of the day was keenly felt. Old enough to start thinking about settling down.

Yet here he was.

The Apache were moving again. Red Buffalo had managed to coax at least the majority of the group to stay on his tracks as opposed to seeking out Stark's or Johnny's. Perhaps, they reasoned, the pair that had split off on their own would link up again with the man they now pursued. Either that or they figured a bird in the hand was better than two in the bush. Regardless, they were coming.

Red Buffalo resumed course, beginning with a light canter. He didn't want to make noise or raise a dust plume, not when they were this close to him. He would put some distance between them first. Once he was well clear, he would push the horse into a hard gallop and go for as long as his horse could hold up before slowing again. He would also take care to leave some ambiguous sign, perhaps even conceal his horse's hoofprints for a mile or so. Anything to keep the pursuers occupied.

He continued on, so concerned with the men behind him that he had no idea what lay before him.

Taza studied the sign. It was a single rider they followed now, not the group that had started this journey. For whatever reason, this one had continued alone while the others dropped away. Had they quarreled and split up? Or had the others become lost? Died? He did not know. But he had one clear set of tracks to follow and follow them he would.

"Taza" — Chayton had ridden up beside him — "why do we follow these tracks? The others left some time back. Why aren't we hunting them?"

"Because this set of tracks is clear and fresh." Taza spoke in a clipped tone to hide his irritation. Chayton had been worrying away at this topic for some time now. "We must take advantage of the opportunity put before us. We cannot go chasing ghosts."

"But they're not ghosts — they were part

of this trail! Now they've gone." Chayton's voice rose in a panicky tone. "What if my sister is among them? We could be —"

"*Enough.*" Taza did not raise his voice. He did not need to. His tone was flat and determined, and it contained an undertone Chayton had learned early on to obey. When Taza spoke that way, he was almost ready to lose his temper. It was usually a good idea to let the topic of conversation drop. So Chayton did.

He dropped back among the warriors of the pursuit party. They either ignored him or watched him with carefully composed expressions of indifference. He knew he was not welcome among their number, was considered a nuisance and a distraction. Yet here he was.

I'll show them, he thought.

Red Buffalo was so focused on bringing along his group of pursuers that he didn't register the dust cloud rising ahead of him until almost too late. He happened to glance ahead for a random moment, and that's when he saw it: a tower of dust climbing into the sky just ahead. He yanked on the reins and brought his horse to a complete stop.

The quantity of dust rising against the

blue background was massive. There was no question in his mind that he was riding into a large body of men. And not likely Indians, given the amount of dust, enough to block out the sun.

There can't be cavalry out this way, he thought. *We would be aware of it. And that group is too large to be a bunch of wild Apaches.*

Behind him, a small group of approaching riders. Ahead of him lay this much larger threat. It would be here any moment.

Red Buffalo slid down off his horse, grasped the reins, and moved into the trees beside the path. This was no forest, not yet, at any rate. It was a bunch of baby pines, spread out from each other across the sand and dirt floor. But Red Buffalo knew if he advanced far enough into their midst, he would be just a blur to anyone on the path. If he and the horse kept still, the two groups would pass without noticing him and likely run into each other.

He pulled a branch from one of the young trees, carefully brushing over and hiding his tracks. Within a short time, he had become a shadow in the distance.

Captain Diego Nuñez of the Mexican army called a halt to his column of caballeros and studied the landscape ahead of them. He had a column of a hundred *soldados* riding at his back, a large formation for this far north of the border. One of Geronimo's generals had attacked a settlement in *el estado de Sonora,* and a response was mandatory. Nuñez and his cavalry had been dispatched on a mission of retaliation.

Now it seemed events had taken a surprising turn. Twisting in his saddle, he motioned for his second-in-command, Lieutenant Torres, to ride up beside him.

"What do you make of that, Torres?" he asked, motioning toward the dust plumes moving toward them through the desert.

"Do you think they are our raiders, *Señor Capitán?*"

Nuñez considered this briefly. "Possibly," he said. "It was not a large force. It could be, now that they are back in the *Estados Unidos,* they feel confident enough to turn and confront their pursuers."

"*Sí, capitán.*" Torres considered it a possible but unlikely scenario.

"Or they could be a different party from the one we seek. A party out hunting or scavenging."

"*Sí, capitán.*"

"But if they are this far south of Tucson, this close to the border . . ." He shook his head. "There is no doubt they are Apache."

"*Sí, capitán.*"

"Go back. Tell Revulcaba to break the column into two teams." He looked up at the rocky slopes to either side of him. "Have them post up behind rocks on high ground, either side of the trail, and await my signal."

"*Sí, capitán.*" Torres saluted, wheeled his horse around, and went to convey the order.

Taza noted a quantity of dust in the air ahead. He assumed it was from the one they pursued. It never occurred to him that it could be a large amount of dust settling from a force that had suddenly stilled its progress.

"We are getting closer," he whispered to one of his lieutenants.

Chayton rode up. "Father, look!" He pointed.

Taza and the lieutenant nodded. Neither spoke, not wanting to encourage Chayton's adventurism.

"Well, are we going to attack?" The boy sounded impatient.

"We are." Taza spoke with a weary sigh. "But we are going to be careful."

"*Why?*" The boy was fairly quivering with rage. "We are many! They are few!"

"*Enough.*" Again, Taza's tone forbade argument.

Chayton bit his tongue and returned to the other riders.

From his vantage point among the trees, Red Buffalo could make out the shape of the approaching horses. To his surprise, he recognized the long blue coats, the white sashes, and the European-style peaked caps. This was a column of regular Mexican cavalry, not *rurales,* riding north.

They're a long way from home, he thought.

What had brought them up this way was anyone's guess. They certainly weren't hiding their presence. Riding in tight formation, they flew Mexican standards and conversed in Spanish that was audible even at this distance. As he watched, the one in command gave an order and the remainder of the men began to post up with their horses behind the rocks up slope.

The Purgatory Crossing Apaches were about to ride into an ambush.

Captain Nuñez waited until the last of his men were in position before going to join them. He dismounted and guided his horse up the stony slope, secreting himself behind the rocks near the front of the men on the lefthand slope. He handed off the reins to a private, drew his sword, and waited.

He heard the clatter of hooves. Voices rose as the Apaches entered the narrow cut.

Nuñez began counting slowly in his head.

Taza rode up in front, Chayton cantering along right behind him. A dozen yards behind lay the dozen men of his search party.

Taza was getting tired of having Chayton along with them. His warriors had been correct about the boy having a right to join in the hunt — Chayton was certainly the proper age to begin gaining experience in such matters.

But in addition to being smaller than the other boys, he was also less mature and more given to whining and complaining than Apache boys.

Taza had hoped this journey might provide him with the opportunity to do a little growing up. It occurred to him that perhaps it was too late. Perhaps he had allowed his wife too much time with the boy and she had spoiled him. It certainly explained a great deal of his behavior.

"Father," Chayton said. "When we find Mosi, perhaps —"

That was as far as he got before the air

was split with a single shriek:
"*Fuego!*"

The caballeros of Captain Nuñez's squad leaped to their feet, trained their rifles on the small group of Apache down in the cut, and opened fire.

It was like a thunderstorm had suddenly erupted over the desert. The scream and stench of gunfire filled the air, and bullets rained down on the Indians. At first taken by surprise, a few fell. Others attempted to get off the path and take cover, but they were swiftly mown down. The men were well and truly trapped in a deadly field of fire.

Two rallied and started up the cliffs on horseback, full of fight. One made it partway up the slope before being blasted from the back of his pony. He fell backward, tumbling through the rocks to the desert below. The second made it a few feet higher than his comrade before a bullet found him and killed him instantly. He slumped forward on the horse, which wheeled and escaped, carrying the dead rider along with him.

Unobserved by Nuñez, the two Apaches at the head of the column managed to escape.

∎ ∎ ∎ ∎

Red Buffalo watched the carnage unfold until he could watch it no more. He turned away until the sound of gunfire subsided. So far as he could determine, their pursuers were finished.

He mounted up and rode away, leaving the death and chaos behind him.

Chapter 36

Stark was tired and hungry. This was an uncomfortable blind, and his physical position, barely tenable. But it was as close as he was likely to get under the circumstances.

Stark wondered why they didn't just scalp the two captives. He was glad they didn't, of course, but it seemed odd they had gone to the trouble of keeping Johnny and Mosi alive this long.

Johnny and Mosi cowered in their corner of the campsite. They were still trussed up, with lengths of rope binding their wrists and binding them together. Tying them up was the one smart thing the scalp hunters had managed to do. Even if they were able to evade their captors and flee the camp, they were tied facing one another, making a swift escape all but impossible.

Stark didn't have to wait long for the first full-blown argument to break out among the scalp hunters. After a confused half hour spent gathering wood, a messy fire was laid and lit. The smoke it exuded was, for some reason, dark and foul. Despite this, Graybeard was anxious for some dinner. He hollered at the Kid to put on some beans, for God's sake. The Kid fired back that he was no cook and began ragging on Shotgun Momma to stop swanning around camp and get to work on their meal.

Shotgun Momma was having none of it. She rounded on the Kid and began cursing him up one side and down the other. He and Graybeard found this absolutely hilarious and responded with mocking and teasing. When she shrieked a curse at Graybeard, he mimicked her back so accurately that the Kid broke up laughing. Shotgun Momma produced a knife and lunged at Graybeard but overbalanced. She went down. The knife clattered away among the rocks. The answering laughter that rose caused her to rage all the more. But instead of picking up the knife, she went for what appeared to be a laudanum bottle, took a sip, and calmed right down.

The liquor came out soon afterward. It was the Kid who drew a bottle from his saddlebag. Graybeard whooped when the cork was pulled. Soon whiskey was flowing. The two men sat together, passing the bottle back and forth, while Shotgun Momma dug through their supplies for food and cooking implements. She knocked over more things than she gathered and required several efforts to assemble everything she needed. But eventually she got dinner started, and the mood of the camp relaxed toward evening.

"What are they going to do with us?"

Mosi's whisper, cautious and breathy, came to Johnny's ears, and he acknowledged it with a glance. He immediately followed this up with a sidelong look at their captors, as if to say, *Quiet, or they'll hear you.* He waited until the argument between them flared up again to answer.

"I don't know."

And the truth was, Johnny had no idea. Nothing this group did made any sense. They seemed like a bumbling, disorganized bunch of drunken fools. That they had managed to get the drop on him and Mosi was a complete shock to Johnny.

He had figured out they were scalp hunters by the paltry quantity of booty dangling from Graybeard's saddle horn. He imagined that this group of would-be ne'er-do-wells probably drifted around, picking up the low-hanging fruit missed by more organized gangs. No doubt they preyed upon the lost, the vulnerable, the injured. Seeking to create their own little paradise of booze and drugs, they approached their chosen career with a kind of lazy, half-hearted campaign of terror. If better opportunities ever presented themselves, this trio likely slept through them.

"Are they going to kill us?" Mosi's voice, while quiet, contained a stormy edge of desperation that she had difficulty controlling.

Would they kill them? Scalp them? Rape them? All three? It was impossible to tell. And the drunker the scalp hunters got, the more unpredictable their actions became. When he finally answered, it was with a weary dismay that carried into three simple words:

"I don't know."

Stark watched them eat. He felt the darkness settle over him like a blanket and was grateful for its embrace. The firelight did not touch his position, so he felt relatively confident that he could move around the distant environs of their camp unnoticed. But he took care to conduct a test first.

He waited until the last of the daylight was gone, then raised an arm above the edge of his blind. It remained aloft for a few minutes without eliciting any notice from the scalp hunters. Then he gathered his courage and came to his knees. Still no response. He was invisible to them out here, and he intended to take full advantage of that.

The Kid was singing now: an out-of-tune rendition of "The Alabama Blossoms." He paused several times, stumbling for lyrics, only to be egged on by Graybeard's cries of encouragement.

Stark crept closer to the camp, enduring the awful singing, while keeping cover between himself and the immediate line of sight of the scalpers. The Kid eventually finished his rendition to the applause of his friends. He took a clumsy bow, tilted the whiskey bottle to his lips, and drank one more time before passing it over to Graybeard.

"That was mighty terrible!" Graybeard enthused. "You're an awful singer!"

"Oh, go to hell, you ol' goat," the Kid replied. "I gotta go relieve myself."

"That's a relief to us!" cried Graybeard, as the Kid meandered into the shadows at the edge of camp.

Stark went to meet him.

■ ■ ■ ■

The Kid stumbled out of camp into the darkness beyond. He was drunk, unsteady on his feet, and only vaguely conscious of his present location. They were somewhere in the desert. They had a couple of prisoners. He was drunk. And he had to relieve himself.

He limped toward a stand of mesquite bushes, unable to walk in a perfectly straight line. He compensated by tacking, finally stumbling up to it sideways, dropping his hand to the fly of his trousers. He was drunk, he told himself again. Somewhere in the desert. And about to relieve himself.

He was blissfully engaged in doing just that, when he sensed movement behind him. "Leave me be," he muttered, assuming it was the others come out to bedevil him. He finished and did up his pants. He was just turning around, when the hand closed over his mouth.

The Kid's eyes widened in alarm. He was too drunk and tired to struggle much but managed to work up the gumption to make a halfhearted effort. That was exactly what he was doing when the keen steel of a blade sank into his back, ending for all time any question about where he was and what was going on.

"Gimme a drink of that!"

"No," said Graybeard to Shotgun Momma. "You've already had enough of your evil juice. You don't need any whiskey."

"I said gimme a drink of it!"

Graybeard extended the bottle with a sigh and a resigned gesture. Shotgun Momma seized it and chugged from it, then handed it back, stifling a burp with the back of her hand.

"Ain't much left," Graybeard lamented, holding the bottle to the light and checking its level. "Best leave some for Billy."

"Where's he gotten to, anyway?" Shotgun Momma demanded. "Billy?"

She stood and went to the edge of the firelight, calling into the darkness.

"Billy? You out there?"

In their corner of the campsite, Mosi and Johnny exchanged a look.

Stark heard Shotgun Momma cry out — heard her use the name Billy and figured that must be the Kid's real name. He hunkered in the shadows and loosed a grunt aimed her way.

"What was that?" she asked, silhouetted

against the firelight.

Stark grunted again. This seemed to mollify her because she gave a dismissive wave of her hand, turned and stumbled back toward Graybeard. "Gimme another sip of that," she demanded.

"Nope," he said. "Got to leave some for Billy."

"I said gimme more!"

Stark judged that the time had come to strike. He drew his Colt and began moving out of the shadows and into their camp.

Johnny and Mosi saw him before the others did. Johnny immediately looked down in case Graybeard glanced over and followed the direction of his gaze.

Stark walked right into the camp. Graybeard was dozing, hands clasped loosely around the whiskey bottle, snores rattling around the spittle dribbling from his mouth. Shotgun Momma stood with her back turned, engaged in vigorous examination of her laudanum bottle. As Stark watched, she abruptly stiffened and tilted her head toward one shoulder.

"I believe I've got you covered," he said quietly.

Shotgun Momma whirled around, the surprise in her eyes transforming to rage.

She was on the brink of a major conniption, Stark could tell. Nevertheless, she was careful to pocket her laudanum before opening her mouth.

"And just who in the dad-blamed world are you, mister? And where the hell do you get off sneaking into our camp in the middle of the night?"

"Oh, just a traveling salesman." He smiled and pointed the Colt at her. "You in the market for a little snake oil?"

"Oh, you're a real wiseacre, aren't you?" Shotgun Momma was not amused at his joke. "You from Jerome?"

"I don't know anybody named Jerome."

"I mean the *town,* not the *person,* numbskull!"

"Well, you're standing here in the sight of my Colt and not vice versa, so who's the numbskull here?"

Stark caught motion out of the corner of his eye. Just a flicker, but enough to catch his attention. He wheeled and fired at Graybeard just as the old man was lifting his pistol. Stark's bullet caught him between the eyes, knocking him back into a resting position where he remained, to doze forever, his other hand still around the whiskey bottle.

Shotgun Momma took this opportunity to

produce a pocket derringer from her skirt, raise it, and fire. The shot went wide, but Stark threw himself to the ground and rolled. An instant before her second shot sounded, Stark raised himself quickly and shot her twice in the chest. Her second bullet hit in the dirt next to Stark.

"That wasn't very neighborly of you," he said quietly. Shotgun Momma went down to strike the ground with a hard smack.

Stark peered around the camp, holstered his weapon, and drew his knife.

"Johnny," he said, "you are one stupid so-and-so."

He knelt, working the blade between Johnny's wrists and cutting upward, severing the bonds. Next he went to work on Mosi, loosening her ropes. At length, they both stood, massaging circulation back into their limbs.

"What the hell were you thinking, boy?" Stark was furious. "You two were just going to ride off into the sunset together like in some cheap dime novel?"

Johnny, miserable, peered at the ground and said nothing.

"And you," he turned to Mosi. "What were you thinking? Don't you want to see your family again?"

"I don't know," she confessed. "Johnny is

handsome, and he likes me. I just . . ."

Stark sighed, staring at these two sorry specimens of young love. He had to admit that he had done some dumb things where women were concerned, so he couldn't stay too angry.

"Come on," he said. "Let's get out of here."

Chapter 37

Stark led the way back to Fort Lowell. He set a punishing pace, not because he wanted to punish Johnny and the girl, but simply because time was running out. The sooner they got back, the better.

They trekked north through the rolling hills, encountering nobody for several hours, yet smoke plumes dotted the horizon, more evidence of Geronimo's campaign of terror. Whenever they saw one up ahead, they left the path and found an alternate route, to avoid encountering the raiding parties.

On a few occasions, it was a close call. Once they nearly came face-to-face with a large party of Apache scouts. It was only by some quick thinking and hurried detours that they were able to avoid detection and capture. Screened by the leaves of a wooded grove, the passing raiders came within five hundred yards of them. Stark breathed a sigh of relief as they swept past and continued south.

"They'll be part of a larger group," Johnny noted. "Probably going to rendezvous with them now."

"Well, they're headed in the right direction," admitted Stark. "Away from us. Let's go."

They resumed the journey. For the next few hours, they traveled without incident. No Apaches crossed their path. And Stark saw no further evidence of scalp hunters or marauders. Somewhere ahead in the distance lay the comparative safety of the fort and General Miles's troops. One league at a time, they pressed on.

Red Buffalo, too, was headed north. He figured that once Stark found Johnny and the girl, they would make for Fort Lowell as quickly as possible, so he turned his steps in that direction and moved fast, to make up for time lost distracting the Apaches.

Like Stark, he saw plentiful evidence of Geronimo's raids. On a dirt road that led north from the border, he passed a stagecoach that had been set upon by raiders. It was a Wells Fargo coach, heavily built and guarded by an armed agent. The Apaches had ambushed the vehicle in broad daylight, forcing it to the side of the road, and then slaughtering the driver and his guard.

When Red Buffalo found it, the horses had been loosed from the traces and the arrow-riddled bodies of the two men left where they had fallen, one on the ground and one still on the driver's box. No effort had been made to rifle the contents of the coach, which were likely valuable. Instead, the raiders had been content to waylay, kill, and be on their way. The waste of life was horrific. Red Buffalo paused by the men's bodies to say a prayer. Then he pressed on.

An hour later, he came across an old man, in a ten-gallon hat, leading a mule loaded down with prospecting supplies. Red Buffalo paused to ask the man what news he might have heard.

"News?" The old prospector spat. "Geronimo's got a bee in his bonnet so bad I can't even work my claim. Heading home to Tucson. No amount of gold is worth getting your head blowed clean off."

Red Buffalo couldn't disagree.

When the heat of the day grew unbearable, Stark found them a cool place to dismount and rest awhile. Located by a running stream in a forested area of the hills, it was an ideal spot to steal a few hours of relaxation. As Stark was dismounting, he saw Mosi move into the trees and begin gathering wood for a fire. When she had a sizeable bundle, she returned and immediately set about getting it lit.

"She's a good woman," he said quietly to Johnny. "I can see why you like her."

Johnny seemed on the point of taking offense at this observation. Then he calmed himself and examined the girl where she was bent over the fire, feeding wood into the flames.

"She *is* a good woman," he agreed. "And she has been through a great deal. She's been telling me about her life in the camp. How her adopted father is overbearing, and her adopted mother is jealous. Her brother doesn't help matters. And then there are all those men in the village who want to marry her. She says she thought about killing herself."

Stark paused at this. It was an alarming statement coming from someone so young.

Hell, it was an alarming statement coming from anybody.

He put on a pot of coffee and thought more about what Johnny had just told him. He had never much reckoned Indians had much of an inner life. For so long now, he had merely hunted and killed them, and that had blunted his perception of them. Knowing Red Buffalo had changed that some. Knowing Mosi and Johnny was changing it further.

She seemed to like Johnny, seemed grateful for his attention and protection. They traded glances and private smiles, as the coffee ran out and the fire died down. Stark checked the angle of the sun. It was getting late.

"We should think about getting back on the trail," he said, rising and stretching. "We —"

Abruptly, he stopped, his hand dropping to his Colt and drawing it in one smooth gesture. Johnny's and Mosi's eyes widened. Johnny seemed on the point of speaking up when Stark silenced him with a raised hand.

Somewhere in the trees, a twig snapped.

They were being watched.

Stark moved to the edge of their camp and peered in the direction of the noise. He felt sure it was a man but made allowances for the possibility it was some desert critter, possibly a hog or coyote. He was squinting into the shadows behind the trees when the twig snapped again, this time closer, followed by a man's voice.

"Nathan Stark? That you?"

Red Buffalo.

Stark grinned and holstered his iron. "Right here, Red Buffalo," he said, and grinned as the Crow rode out of the trees. "You're a sight for sore eyes, man."

Stark was happier to see Red Buffalo than he would have ever thought possible. Darned if he wasn't becoming fond of that stupid Indian, he thought.

A second pot of coffee was brewed, and they traded news of their adventures since they parted ways. Red Buffalo described his efforts to lure the Apaches away from the direction of Stark and those he pursued, and the ambush laid upon them by the Mexican army.

Stark told the story of tracking Johnny and Mosi to the scalp hunters' camp, and of his encounter with Graybeard, Shotgun Momma, and the Kid.

Johnny and Mosi stayed quiet throughout most of this exchange, trading glances with each other. Red Buffalo listened to Stark finish his tale and then sucked down a healthy shot of coffee before turning to them.

"So," he said quietly, "did you two learn your lesson?"

The pair said nothing. After a short pause, Mosi nodded to him humbly.

"That's good." Red Buffalo flung the dregs from the bottom of his mug. "We put in a lot of time to find you. Risked our lives. Would be a shame if all that effort went wasted because you decided to go off and have an adventure. There are people counting on you, you know."

Again, silence. Stark touched his partner's shoulder.

"Come on," he said. "Let's cut trail."

They resumed their journey toward Fort Lowell, wending their way through the hillocks. An hour before sundown, they encountered some railroad tracks, the first real sign of civilization in miles.

"We're within a day's ride, I figure," Stark said. "If our luck holds, and we don't bump into any more Apache raiders, we should get there sometime tomorrow afternoon."

"I could use some shut-eye," Red Buffalo confessed.

Stark had to agree. They found a sheltered spot to camp at the base of some cliffs. Having not seen any smoke plumes for several hours, they risked a fire. Mosi whipped up dinner from their rations. She and Johnny ate silently, keeping to themselves. While Stark and Red Buffalo stayed up late to talk, the young couple went off to a quiet corner and bundled together in Johnny's bedroll.

Stark and Red Buffalo traded an amused look but said nothing. An hour or so later, they turned in themselves.

Stark awoke in the predawn cold. Shivering, he looked toward the fire where Red Buffalo was making some coffee. On instinct, he turned to Johnny's bedroll.

It was gone. And so were both of them.

"What the hell?" Stark sat upright and kicked off the blankets. "Where are they?"

"No idea," said Red Buffalo. "They were gone when I woke up."

"I can't believe this." Stark clutched his head in his hands. These two kids would be the death of him. "We'd best be getting after them."

"Coffee first," said Red Buffalo, handing him a cup. "Reckon we've got a long day ahead of us."

Chapter 38

Although fierce, Taza had a gentle side. He tended to conceal this aspect of his nature, which was much in evidence only in his dealings with animals and small children. Like many charged with the great responsibility of defending his people, he ordered his private world with the values of harmony and peace. For this reason, Taza prided himself on his self-control, tolerance, and patience. Particularly, the latter.

But now his patience was running out. He had sustained the loss of his warriors in the ambush. Had narrowly escaped with his life. And the one person who had managed to escape with him was none other than Chayton.

The boy had not shut up since the ambush. Not once.

"Father, I think when we get back with Mosi, you should arrange for her to marry. I think the marriage should be with

Chama." Chayton paused. "Chama has a sister. If he marries Mosi, then I can marry his sister. A strong marriage is important for a warrior to have. And I want to be a warrior. I want to serve the people as you do, Father. I hope to one day become a war chief like you. So I should get married, and I think that's the way we should do it."

Taza said nothing, scanning the ground before him for sign. The tracks they had been following had led them into the ambush that killed his men. He was having trouble locating them among the scatter and chaos of the sign left by the Mexican soldiers. But now he was clear of that confusion. And still there was no evidence of their quarry's passage.

Something was wrong.

"When I am married, I shall have Chama as my brother-in-law," Chayton was saying. "And because of that, I —"

Taza held up a hand for silence. Chayton immediately quieted.

"The trail sign is gone," Taza said quietly. "Something happened. We will go back and pick up the trail where it left off."

"But I don't understand," protested Chayton. "There are tracks everywhere and —"

"Those are tracks the soldiers left," Taza said through gritted teeth. "I speak of the trail we were originally following."

Taza took a deep breath when he was finished. The boy was an absolute idiot.

He led them back through the chaos and scatter of tracks, back through the narrows where their group had been ambushed, back through the bodies of their dead comrades. It took some doing, but Taza was eventually able to find where the tracks left off. It was right before the entrance to the ambush site. And they inexplicably vanished.

Taza looked around. The rider who had left these tracks was crafty, probably a tracker himself. There was no point at which —

There.

A disturbance in the soil. Something not left by animal or horse. A pattern in the dirt, as if someone had brushed the sand with leaves. Taza followed this pattern into the grove of nearby trees. The disturbance continued for a hundred yards before suddenly vanishing. Discarded nearby, he noticed, was the leafy branch of a tree. And not far from it was —

There.

He saw the footprints of a man. He had been standing beside the horse that had left the four impressions of its hooves. Taza surmised the man had gone into the trees, dismounted, and then held his horse still as the Apaches passed into the mouth of the ambush. And afterward?

"Once Chama is my brother-in-law —"

"Please be quiet." Taza said this calmly, holding his anger and energy in reserve.

Chayton fell silent, as bidden. That was the best choice he could have made.

For Taza was focused now. His quarry had been here, and not too long before. Casting around, he found fresh sign, the line of hoofprints left after the man had mounted up and gone. Back in the direction from which he had come. So the man had led them here intentionally. Led them here to be . . .

Slaughtered. A cold chill wrapped itself around Taza's heart.

He spurred his horse and went after this man, following the tracks, noting the man had made no effort to hide them. Probably figuring Taza and his men were now dead and so, posed no danger to him.

"Father, I —"

Taza spurred his horse to a fast gallop, making continued conversation impossible.

The man, whoever he had been, was crafty.

The tracks continued north. Eventually, they led out of the open desert to a road.

Taza followed the trail. The road remained empty and deserted. Eventually, it led them to a stagecoach. Taza slowed down to examine it.

The horses were gone. Both the driver and another man had been killed, their bodies left to rot in the sun. This would have been the work of Geronimo's raiders, no doubt about it. Taza studied the arrows embedded in the coach and the bodies of the two men. The raiding party had descended, killed, and left in a hurry. Taza, who had no great love of white men, nevertheless viewed this as an act of irresponsible butchery, one completely without honor.

"Dead white men," said Chayton, contemptuously.

"They were travelers. Passing through. They posed no danger to anyone." Taza shook his head. "These men did nothing to deserve this. It is nothing to praise."

Before Chayton could reply, his father urged his horse forward, continuing to follow the tracks north.

The longer Taza tracked his quarry, the more convinced he became the man was an Indian, like himself. A warrior. Someone who knew when to attack and when to retreat, when to expose himself and when to take cover. This craftiness, while admirable, had led to the needless death of his warriors and a great loss to his tribe.

Taza steeled himself. He was determined to find this man. And when he did, he would kill him.

Chapter 39

By Red Buffalo's reckoning, Johnny's likeliest path would be back toward the unused seasonal campgrounds of the Purgatory Crossing Apache. The tracks certainly seemed to confirm this theory. The longer they followed them, the more Stark grew convinced the young half-breed had chosen a return to the cliff dwellings as their next move. Red Buffalo agreed.

"It's a good place," the Crow said. "The horse can be brought inside. The wash fills up with water in the cold season, and there's wood around for the scavenging. They could even spend the winter there." He paused, thinking. "It's where I would go."

"Agreed. And this time, we tie Johnny to his damn saddle and don't take our eyes off him until we reach Fort Lowell."

Red Buffalo chuckled. "There's nothing more fool-headed and persistent than a young man with an itch."

"That sounds about right!"

They were approaching the cliff dwellings from an alternate direction, wending their way through a forest of saguaro cactus. This was the classic desert land of the Arizona Territory, a rocky territory of buzzards and bleached bones. The sun was unforgiving, pouring onto the land, wilting vegetation, searing and, more often than not, killing the wildlife all around.

"Amazing anything can survive out here," Stark muttered.

"Depends on what you are accustomed to, I guess," offered Red Buffalo. "Apache people. Hopi people. Navajo. All been out here since the beginning. Somehow, they make it work."

"Can't imagine how."

"The secret to enduring the heat is not to fight it, but to accept it."

Stark tried. It wasn't easy. Shade was scant. When they finally did find some, they rested in it. One siesta's cover came in the form of a shadow from some tall cliffs enclosing the trail. Within its borders, the temperature was lessened by a few degrees. Even the horses seemed to appreciate the respite.

They shared out water from their canteens. Red Buffalo was watering his horse when he spoke softly.

"We have visitors," he said. "Don't look just yet, but they're on the ridge behind us. They just showed up a second ago."

Stark pretended the Crow hadn't spoken. He moved around to the saddlebag on Buck's right side and drew out a shaving mirror he packed along. Holding it down against his belly, he could focus on the ridgeline above without craning his neck.

There were four of them. One was an Apache, complete with bone breastplate and feathers, but he also wore a white man's blue jacket. Beside him was an elderly black man clutching a shotgun. Two dark-haired white men with curly black hair and pale skin startled Stark until he recognized them as twins.

"Who do you think they are?" Stark asked.

"Likely scalp hunters. Or thieves."

"They're fixing to make a play on us, I reckon."

"Reckon so," Red Buffalo agreed.

They took their leisurely time getting back on the trail.

At some point, the four intended to strike. It occurred to Stark that he and Red Buffalo should set up a plan to ambush the ambushers.

They were clever, this quartet. As Stark

rode along, he paused periodically to turn back and check the trail behind them. He saw no silhouettes of men, no plumes of dust from plodding horses, no signs at all that they were being followed. But they were — Stark could feel it. So could Red Buffalo.

"They are there," he said the next time Stark turned to peer over his shoulder. "That one in the blue jacket. He's the one who worries me."

"Why?"

"He's a sorcerer," Red Buffalo said crisply.

"How can you tell?"

"His mode of dress. The Indian leggings and breast plate, but the white man's coat. That's common among witches and the like. But it's those two white boys in particular."

"The twins?"

"Yes." Something in Red Buffalo's tone took a distinctly uncomfortable turn. "Twins are powerful medicine among sorcerers and witch doctors. Those two back there? They are likely mindless slaves to the Indian man, doing whatever he tells them. The older black man with the gun, he's the muscle."

"Why do you say that? That they're mindless slaves." Stark's mind was racing. "How is that possible?"

"A pinch of grave dust. An owl feather. An oath sealed with a drop of blood." The Crow scout's voice grew cold. "It's the Magic of the Jar. Trapping a man's soul. They say it's easier to do with twins, white twins in particular. I met a black man from the islands who talked about his people's witch doctors doing the same thing. Turning living people into soulless slaves by trapping their inner essence."

Stark was not a man for superstition or magic. He disbelieved all that sort of thing, had seen ruin befall soldiers who trusted in their rabbit's foot or a medicine pack worn around the neck into battle. But he also knew that there were strange and unexplained things in the world, things not understood by science.

"Well, whether mindless slaves or not, those two white boys bring the number of our shadows to four." Stark set his gaze on the trail ahead. "I'd still rather face two than four."

"We have to figure out what to do about them."

Stark pondered for a long moment before something occurred to him. It was an idea as outrageous as any he had ever conceived.

"How sure are you about the man in the coat?" His tone was serious. He had to be sure about this. "Say on a scale of one to ten. How sure are you that guy is involved in some sort of hoodoo?"

"Eleven."

"All right." Stark grinned. "Let's have a little fun with our friends."

Now it was Red Buffalo's turn to feel a little nervous.

"This is stupid, Nathan Stark!"

"Here. Here's another stick. Do you need more thread?"

Red Buffalo grunted in frustration and continued lashing together the twigs Stark had given him into figures resembling human arms and legs. They were literal stick figures: two sticks bound together in a X, with a single third stick joining the top two points. He and Stark had already lashed together about ten of the things.

"Okay." Stark paused and looked back. As ever, he saw no sign of their pursuers. Yet they were back there, he felt sure of that. Up ahead, a flourishing mesquite tree leaned out over the trail, its bare branches forming a sort of natural canopy. "How good is your balance?"

"I'm an Indian. Born on the back of a pony. Fearless."

"That's not what I asked. I said, how's

your balance? Can you still stand in the saddle?"

"Like I said, I'm an Indian. But an old one."

"Meaning what?"

Red Buffalo shrugged. "Meaning even monkeys sometimes fall from trees."

"Okay." Stark reined to a halt beneath the overhanging mesquite branches. "We've got thread. And we've got ten stick figures. So let's dangle them from the branches. Right here."

"All ten?"

"I was thinking, yeah."

"No." Red Buffalo shifted, brought his hands beneath him and vaulted to an upright stance in his horse's saddle. "Four, Nathan Stark. One for each member of the pursuit party."

"That's spookier. Yeah, I like it."

Stark watched as Red Buffalo set to work. He had to hand it to the Crow. The old man had flair and a sense of symmetry. He hung two large figures, then two smaller ones closer together, obviously meant to represent the twins. When he was done, he slid back into his place on the saddle.

"What do you think?" he asked.

"It's perfect, Red Buffalo. Those two little ones stuck together are a nice flourish. And now, for the finishing touch . . ."

He drew a dead hare from his saddlebag, slit its throat, and laid its body in the middle of the trail, directly below the four stick figures dangling from the branch above.

"What do you think?" he asked.

"Sprinkle some blood on the stick figures," Red Buffalo suggested.

"Nice detail," Stark said, and did just that. Then they withdrew and sought cover to observe the effect their craftwork had on their pursuers.

It didn't take them long to arrive. They streamed up in tight formation, with the witch doctor in the lead. He advanced to the overhanging branches, then turned and waved for the other three to halt a short distance back. Then he dismounted, examined the corpse on the ground and the blood-soaked stick suspended from the dry mesquite branches. Then he turned toward the sky.

A howl escaped his throat, a sound of raw terror and rage. It was all Stark needed to know that his warning had been taken seriously. And that this would end soon.

Chapter 40

The shock of their little display bought Stark and Red Buffalo enough time to steal a march on their pursuers. They galloped hard by daylight and continued for a good part of the night, taking advantage of the swelling moon's light.

An hour or so before dawn, they stopped for three hours, to feed and water the horses, and grab a little shut-eye. Neither man stayed awake on watch; both just collapsed, exhausted. Red Buffalo awoke first, shook Stark out of sleep, and they mounted up to continue the journey.

Stark took care to double back, set up false trails of prints, erase signs of their passage whenever possible. By his reckoning, he had done a good job. Even in full daylight, their path would prove difficult to follow. He felt he had put sufficient effort into throwing off their pursuers to be able to relax somewhat. He mentioned as much to

Red Buffalo, who seemed skeptical.

"With that magician among them, I wouldn't be too sure," he cautioned. "They have a talent for picking up on things other people miss."

Stark said he would bear that in mind.

Soon, they entered the network of washes and arroyos that tapered into the shallow creek that passed by the cliff dwellings. Stark knew it was only a matter of time now. When a bend in the stream brought the cliffs into view at a distance, a lazy spiral of smoke climbing skyward told him Mosi was at work making dinner.

"Only a matter of time now," said Red Buffalo.

Stark gave some thought to what he was going to say to Johnny. He had been furious upon learning the couple had wandered off again, but thought he was beginning to understand a little of why.

They're young, and I'm sure she wants children, Stark thought. What future was there in a desert territory riven by war? He wouldn't be surprised to learn that their plan involved an escape from the Territory altogether. He felt certain Johnny would abandon the Free State of Mescalero if it meant he could be with her. It was a motivation Stark could understand.

But they couldn't be allowed to slip away again. If necessary, he would tie Johnny up. Her, too — if it came to that.

The miles rolled away. The plume of smoke from the cook fire grew. And soon the cliff dwellings loomed.

Johnny was bent over the cook pit, feeding wood into the fire. His back was turned as Stark and Red Buffalo rode into camp, the sound of their hooves muffled by the soft sand of the arroyo. They were sitting there waiting when he turned back from the fire.

"Hello," said Stark.

Johnny seemed on the point of running then and there. But instead, he glanced at the mouth of the nearest dwelling, the same one in which they had taken refuge. As Stark watched, Mosi poked her head out from around a corner. Johnny sighed heavily and then gestured for her to come out. She did, slowly and tentatively, walking down the packed earthen ramp until she was in his arms.

"You two are just determined to go your own way, aren't you?" Stark asked, disbelief coloring his tone.

"We don't want any part of this anymore." Johnny sounded annoyed as he spoke. "We're both sick of the war, the raiding, the killing. We're going to leave."

"And go where?" Red Buffalo demanded. "Your people are here!"

"We can go south," Mosi said softly. "Down into old Mexico. There are Apache down there. We can make a home for ourselves there."

"If you really are against the killing," Stark said, "then the best thing you can do is come back with us to Fort Lowell. Help us get the Navajo guides back working again. *Then* go to Mexico."

But Mosi shook her head. "If what you say about Atsa is true, then he's a chief. I'll have to marry who he chooses. I don't want any part of that. I want to be with Johnny. No one else."

She sounded at once confident and completely childlike in a way that made Stark's heart turn over. It was all so simple in her mind. For years she had lived tucked away among the Purgatory Crossing Apache, knowing little of the outside world. She had no investment there. Running away was a simple, impulsive solution to the shock of discovering there is a world larger and broader than she'd thought imaginable.

Johnny was different. He was angry — about the war, about his own status as a half-breed, about having to live outside the law among those misfits in the Free State. That anger had boiled his insides down to a hard kernel of hate that sat like a lump of coal where a heart should be. Finding Mosi was his one chance to warm that coal and make a life for himself outside of a world where he was not welcome.

"We have no reason to go back," Johnny said dully. "Just leave us alone."

"You know we can't do that," Stark replied. "We're out here doing this under orders from General Miles. You're coming back with us. One way or the other. We'd rather it be with your cooperation, Johnny."

"Back!" Johnny spat. "For more killing? More war?"

"The only way to end this war is to end Geronimo," Stark said patiently. "And the only thing with the power to do that is the United States government. By helping us, by helping the cavalry, you'll be helping to keep those people safe."

"What people?"

"Haven't you been paying attention?" Red Buffalo asked. "Haven't you seen the smoke on the horizon? All those homes being set ablaze by Geronimo and his men? Who do you think lives there? It's just ordinary people, Johnny. They're the ones suffering and paying the price. How can that be fair?"

"Was my life fair?" he bristled. "Hers?"

"You're so full of anger and hatred that you'd let the world burn, even though you could stop it?" Red Buffalo shook his head in disbelief. "You should go then. Go to Mexico! Leave and never come back, because you have no heart, no soul, no connection here. Or anyplace. You're lost!"

"What do I owe them?" Johnny shot back. "What does she owe them? You can't claim we owe them anything. Because we were cast aside. Forsaken, both of us. Did anyone come to get her? Or to come get *me* when *I* was young? No. We were left to fend for ourselves. And we were *kids.* Now you expect us to take on the responsibility for an entire Territory? That's not fair."

"Life ain't fair!" Stark snapped. "We're never ready for the challenges that come our way! But when we can lend a hand, help make the world a better place . . . Well, don't you think we kind of have an obligation?"

"Why?"

"Do you want to have a baby with her?"

"Yes!"

"Well, then. Think about the world that baby is going to grow up in," Stark urged. "You have a chance to change that world for the better by acting now. So for your baby's sake, do it, why don't you?"

Johnny absorbed all of this with stony calm. For the first time, he seemed to run out of arguments. He also seemed to have run out of steam. A moment later, he was drawing Mosi away and speaking to her urgently, in hushed tones.

"What advice do you think she will give him?" Red Buffalo asked.

Stark considered the question carefully. He didn't know much about the girl, but what he had observed suggested she was a person of solid moral fiber. She had the ability to care for others outside of herself. In this simple way, she was extraordinary.

"I think she's going to tell him he has a responsibility. Because she'll recognize her own. They're good people. I think they'll make the right choice."

After a brief exchange, they parted. Mosi went up the earthen ramp to the cliff dwelling's entrance. Johnny stood and watched her go, then made his way over to Stark and Red Buffalo.

"We've had a talk about it," he said. "I wanted to hear what Mosi had to say, but she's too shy to speak up in front of others."

"That's wise," said Red Buffalo. "If you want to marry her, better get used to listening to her."

"She says we should go back," he said flatly.

Stark and Red Buffalo exchanged a look.

"Mosi says she wants to meet her father. But that she's going to be clear that she and I are going to Mexico together to start our family there. It's our choice. She will stay long enough to help resolve the strike. But once we're done, we're leaving the United States. And we're never coming back."

"That's your choice," said Stark. "We'll leave at first light."

Chapter 41

Stark woke in the wee hours, strangely rested. He turned in his bedroll and blinked, knowing from experience that he would not get back to sleep this night. Sighing, he pushed himself to a sitting position and peered through the door of the cliff dwelling to the sandy riverbed below.

The moon beamed a diagonal wedge of light across the wash, illuminating the rocks, causing the bright nuggets in the sand to twinkle, just like in daytime. The shadows, though, were darker, their edges brighter and more sharply defined. It was the stillest part of the night. Lost in dreams, no living things stirred.

He was thinking this when the scalp hunters rode out from the cover of the trees into the moonlight.

He could not have awakened at a better time.

It was them, the same group they had just narrowly avoided and escaped from a day or two before. The Indian man in the blazer rode up front, followed by his elderly black companion. The milk-white twins brought up the rear, riding side by side. Stark could tell they had not yet looked up and seen the cliff dwellings. But that would happen any moment.

Without taking his eyes from the group, he stretched out one leg and, with the toe of his boot, tapped Red Buffalo, sleeping nearby. The Crow roused instantly and without a sound.

"Scalp hunters," Stark whispered and pointed.

Red Buffalo looked, nodded, and rose, moving quietly to where Mosi and Johnny slept. He roused Johnny and bid him to be quiet, as Stark rose and drew his gun.

The scalp hunters had stopped in a loose cluster at the base of the cliffs. They were staring up. The black man with the gun was pointing, and the low buzz of voices could be heard rising from below.

"They tracked us here," said Red Buffalo, his voice barely a whisper where he crouched beside Stark.

"Will they come now or wait until morning?" Johnny hissed.

"They'll come," Stark said. "They can't afford to pass up the chance that we'll be out cold when they attack."

"Too good to pass up," Red Buffalo agreed.

"Sooner or later, they'll get here," Stark muttered, watching as the group below split up. The twins remained together on their horses in the sand, while the Indian moved to the left and the black man with the shotgun approached the earth ramp leading up to their position.

"We've got company," Stark breathed.

The three of them withdrew into the shadows just inside the entryway. The moment he stepped indoors, their visitor would smell the fresh woodsmoke and know people were hiding here. Stark knew he would signal his comrades the moment he was sure. The trick would be taking the man before he was certain.

He holstered his Colt, drew his knife, and crouched beside the entrance, breath held, waiting.

The elderly man with the shotgun sidled up the ramp, moving silently, eyes on the entrance, a knot of fear tightening at the base of his spine. Of all the sensations he was currently experiencing, it was the fear that he paid attention to. Fear was the currency of their little quartet. Fear was the key in which their song was played.

He thought of the man in the blue jacket merely as the Boss. The twins called him by his Indian name, but to the elderly black man, he was just the Boss. It was a title that suited him. The Boss was the best with a knife, the fastest with a gun, the sharpest with his wits. And he had something else going for him, too . . .

The Hoodoo.

It was the Hoodoo that motivated them, that impelled them to stick together and do the Boss's bidding. It was the fear that impelled him and the twins to feats of strength and courage beyond anything they might imagine possible. Like clambering up this earthen ramp in the dark. Who knew what lay beyond the entrance? Probably nothing. But it wasn't the sort of thing he would normally do.

Except that the Boss had asked him to.

The man reached the entrance to the cliff dwelling and flattened himself against the wall by the door. If there was anyone in there, he would clear the room. Two blasts from the shotgun should be enough. And even if it wasn't, the sound of its report would bring the others running.

Gathering his courage, he lifted the gun and began edging into the doorway.

Stark saw the shadow move, saw it flatten and shorten as the man approached, then saw the twin snouts of the shotgun edge into the dwelling. He bided his time, waiting until the shape of the man clutching the weapon became plain before moving.

Stark lunged forward, one hand seizing the shotgun low on the barrels while the other whipped around, driving the blade into the man's throat by his Adam's apple. Stark clenched his teeth against the expected roar, but none came. He had snuffed out the man's life before he could squeeze the shotgun's triggers.

He held on to the gun, keeping a grip on it, as the man fell, his life gurgling out of his throat in soft gouts of blood and breath.

"That's one down," Red Buffalo breathed.

Down on the sand, the Boss waited impatiently for a report back. He had sent his man up to the cliff dwelling and expected either an all clear or the sound of a weapon. Instead, he heard silence. And it displeased him.

The Boss was not a man to show patience or accept failure. He demanded obedience.

He demanded success. One led to the other. Now his man was not obeying.

The Boss raised his face and gave a throaty birdcall, then waited for a response.

None came.

Something was wrong.

"What's he doing?" Red Buffalo asked.

Stark peered out the doorway at the man who had just uttered some sort of birdcall. Obviously, a signal of some kind that the man with the shotgun was meant to return. Because when he did not, the Indian tried again. Receiving no reply, he beckoned the twins to come to him.

He's making plans for an attack, Stark thought. *No point in letting him make too much progress.*

He hefted his Henry rifle, figuring the distance. Two hundred yards at most. It would be an easy shot.

Stark knelt, carefully positioning the rifle, right hand on the trigger, left elbow balanced on his raised knee. He had just centered the sight on the man when suddenly he moved.

With a clipped command, the man galloped his horse toward the earth ramp leading to the doorway, where Stark and Red Buffalo crouched. Then he was tearing up the incline at full speed, crying out at the top of his voice, the twins behind him.

Stark stepped out of the doorway.

The abruptness of his appearance must have startled the Indian because he pulled back on the reins, causing his horse to come to an abrupt stop. The twin closest behind him collided with the back of the leader's horse, knocking them both from the saddle to the ground.

Stark shot the medicine man in the blue jacket as he rose to his knees. He flew backward to splay out on his back on the soil. The unhorsed twin saw his partner's body flung to the ground, took one look at Stark, and turned to run.

The other twin, meanwhile, bolted past them and into the cave dwelling.

It was an unexpected — an insane — move, all things considered. This twin was either stupid or absolutely determined to rescue the black man with the shotgun.

Stark and Red Buffalo sprinted into the cave after him. They saw Johnny's shadow collide with the horse and get bounced to one wall. Then there was a rush of action that blurred in the shadow. Hurriedly, Red Buffalo lit a match. It took time for the light to expand enough to fill the cave. But as it did, they heard a scream.

Once the light grew to full strength, Stark beheld a grim sight.

The second twin was crawling along the ground, one hand trying to stem the blood pouring from his neck. He made odd, grunting noises as he crawled, pausing now and then to reach for something — perhaps an enemy, perhaps a plea for help. But he only managed to crawl a dozen feet or so before he collapsed, dead.

Mosi stood trembling, a bloody knife dangling from her right hand.

"Mosi!" Johnny rushed to her side. "Mosi! Are you all right?"

Mosi struggled to speak. But in the end, she merely flung the knife to the ground, gathered Johnny in her arms, and wept.

Chapter 42

They lit out for Fort Lowell at dawn the next morning. It was obvious right from the start that Mosi was not doing well. She emerged from the doorway draped in a blanket, its topmost section drawn down over her head and face like a hood. With Johnny's help, she mounted clumsily behind him on his horse. Stark wasn't sure but thought he might have heard a sob as she settled herself.

"She's in rough shape," Stark muttered to Red Buffalo, as they set out.

"She killed a man last night." The Crow sighed. "You remember your first one?"

Stark did. It was during the War Between the States. While serving a stint, under General Stuart, in the cavalry, his party had surprised a small group of Union soldiers caught behind the lines and attempting to straggle back to their command. Stark's unit had attempted to encircle and capture them, but the Yanks had put up one hell of a fight. Stark's horse had been hit and a red raging mist had befallen him. Rather than break off the attack, he had spurred his wounded mount forward to trample the man responsible. The Union private had died, screaming and choking beneath the bloodied hooves of Stark's horse. Stark had dismounted and finished him with a bullet. It was the kind of thing one tends not to forget.

"She's just a girl," Stark said quietly. "No girl should ever have to do what she did."

"No girl," agreed Red Buffalo. And left it at that.

They were coming out of the rolling hillocks now, crossing the barren stretch between the frontier and the outskirts of Tucson. They saw no smoke plumes on the horizon. It occurred to Stark that perhaps it was too early for raids. The chances were that Geronimo and his men had worked late into the night and possibly into the wee hours. Now was the ideal time to go flat out, to risk traversing the wide-open desert with its lack of cover for the safety of the fort.

The sun climbed relentlessly into the sky, first breaking the night's chill, then igniting the spark of the long, slow burn that would be that day's weather. Stark saw the last traces of the nocturnal animals scampering home to their lairs. The day's temperatures would bring punishing heat of the kind only bearable to lizards and snakes.

And Apache, he thought, ironically.

"How much further, you reckon?" he asked Red Buffalo.

"A few hours, we should be there." Red Buffalo heaved a weary sigh. Stark had never seen the Crow so tired before. It had been a long road, with many a detour and much bloodshed. They could both do with a long rest after this. Stark, despite loving the open trails, was starting to think fond thoughts of a quiet few days holed up in some comfy hotel, with good food and a quiet parlor. It would be, truly, what the doctor ordered.

Two hours into their journey, the ground beneath them began angling slightly downward. A scraggly line of stunted cottonwoods knelt by the edge of an arroyo. Johnny brought them to the banks, then slid down from the saddle to step into the dry riverbed. Bending, he drew out his knife and began hacking at the sand in the middle of the dry wash. He went at it hard for ten minutes before looking up with a satisfied smile.

"We've got water," he said brightly. "It's a slow flow, and muddy. But it's there."

His was a welcome discovery. For, although they had enough water for themselves for the remainder of the journey, the horses needed moisture. Red Buffalo and Johnny worked together to fill a small clay pot Johnny produced with wet sand, which they strained through cloth to remove the worst of the dirt. They repeated the operation three times before they had perhaps half a bucket's worth of pale gray water.

"Better than nothing," Red Buffalo muttered, holding the pot up to Buck's face. Stark's horse took several deep, grateful drafts before Red Buffalo moved on to his own horse.

"Johnny," said Stark. "This land here. Whose territory?"

"Here?" Johnny frowned. "Used to be Pima territory until the Apache began their raiding. It's dead land, now. Cactus land."

"Cactus land for sure," Stark agreed. He looked around. There was no one in evidence. He felt certain they were not being watched.

He was wrong.

"Father."

Taza turned his attention to where Chayton lay spread-eagle in the wild grasses wrapping the side of a hill near where the quartet had stopped. His adopted son had kept the group in view since their arrival, convinced that Mosi was among them.

"I recognize both of them, father," he said. "Both of the Indians who came out of the forest and enticed Mosi away. I see them there, along with Mosi and a white man."

Taza breathed heavily, calming himself. He knew what was to come.

They would attack, of course. There could be no other response at this point. His daughter had been taken, his warriors slain. The men responsible would die. And Mosi would be returned to Taza's family. Then married off, quickly, because Taza no longer wanted the responsibility of caring for her.

He looked at Chayton.

Taza was done with the boy, too. It was time to be shed of him. Time to send him on his way with a group of warriors on some minor task and, upon his return, show him to a separate tent. Make him go live on his own. That would help him to grow up and leave Taza in peace.

But for now, Taza had to steel himself. He would have to lead this impulsive, unsteady boy on a difficult and emotional mission. They would face great peril. There was a

high likelihood one of them could perish.
   But it was what it was.
   Now it was time to go.

Chapter 43

The water they retrieved from digging and filtering was brackish and dirty. Not the sort of thing they'd drink themselves, but it was sufficient for the horses. With their tough gut worms and hearty constitutions, the animals could survive on just about any sort of fodder or moisture. Taking time to water them now would ensure a smooth journey the rest of the way to Fort Lowell.

Stark knew they were at the rump end of their trip. In less than a few hours, they would be back among Miles and his men, in relative safety.

But he knew from experience that overconfidence toward the end of a trail could lead to disaster, so he took the opportunity to check over the horses, their rations, their ammunition. He was determined to leave nothing to chance.

"How do you think Mosi will get along with her real father?" Red Buffalo asked.

"Hard to say." Stark shrugged. "Fathers and daughters are a tough relationship, even at the best of times. And this doesn't qualify as the best of times."

"True." The Crow gave Mosi a long, measuring look. "She's been through a lot. Hopefully, Johnny will make a good husband and take care of her."

"He's done a good job, so far," Stark said.

"She has certainly been the focus of his attention," agreed the Crow.

Johnny was gathering up his knife and clay pot, and kicking sand into the hole he'd dug in the riverbed —

Mosi was guiding Johnny's horse back toward him by the reins —

Red Buffalo was mounting up — when the first shot was fired.

Stark dropped and rolled, drawing his Colt, as Red Buffalo crouched, drawing his own gun. An arrow sang out from the mesquite bushes along the river's edge, narrowly missing Johnny. Stark looked left and right, left and right, trying to assess how many attackers they faced.

Chayton could see Mosi. His sister was crouching beside a horse. Nearby was the one Indian man who had grabbed her hand and run into the forest near her village.

Chayton had already tried to kill him once with an arrow and missed. So he set up to try again.

Moving stealthily, he nocked and drew an arrow into position. His sister's kidnappers still had no idea of his position, and he used that to his advantage. Taza was keeping the other two pinned down by rifle fire, so he would deal with this man.

He held his breath and fired.

The arrow flew true, perhaps the best bow shot Chayton had yet made in his young life. The young Indian man in the riverbed saw it coming and rolled away, quick as he could, putting some distance between himself and the projectile. Which also had the effect of putting some distance between himself and Mosi.

Chayton took the opportunity to rush down toward his sister.

Stark came to his knees, Colt extended in one hand, firing toward the place from which enemy fire came. He was only marginally certain of the point of origin but shot anyway, laying down suppressive fire, giving the others time to take cover. Red Buffalo had grabbed his horse's reins, forcing it to the ground before diving behind it.

With a glance to ensure Mosi and Johnny

had not been hit, Stark began advancing on the edge of the wash, resolutely keeping the Colt's iron sight between himself and the sniper's position.

He became aware of a blur of motion off to his left. Someone had broken cover and was moving into the wash. He heard Red Buffalo snap off a shot aimed in that direction and trusted his partner would keep his flank covered. Sensing the man firing from cover was lining up for another shot, he blasted two rounds from the Colt, put his head down, and barreled into the bushes.

It was a tight squeeze, and he fought his way through. But eventually he ripped his way into the center of the thicket, where the gunman had been.

He was gone. He had left his smoking rifle on the ground. Nothing else.

Cursing, Stark began fighting his way back out of the thicket.

Chayton streaked across the riverbed toward his sister.

"Mosi!" he shrieked. *"Mosi!"*

The girl turned toward the sound and started at the sight of her brother. "Chayton!" she cried. "Don't —"

It was as far as she got before Chayton was upon her, grabbing her wrist and dragging her back toward the riverbank. "Come!" he was crying. "Father is here! We've come to rescue you!"

"No!" She yanked at his grip, seeking to escape.

Suddenly Johnny was there, moving full speed, ramming a shoulder into Chayton's chest and driving him backward into the sand. Mosi was flung clear by the impact, but the two young Indian men slammed into the floor of the wash. Chayton scrambled, reaching for his knife as Johnny reared up, hauled back a fist and punched the boy on the face, bloodying his nose and mouth.

"Johnny, no!" screamed Mosi.

But Johnny wasn't listening. He was hauling back again for another punch when Chayton kicked out, driving Johnny back through the air to land with a hard crunch a half dozen feet away.

Then Chayton was grabbing her wrist again. "Come on, Mosi!" he cried. "Let's get —"

Then Johnny was on him again. Mosi watched her lover slam her brother with punches to the neck, the side, the head. And then he was grappling for his knife.

"Johnny, no!"

Chayton's head whipped around and he saw Johnny's knife slide out of its sheath.

He dropped Mosi's wrist and leaped for where his own blade had fallen into the sand.

Johnny whipped his knife hand around, narrowly missing Chayton.

Chayton grabbed up his own knife — just as Mosi stepped between them.

Taza hurtled out of his hiding place, aiming straight for Red Buffalo.

The Crow saw the Apache war chief coming on and drew his gun. He raised it, fighting to bring the sight up, but Taza chose that moment to hurl his left hand forward, fingers opening. A spray of dirt and sand pelted into Red Buffalo's face. Blinded, he jerked the trigger spasmodically, but the shot went wide. A moment later, Taza was on him, slashing with his knife.

Red Buffalo took a cut on the forearm before dancing back, hands raised, shaking his head to clear his eyes. Then Taza was there, knife whipping back and forth. Red Buffalo backed away again, drawing his own knife. Taza swiped at him, missing, the blow going wide. Red Buffalo slipped in, elbowed the Apache in the ribs, then dealt Taza a wide cut across the abdomen.

The Apache chief drew in a quick breath, fighting the pain. He remained upright despite the wound, still furious. He came at Red Buffalo with a scream, bringing the knife in overhand. Red Buffalo blocked Taza's knife arm with his own, punching with his free hand. His second punch connected, driving Taza back with a bloody nose.

"Leave it," Red Buffalo said. "Go now. Back to your people."

Taza screamed and hurled himself at Red Buffalo. The Crow sidestepped the advance, brought up the knife, and drove it squarely into Taza's throat, killing him.

Johnny reached for Mosi, pushing her out of the way. Chayton bounded into the space she had occupied, slashing at Johnny's face with his knife. Johnny retreated, his own knife out, biding his time. Chayton came again, his face contorted in fury. Johnny met him with a shock of impact that staggered both of them. Chayton punched out, hitting Johnny in the face. But that didn't stop Johnny. He slashed, opening a wide cut on Chayton's forearm.

At the sight of the blood, Chayton became hysterical. He screeched and rushed Johnny. The half-breed retreated. One step. Two — And then his bootheel connected with something and he went down, Chayton looming over him.

"Chayton, no!"

Mosi's scream was lost in the ferocity of Chayton's attack. He was hacking at Johnny now, knife point flashing. He would *kill* this man who had dishonored his family! He would make a name for himself as a warrior! He would —

"Chayton!"

Mosi screamed and threw herself onto her brother, grabbing for his knife arm. But Chayton, enraged, and focused entirely on Johnny, failed to register that it was his sister. He whipped around, knife out.

It sank, hilt deep, into her stomach.

Mosi screamed and sank to her knees.

Red Buffalo turned. "No!" he cried.

Stark stumbled out of the bush into the riverbed just in time to watch her die.

Chapter 44

Finally, Stark thought. *We get to bury one of the dead.*

He had seen so much death on this journey — the scattered bodies of ranchers, stagecoach operators, guards, marauders, and scalp hunters — and been forced to leave them, lest disturbing the remains revealed their presence to the Apaches.

But now, with Mosi's death, they would do right by one who had fallen on the trail.

Stark thought all these things as he watched Johnny and Red Buffalo prepare Mosi's body for transport to Fort Lowell. Her brother, having fled after the battle, would probably return to claim the body of the other man, the one Red Buffalo had killed. And despite the Crow and Johnny being from different tribes, they worked together to purify and wrap Mosi's corpse. Somehow, instinctively, both knew what to do.

Stark stood to one side, watching respectfully, grieving for all those lost to the Apache Wars. He was not much of a God-fearing man, but one thought did occur to him.

One day these wars will be over, and this harsh and rocky land will become home to those who wish to live in peace.

That, along with Mosi, was worth praying for. And so he bowed his head and did just that.

The return journey to Fort Lowell passed without incident. Red Buffalo rode alongside Johnny, the two talking quietly while Stark rode up ahead, taking point. They passed out of the flatiron of the desert and into the more hospitable climate of sluicing washes and cottonwood trees that signaled the outskirts of Tucson. Then the fort and its outskirts sharpened into visibility on the horizon ahead. A single rider was coming out to meet them. Stark chuckled when he recognized the man.

"Corporal Buell!" He reined to a stop. "Good to see you."

"We were starting to worry about you, Mr. Stark!" Buell's walrus mustache spread in a warm smile. The smile vanished when he craned to look over Stark's shoulder. "A body?" he asked. "Who — ?"

"It's Chief Atsa's daughter. We found her." Stark's jaw firmed as he added, "Her brother killed her."

"Oh, good Lord," muttered Buell. "Atsa and his men are at the fort now, meeting with General Miles. This won't go over well."

"Understood." Stark shrugged. "We tried our best. There was much we didn't count on. And a few surprises. None of this turned out like we expected."

"Things rarely do," Buell sighed. "Come on, let's get you fellas squared away."

With that, Buell turned and led the party back to the safety of the cavalry outpost.

Buell was right. News of Mosi's death at the hands of her own brother was not well received.

Miles kept them cooling their heels outside his office for several hours. The activity of the fort passed around them as they waited — the usual business of troops, support staff, family members of officers, and the many Navajos who were visiting along with their chief.

It was one of these who, in stopping to chat with Johnny and Red Buffalo, informed them that Atsa was inside. He had been meeting with General Miles all morning.

Buell had seen to Mosi's body, removing it to the infirmary for storage. He returned now with three lunch buckets in hand.

"Lampkins sent these," he said, putting them down before Stark. "Nothing fancy. Just some bread and chicken. General's still keeping you waiting, I see."

"Apparently, he's finished meeting with the Navajo chief now." Stark parted the folds of the checkered napkin atop one bucket and peered in. Delicious odors wafted out. As usual, Lampkins had outdone himself. "Atsa left by the back door, I reckon. They were in there a long time."

"General Miles was trying to get Atsa and his scouts back on our side," Buell said. "The negotiations were rocky. Miles has been informed of your arrival with Mosi's body. I expect Chief Atsa has likewise been informed."

As Buell toddled off back to his duties, Stark brought two of the lunch buckets to Johnny and Red Buffalo where they sat talking quietly. Red Buffalo rose and stepped over to intercept him.

"If that's food from Corporal Buell, please return it with our thanks," Red Buffalo said. "We won't be eating today. We're in mourning. It's our way."

Stark looked to Johnny. The young half-breed sat staring impassively into nothingness. Mosi's death had left him desolate. Red Buffalo had chosen to accompany Johnny on that journey. Stark couldn't help but feel a swell of admiration and respect for his partner.

"I understand," he said quietly. "You're a good man, Moses Red Buffalo."

"Even for an Indian?" A hint of amusement twinkled in the Crow's eye.

"Yeah." Stark smiled sheepishly. Red Buffalo returned to Johnny and resumed talking.

Stark took his lunch bucket to the porch steps of Miles's office and took a seat. He was tired and hungry. He reached in and hauled out a fresh biscuit, taking a bite and savoring its flavor. As he ate, a small group of Navajos emerged from the infirmary and approached Johnny and Red Buffalo. They conferred briefly before the two men rose and accompanied the group back to where Mosi's body was being held. Soon afterward, an aide poked his head out the door and spoke.

"Mr. Stark? General Miles will see you now."

"Thank you." Stark rose and put the lunch bucket aside, then accompanied the aide into the building, wiping chicken grease from his hands on his trousers as he went.

Miles was standing by his desk when Stark arrived. "Welcome back," he said tonelessly. "Apparently, the mission did not go according to plan."

"No, sir," replied Stark. "We encountered resistance from Mosi's brother, Chayton. He refused to leave with us and fought against our efforts to return Mosi here. He helped lead a raiding party that ambushed us in a wash a half day's ride from here. Mosi was killed in the resulting action."

Miles sighed and went to the window, shaking his head. "A damned shame," he said quietly. "Atsa is with his men at the infirmary now. I told him of your mission when he arrived. At first, he seemed pleased. But now . . . who knows?" He turned to Stark. "You men did your best. You rode into rough country, on a difficult mission, with little chance of success. Frankly, I wasn't sure you'd make it back. But you did. And you brought Mosi's body with you. That could be construed as a kind of success. If nothing else, it provides Atsa with some satisfaction."

"Yes, sir."

A knock came at the door. Miles bid the visitor enter. It was the same aide who had conducted Stark inside.

"Sir," he said. "The other two native guides, Red Buffalo and Johnny Two-Face, are here."

"Send them in." Miles took a seat behind his desk.

Both men entered somberly, bereavement weighing on them heavily. Johnny was taking it especially hard. Red Buffalo placed a hand on Johnny's shoulder briefly and squeezed before dropping it to his side.

"We have spoken with Atsa," he said simply. "He and his men are purifying Mosi's body now. It is their intention to return her to Navajo land for burial."

"Of course," Miles said. "Please inform him that we would be happy to offer a wagon and an armed escort for the journey."

"I will." Red Buffalo nodded. "There's something else, too." He turned to Johnny.

"Atsa has sworn a blood oath to avenge Mosi's death," Johnny said. "He has vowed revenge on the Purgatory Crossing Apache, and all Apache. He says that his scouts will end their strike and return to work assisting your cavalry. He vows to fight by your side for as long as it takes to eradicate the Apache from this land forever."

Miles listened impassively. When Johnny finished, he nodded soberly. "Please thank

Chief Atsa on my behalf," he said. "And offer my personal condolences for the loss of his daughter."

"We will," said Red Buffalo. "We're going to go help them ready Mosi's body for the journey."

"Of course."

The two men left, closing the door behind them as they went. Miles sat perfectly still for a long moment before rising and moving to a side table, where a decanter and some glasses rested.

"It was the outcome we wanted. But not in the way we were hoping for," he said, taking up the decanter.

"No, sir," Stark said.

"Yes, I suppose it's a kind of success." Miles poured two glasses of whiskey and handed one to Stark. He raised his glass. "To Mosi. And to the end of this damned war."

"I'll drink to that," Stark said. And did.

Stark accepted General Miles's invitation to remain at Fort Lowell for a few days before beginning the trek back east. To say he was grateful for the hospitality was an understatement. After his time on the trail, he needed a bath and a shave, a soft bed and good food. After another drink, they ended their meeting, and Stark emerged to stand on the porch in time to see the Navajo delegation beginning their preparations for departure.

Atsa had accepted the offer of a wagon but turned down the escort. From the look of things, the Navajo had plenty of guns to secure the journey back to their homeland in safety. Stark could see Johnny, already in the saddle, ready to ride with them. Red Buffalo talked to Johnny briefly before coming over to bid farewell to Stark.

"We're going now," Red Buffalo said. He extended a hand. "Thank you, Nathan."

"Sure thing." Stark shook warmly. "It was good to work with you again."

"And you." Red Buffalo paused for a moment before adding: "Atsa has offered to adopt Johnny and welcome him into the family. The Navajo warriors are especially pleased with this. It's good for them. And for Johnny."

"It is," agreed Stark. "What are your plans?"

"I have always wanted to see Navajo country," Red Buffalo said. "This will be my chance. I will journey to their territory. And along the way, I may learn more about the Prophet and the Ghost Dance."

"I hope what you find is a comfort to you."

Red Buffalo nodded. "And you?"

"I'm going to stay here for a few days, then start heading back. Buck and I will board the train in Tucson. Should be back on the plains in a few days."

"Perhaps I'll see you out there again someday," Red Buffalo said. "Or perhaps back here. Who knows?"

"Yeah. Who knows?" Stark smiled tiredly. "Safe travels, my friend."

"And you." Red Buffalo nodded and turned back to join the departing Navajo. Stark watched as he mounted up. Shortly afterward, the party began moving out of the environs of the fort into open desert.

And that ends it, Stark thought. He looked to the sky. Circling overhead, a lone vulture patrolled the thermals, scanning the land below for game. Perfectly adapted to the heat and privations of the desert, he was home. As Stark would soon be.

But for now, he needed to rest.

As the dust settled from the departing Navajo, he turned and headed wearily for his bunk.

ABOUT THE AUTHORS

William W. Johnstone is the *New York Times* and *USA Today* bestselling author of over three hundred novels of Western adventure, military action, and chilling suspense, and with over 35 million books in print, he is the bestselling Western writer in the world. Born in southern Missouri, he was raised with strong moral and family values by his minister father, and tutored by his schoolteacher mother. He left school at fifteen to work in a carnival and then as a deputy sheriff before serving in the army. He went on to become known as "the Greatest Western writer of the 21st Century." Visit him online at WilliamJohnstone.net.

J.A. Johnstone learned to write from the master himself, Uncle William W. Johnstone, who began tutoring J.A. at an early age. After-school hours were often spent retyping manuscripts or researching his massive American Western History library as well as the more modern wars and conflicts. J.A. worked hard — and learned. "Every day with Bill was an adventure story in itself. Bill taught me all he could about the art of storytelling. 'Keep the historical facts accurate,' he would say. "Remember the readers, and as your grandfather once told me, I am telling you now: be the best Johnstone you can be." J.A. Johnstone has co-written numerous bestselling series with William W. Johnstone including The First Mountain Man, The Brothers O'Brien, Preacher, and The Last Mountain Man.

The employees of Thorndike Press hope you have enjoyed this Large Print book. All our Thorndike Large Print titles are designed for easy reading, and all our books are made to last. Other Thorndike Press Large Print books are available at your library, through selected bookstores, or directly from us.

For information about titles, please call:
 (800) 223-1244

or visit our website at:
 gale.com/thorndike

www.ingramcontent.com/pod-product-compliance
Lightning Source LLC
Jackson TN
JSHW020931040625
85341JS00001B/1